PLEASANTLY PURSUED

Book #2

9-4-24

ALSO BY KASEY STOCKTON

Regency Romance

The Jewels of Halstead Manor

The Lady of Larkspur Vale

The Widow of Falbrooke Court

The Recluse of Wolfeton House

The Smuggler of Camden Cove

Properly Kissed

Love in the Bargain

His Amiable Bride

A Duke for Lady Eve

A Forgiving Heart

All is Mary and Bright

Myths of Moraigh Trilogy

Journey to Bongary Spring

Through the Fairy Tree

The Enemy Across the Loch

Contemporary Romance

His Stand-In Holiday Girlfriend

Snowed In on Main Street

Melodies and Mistletoe

PLEASANTLY PURSUED

KASEY STOCKTON

GOLDEN OWL
PRESS

Copyright © 2022 by Kasey Stockton
Cover design by Seventhstar Art

First edition: September 2022
Golden Owl Press
Fort Worth, TX

Library of Congress Control Number: 2022915368
ISBN 978-1-952429-28-6

For Susie, who in no way embodies the stereotypical mother-in-law.
I'm lucky to have you, and I love you!

CHAPTER I

THEA

I had always believed myself rather adept at hiding, but this time, I wondered if I'd gone too far in my disguise. Flour dusted my nose, hiding my faint freckles and pale skin beneath a coating of white powder and effectively disguising what dark hair was peeking from beneath my maid's cap. I surely looked as though I'd lost a round of bullet pudding, and while that game was enjoyable during Christmastide, it was November now, and Cook was not going to be pleased to discover the mess I'd made.

Baking appeared so much easier when someone else was doing it. But when I was asked to knead the dough, the particulars of the act evaded me. It could not be so complicated, though. Roll the lump, punch the lump, roll it some more . . .

"Gracious heavens, child," Cook said, bustling back into the workroom. Her brown hair was hidden beneath a cap, an apron tied about her ample waist. "What are you trying to do to that poor loaf?"

"Knead it?"

"Beat it to death, more like," Cook muttered under her breath. She scooted me aside with her hip, and I leaned back against the counter and wiped the back of my wrist over my forehead. I had only been working as a kitchen maid in the Fuller household for a fortnight, but even now I could not properly prepare the dough for rising.

"Get working on those peas," Cook said, pointing to an empty bucket in the far corner.

"Yes, ma'am." I picked up the bucket and let myself outside.

"Gather some beets while you're out there," Cook called through the closed door. "And wipe your face, child. You look a mess."

I opened the door to acknowledge that I'd heard her.

After spending the last few years in Mrs. Moulton's finishing school for young ladies, I felt extremely out of place in the belly of a grand house, helping prepare dinner and clean up after Cook. Mother would be aghast, were she alive to see me now, and I spun my ring on my finger at the thought. Discomfort aside, the anonymity of my current position lent me a degree of security. It would not matter who the Fuller family had to dine, for I would never find myself face to face with any guest of theirs.

After doing my utmost to establish a career as a governess— the children were too young and disobedient—and then a modiste's assistant—she had appreciated my fine manners, but my stitches were abysmally wide—I'd stumbled onto this kitchen maid opportunity at a market in Brumley. I found it a sign of good fortune after a streak of ill luck. It was the ultimate hiding place. I would never be discovered in this capacity, and Cook was determined to teach me what I needed to know. Though it did seem I tried her patience more often than not.

But more than anything, I valued my current position because I had only myself to depend on. My safety and success were reliant upon no one but me, and it was not as though I could break my own trust. It was a comfortable position to be in, welts on my hands and cracked knuckles notwithstanding.

My knees grew damp on the hard, cold ground while the late

autumn sun warmed my bent neck. I leaned forward and picked peas, snapping them at the base of the vine and dropping them into the bucket. Residual powder from my kneading mishap tickled my nose, and I lifted the bottom of my apron to wipe the flour from my face.

It had been nearly six months since I'd slipped out of my finishing school and run off to find refuge from the unpleasant future looming ahead of me. In that time, I had yet to find a situation as happy as this—which was perhaps a poorer reflection on my previous two positions than praise for this one. Cook's mannerisms were harsh and the work grueling. I fell asleep every night before my head reached the pillow, and my hands were slowly turning to leather. But brief moments outside like this were small fortunes I could tuck away to help me through the long days.

I knelt in the kitchen garden, the sun beating on my back and warming my skin through the coarse maid's gown I was required to wear. The uniform was a far cry from the lavish ballgowns and silk stockings I was accustomed to, but finery was worth sacrificing for a life I could call my own.

I did not intend to remain a servant forever, just long enough to meet a man and carve out a future for myself of my own choosing. Though meeting men seemed increasingly difficult in this position. Perhaps my goals would be better achieved were I to find a position as a shop girl or assistant—so long as it did not require sewing.

My parents had spoiled any desire to claim a gentleman for a husband. In my experience, gentlemen were the very worst of creatures, and I would be much happier with a humble man.

Hoofbeats pounded the hard-packed lane that ran alongside the garden. A drystone wall separated me from the road, but still I bent away to avoid the cloud of dust that would soon billow in my direction. The gentleman atop the horse wore a decent set of finery, and a scowl marred his handsome fa—oh, *dear heavens.* A chill washed through me when my gaze fell upon his familiar countenance. I knew him.

Either this man was Benedict Bradwell, or the sun had played a trick on me by assigning him the face of the last man in England I ever wanted to see again. A man I had begun to call handsome, even. My brain deserved a scrubbing with soap for entertaining such a thought.

His bored gaze dropped to me, and before I could fully dive behind the stone wall for cover, recognition lit his blue eyes.

Drat. He'd seen me. I listened to the pounding of his horse's hooves fade down the road a bit, clutching the bucket tightly and hoping he would continue on his way. To my dismay, the horse slowed. I could hear Benedict turning about, but I could not face him. If he was to discover me—to confirm it was truly *me* he saw in the bedraggled maid's gown bent over a garden patch—he would surely drag me from my safe situation in Brumley and deposit me at my lecherous chaperone's house. Or, worse, Benedict would take me home with him.

I jumped to my feet and ran for the house, alarm lacing my stomach and lighting fire beneath my quick steps. Benedict called my name, which only made me run faster. I slammed into the kitchen, and Cook startled, looking up from where she was shaping dough into loaves.

"We'll have none of that, now," she said, scowling.

"Of course, ma'am." My heart raced and my cheeks flushed. Surely Benedict would not follow me into the kitchen of a stranger's house.

I moved to the corner of the worktable and started peeling open the pods and separating the peas from the shells, my heart doing its utmost to beat directly out of my chest.

The door rattled from a quick knock, and Cook looked at it with a questioning brow. He'd followed me? Panicked, I reached over the table while Cook's head was turned, took a fistful of flour, and threw it over my face.

I coughed. Gritty powder snuck into my nostrils, drying my skin, and I blinked away the excess from my eyes. I focused again on my task separating the peas, keeping my gaze lowered.

A heavy knock rattled the door again, and Cook bustled over to answer it. She swung it open and drew in a breath of surprise. I had to admit Benedict could strike a dashing figure when he so chose, but Cook's breathlessness felt disloyal all the same.

"This isn't the main entrance, sir," she said, as though Benedict had come to call and mistaken our tiny door for the way into the house.

I dropped my gaze to the peas in my ever-moving hands, willing him to leave. He did not obey my internal pleading, of course. Not that I would expect him to do anything I asked of him.

"I am looking for Miss Northcott." His deep, calm voice rumbled through the room, driving prickles over the back of my neck.

"Don't have anyone here by that name."

Dear heavens, I was glad I'd thought to give my employers a false name.

"Is that not her, right there?" Benedict must have gestured toward me, for I was the only other person present. "Miss Dorothea Northcott."

"No, sir. That's our Mary."

Bless Cook and her sudden confusion. It sounded like she spoke with affection, and Benedict would not believe anyone capable of having that emotion in regard to me.

I hazarded a look up and found Benedict analyzing me, his eyes widening when they reached my flour-covered face. A questioning look passed over his gaze, and I hoped it meant he was second-guessing himself and not the oddity of finding me covered in white powder.

"Thea," he said, calling to me. I fought the impulse to react to the shortened form of my given name. It had been so long since I'd heard it. Years, in fact. It was a connection to my lost parents and to Benedict's mother—Lady Edith, my godmother—who had taken me under her wing and given me a home shortly after my mother died.

"Why are you doing this?" he asked.

Cook glanced at me and a startled expression flashed over her face. *Please do not comment on my floury cheeks.* She seemed to shake herself. "Can I help you with anything else, sir?" she asked him, apparently finished with having this nonsense in her kitchen. "This is not the woman you seek."

Benedict's jaw flexed. He looked from me to Cook. "No, I thank you. It would appear I have been mistaken." He lifted his gaze to me. "I shall leave you in peace."

The expression on his face spoke the opposite of his words, and I was suddenly very certain he had no such intentions.

The door closed behind him as Cook let out a strange scoff. "Some men think all women look the same. Sure as anything, you have the same color hair as this Dorothea Northcott and nothing else in common."

"More than likely," I agreed.

She returned to the loaves, looking from my bucket of peas to the work counter between us. "Where are my beets?"

I fought a smile. It was a relief that Cook was able to move on so swiftly, for it meant she did not hold any suspicions that Benedict knew whom he was looking at.

"I forgot them."

"Well, fetch them, child."

Not until Benedict had ridden far, far away. "Of course. I'm nearly finished with these peas."

She harrumphed.

I commanded my fingers to slow. I took the pods one at a time and peeled them open, removing the peas in an exaggeratedly sluggish manner. The windows set high on the walls were not facing the proper direction for me to watch Benedict ride away, so I would have to content myself with supplying him ample time to leave.

Nearly a half-hour later, Cook slammed her hand on the wooden table top, jolting me. "Hurry it up, girl."

"I'm nearly there. I only have two left." I shelled them both quickly and shoved the bowl of peas toward Cook, then gathered the casings in my apron to deposit in the compost outside. The sun shone in my eyes, and I lifted my hand to shield them while I dumped the pea pods, then made my way through the kitchen garden toward the beets.

"I was beginning to wonder if I would be forced to wait out here for hours."

The deep voice came from behind me, and though I knew at once that it belonged to Benedict, the sudden nearness startled me and I jumped.

Forced to wait out here for *hours*? He could not truly believe I came out with the express purpose of speaking to him. I shot him a glance over my shoulder, glad I'd not yet fully wiped the flour from my face. "I'm Mary," I said, affecting the lowest-born accent I could muster. "I don't know the woman you're looking for. It isn't me."

His flat lips proved how little he believed me.

"What is the matter with you, Thea? You've worried my mother half to death, and if you aren't careful, you'll incite all manner of rumors, too."

My stomach clenched in discomfort. Was my fear of facing a bad reputation not part of the reason I'd fled? It was never my intention to attach further scandal to my name—my parents had done enough of that for me already. But I would not allow Benedict to unbalance me now. I stood my ground. "Truly, sir. I am not this Miss Northcott of whom you speak."

"Devil take it!" He ran a hand over his face. "A little white powder will not hide you from me. Drop the facade. I know it's you." His chest heaved in frustration.

The way I understood this situation, I now had two options: I could admit the truth, or I could keep pretending I didn't know what he meant until he began to second-guess himself and left me.

Truly, I never had a choice to begin with. There was no situation in this world that would ever entice me to allow Benedict to win.

"It's flour, sir, and it's not a disguise. It is a product of my occupation. You must be on your way now or my employer will be out here soon, and she will surely report you to the constable."

"For standing in the garden?"

"For pestering her kitchen maid."

"I was correct. You've gone and found yourself a position." He scoffed. "I never did realize you were capable of such work, Thea. Though I suppose you feel the need to exhaust yourself daily in order to cover the guilt you must surely feel."

"I have no guilt, sir."

"Of course not," he muttered. "You would have to be possessed of a heart first."

That stung a little. I tried not to think of his mother and what my absence had done to her. In truth, I hadn't much considered Lady Edith or what she would think. It was something of a surprise to learn that it had affected her to any great extent. "Go on your way, Ben—" *Blast*. He had me now. I hurried to cover my blunder. "*Be* on your way, please. I have nothing more to say to you."

The gleam in his eye proved that I hadn't been able to cover my blunder well enough. Time for a distraction. I picked my way through the garden and dropped to my knees, digging beets from the earth and piling them in the bottom of my apron. Benedict quietly watched me work, his attention unnerving. When I stood again, it was with a renewed determination to have the man far from Brumley.

Benedict's hand on my arm gently stopped me from escaping. I held my breath, aware of the warmth that permeated his touch. It was likely the heat of boiling rage transferring from his hand to my arm, but it gave me pause, nonetheless.

"I will not press you further today, Thea. But know these two things: I will not leave Brumley until you agree to come with me, and you could never fool me into believing you are someone else."

I said nothing in response to this bold declaration. What would be the point? It implied a depth of intimacy I was unable to validate. He had caught me nearly calling him by his name, so we both knew exactly who I was.

Yet I was far too stubborn to admit defeat so squarely.

"I hope you find comfortable accommodations, then. If you are waiting for me to come with you, you will never be leaving Brumley again."

He dropped my arm, and his mouth ticked up into a half-smile. He looked to the tall house looming behind us. "This is the Fullers' residence, is it not?"

Cold dread pooled in my stomach. We were in Leicestershire, miles from York, where I had been previously attending school, and even further from Benedict's home in Cumberland. How the heavens did he know a genteel family from *Brumley*?

His smile was snake-like and frustrating. "I rather think I will just stay here."

CHAPTER 2
THEA

I did not catch another glimpse of Benedict for the remainder of the day, but when the footmen came downstairs to retrieve dinner dishes for the Fullers, they were exasperated.

"They've had a late addition to dine," Tom said. "A gentleman."

Benedict. It must be. How had he managed it? When he'd known the name of my employers, I had been surprised. But that he knew them well enough to receive an invitation to stay? That bordered on ludicrous.

There was nothing for it. I would need to escape in the middle of the night.

But where would I go?

"What does the gentleman look like?" I asked Tom while Cook dashed madly about the kitchen to ensure the tureen had enough soup and the platters enough bread and ham.

"Tall chap," Tom said. "Curly hair. From the look of his clothes, he comes from money."

It sounded like Benedict. I gritted my teeth. If he was dining, that gave me plenty of time to clean the rest of the kitchen and pack my measly belongings before I could escape. I looked at

Cook; her harried expression tugged at my heart. I couldn't leave her without notice, not when she had so many tasks and no one else to help. Deserting her now would be beyond the pale.

Once the footmen left and silence descended on the kitchen again, Cook looked at me and screwed her brown eyebrows together. "You still have flour on your face."

"I will clean it off." Outside, perhaps, after I had the chance to gather my belongings . . . if I could bring myself to leave her.

She looked at the soup-encrusted pot and the smattering of other dishes waiting to be cleaned. "Aye, once you've cleared this mess."

"Of course, Cook." It was to be expected. Cleaning the dishes was hard, time-consuming, and the least favorite of all my duties. My finer upbringing displayed itself most egregiously in my incompetent scrubbing of pots.

Cook left me to tend to the dirty dishes while she sipped her tea at the long table, then took herself off to bed. She walked with the slow gait of a woman who had been too much on her feet for far too many years.

The meal upstairs had long since ended and I was alone now —the only time I was able to completely relax, despite the mountain of dirty dishes looming before me. Mr. and Mrs. Fuller never required anything after dinner, and their meals—for a genteel family—were blessedly without fanfare. That had the potential to change if Benedict intended to remain for long. In my fortnight of employment here, I'd yet to work a dinner where the Fullers had anyone to dine—until tonight.

I looked to the ceiling and scowled.

Why *him* of all people? Why did Benedict Blockhead Bradwell have to ride past the garden the precise moment I was in it? I could not appreciate fate's intervention here. But stranger still was the man's stubborn insistence on bringing me home with him. Despite his mother, Lady Edith, taking me in and giving me a home when I had first returned to England, she had no legal obligation to me. When my mother died one year after my father's death, I was sent immediately to my uncle, who had turned me around and sent me to my godmother's house— Lady Edith. She'd taken me in and given me a family and a home, but she had no responsibility for me. No, the only person with any claim on me was my legal guardian, Uncle Northcott, who hardly cared where I was or how I was managing. I was alone in the world, making my own way in the manner I wanted to.

I shoved a bowl into the basin with too much zeal, and sudsy water splashed over my face. It dripped from my cheeks onto my apron in globs, the water mixing with the residual flour on my skin and forming a soapy paste. The dark windows and quiet kitchen proved the late hour, and I was grateful not to have an audience. Footmen had already come and gone, delivering the meal's dirtied dishes and taking themselves off to bed.

I filled a fresh bowl of water from the pump and dipped a clean rag in it, meticulously working to scrub off the pasty goop. What was I doing here? Whom was I trying to fool? I wasn't cut out for kitchen work. A proper genteel husband was not an option for me, and a decent husband—perhaps a farmer or a shop owner—would never be obtained in the belly of the Fullers' house.

A shadow darkened my peripheral vision. Benedict leaned lazily against the wall, and my inner defenses immediately rose, as if my body itself was preparing for the impending battle.

My shoulders tightened, and I slipped into an awful rendition of a low-born accent. "You should not be down here, sir. If you have a request from the kitchen, you ought to ring the bell."

"It would appear strange if I rang for help and requested that the kitchen maid be brought to me, would it not?"

I sent him a withering glare. "It would hardly matter, for I would never come to you."

"You would deny a guest in your master's house? Is it not a servant's objective to *serve*?"

I swallowed the disgust rising in my chest. And to think at one point I'd actually had something of a *tendre* for this man. Repulsive. "What do you need, Benedict?"

Surprise passed over his face, followed swiftly by relief. "We're to drop the facade, then?"

"It is obvious that you know who I am. I've gone to great lengths to hide, so it feels a rather cruel trick of fate that you've stumbled upon me. What is less obvious is why you remain. Except I realize how much you take delight in vexing me." I dropped my voice. "Never mind. Perhaps your reasons for not leaving me in peace are clear, after all."

He straightened, ignoring my quip. "I did not stumble upon you, Thea. Or, rather, I *did*, but only after searching all over the blasted countryside. My search led me to Brumley nearly a week ago, but finding you was another matter."

He'd been *searching* for me? That could not be true.

I returned my attention to scrubbing the dishes. I needed to continue working or I would be in the kitchen all night. "You expect me to believe that you have put forth effort to find *me*?"

"It is the truth. Though you needn't be so suspicious. I did not do so out of the goodness of my heart."

"Well, of course not. You would need to possess one of those first."

Benedict shook his head and rubbed a palm over his face. "I deserved that. You must know I regretted my harsh words from the garden as soon as they left my lips. I have been searching for you for months, following all manner of tips from your friends and acquaintances that led to dead ends, and I have been ready to give up."

Guilt slithered into my stomach and coiled, tightening it, and I bent my focus to scrubbing a particularly crusty soup tureen. In all honesty, I had not realized anyone would care about my absence enough to require such searching. Anyone except Lord Claverley, of course.

I stilled, looking up into Benedict's blue eyes. "Who sent you?" If he mentioned his cousin by name, I would be sorely tempted to splash this soapy water on him.

"No one."

"But you said—"

His blue eyes focused on me, though he seemed to deliberately remain casual in his bearing. "I did not look for you out of the goodness of my heart, but no one sent me. My mother has been worrying herself ill since we received word from Mrs. Moulton that you left her school. Mother did not understand why you couldn't seek the refuge you needed with her, and though she is too well-mannered to say so aloud, I'm certain she blames me for it."

If that was true, Lady Edith would not be entirely wrong. But that was not the whole of it. I cleared my throat. "In that case, your motives were far more selfish than you let on. As usual."

"Finding you in order to please my mother?"

"Finding me to appease your guilt."

He leaned against the counter beside me, folding his arms over his chest. His forehead puckered. "I suppose you are not wrong, though I would like to think my ceaseless hunting has been more altruistic than self-serving. I cannot deny that my guilt propelled me into action."

This side of Benedict was much harder to remain angry with. The seldom seen moments he lowered his sword and was willing to partake in rational conversation were the only times I did not wish to stomp on his foot and shout my frustration.

Yes, it was a childish response. We'd met as veritable children and I do not believe our relationship matured much beyond it.

"Will you return to Chelton with me?" he asked. "My mother would be happy to see you. James has married now, so there is another young woman in residence. You would like her."

The picture he painted was enticing beyond all measure. My hands ached from the relentless scrubbing of dishes and hot water and kneading dough and working in the kitchen garden and all the other tasks required of me. Exhaustion slipped through my shoulders, bending them forward in defeat. It was an impossible situation. If I returned to Chelton, I would be delivered to Lord Claverley, and *that* was out of the question.

"I cannot leave. I have a position here and people are depending on me."

"Under a false name," he said. "Surely they could never trace you back to Chelton."

"That is unlikely, yes, but it would not be right to leave them without notice." I cleared my throat. "Which matters little, anyway. I do not intend to leave. I am content here."

He scoffed.

"I *am*," I insisted. "It is good work. I remain in the kitchen mostly, so no one in the house truly knows me, and I am . . ."

"Yes?"

I pried the word loose, and it ripped from me, like a bird set free. "Safe. I feel safe here."

"Gads, Thea. You would be safe at Chelton. It is nearly a fortress."

I shook my head. I could not explain to him my numerous reasons for finding safety in a Leicestershire kitchen, for he would not understand any of them. Least of all the way Lord Claverley's pudgy fingers had run down the ribbon of my dress and made my chest run cold during my final dinner at Chelton, before I'd gone off to school. That disturbing experience had occurred in the drawing room, surrounded by other people. How would the earl behave in the privacy of his own home, without company? I knew how men of his ilk acted. I'd watched my father act in much the same way, and his friends were no different.

I wanted a husband. A *humble* husband. Those were not found in London's ballrooms or Lord Claverley's dining room. I was grateful for Lady Edith's efforts, even when she had gone to the trouble of arranging for Lord and Lady Claverley to chaperone me during the Season. However, I could never accept that generosity, not when it would lead to a life in shackles.

"It is not for you to understand, Benedict," I said at length.

"That is abundantly clear."

"Then you will keep my secret? You will not tell anyone of my location?"

He moved to argue. "But—"

"You may tell Lady Edith I am safe and content. I had hoped my letter to Mrs. Moulton would do that. I would like for her to be at ease."

His face tightened. "That is not enough. She will not be happy until she has seen with her own eyes that you are whole and unhurt. Did you know she sent for Mrs. Moulton and had her brought to Chelton so she could question the woman in person?"

I gasped slightly. That seemed excessive . . . except that Lady Edith could not travel by carriage without growing grossly ill. It was a malady that affected her greatly. I could understand how the better option for Lady Edith was to send for my headmistress, though I found that to be unnecessary and largely excessive.

"I left a note so no one would worry."

Benedict's lips turned into a wry smile. "Perhaps the vagueness of your note only made them worry more."

I leaned forward, resting my elbows on the edge of the worktable. I'd made a mess of things. How was I to fix this? Of all people, I'd never wished to hurt Lady Edith.

I looked at Benedict. "You believe she will be satisfied if she sees me in the flesh and can discern for herself I am well?"

He straightened. "I do."

"If I come with you, I will lose my position."

"You will not need one if you come with me."

I shook my head, standing tall and holding his blue demon eyes—handsome but dangerous. "I might consider a journey to Chelton to ease your mother's worry, but I do not intend to remain there."

His expression hardened. "Why must everything be so difficult with you?"

"Difficult with *me*? Why must you fight me at every turn?"

Benedict shifted toward me, his hand clutching the countertop, his fiery gaze fastened on me. I faced him as well, my soapy hand holding the bowl over the basin for cleaning, my other dripping water on the floor. Our chests heaved in time, and I wondered at the sanity of agreeing to travel *anywhere* with this man.

He spoke as though his words were forced from a tense jaw. "If I wait for you to work out your notice, will you come with me to Chelton and speak to my mother? No one will require that you remain there forever, but surely you would be open to the prospect of staying under her care."

Under her care? Or that of Benedict's blasted lech of a cousin, Lord Claverley? I drew in a breath and nodded. "I can agree to that."

His shoulders visibly deflated. "Good."

"I will come with you," I said, "on one condition."

CHAPTER 3
BENEDICT

I should have known Thea would never make anything so easy as to simply agree and leave it at that. I clenched my jaw and commanded my patience to hold, stretched and thin as it was. Thea squared her shoulders, looking up at me with her round, blue eyes, as though she was just as tall and mighty as I, instead of a wisp of a thing I could easily throw over my shoulder and carry from this room if I chose to.

The mental image that provided was entertaining, and I was certain if I pursued that particular method for returning Thea to my mother, I would have the bruises and scratches to prove her feisty temperament. Convincing her to come on her own would be much better for the both of us. I returned my focus to the task at hand.

Thea's knuckles appeared angrily red, and the perimeter of her thin face was still covered in flour. She looked as though she'd missed a few meals, the shadows beneath her eyes evidence of her lessened sleep. I wanted to dip her rag and wipe the remainder of the white powder from her temples and chin, but she would undoubtedly interpret my actions to somehow mean I had ill intentions of some sort. She was purely incapable of seeing any goodness in me. Instead of allowing that to sting, however, I fortified the wall around my heart.

If Thea was supplying conditions, that meant she was willing to negotiate. I was halfway to reaching my goal.

"What condition is that?" I asked.

"I refuse to go to Lord Claverley's house."

An odd request. "He and his wife are meant to chaperone you for the Season."

"Which I have mentioned time and again I have no desire for. I will not return to Chelton if your mother intends to send me straight to Lord Claverley."

Did I have the authority to promise such a thing? I was the youngest of three sons, the man with the least amount of authority in my house. My mother, Lady Edith, had run our family with precision and total power since my father died, and she was not to be argued with. It was easy to allow her to rule our lives, though, since she seemed to be correct most of the time in her estimations.

After more than a month of searching for Thea, I was willing to promise nearly anything to make her agree to come with me. Her face was too thin, her eyes too tired, and despite her ability to crawl under my skin, I felt she needed rest and regular meals above all else—and soon. "I will do whatever is in my power to make that so."

"No," she said calmly. So calmly, in fact, that my hackles rose. "That is not good enough. You must vow to me that I will not be forced to leave Chelton, and neither will I be forced to remain."

She sought independence? Did she not realize she already possessed it? There was a reason I had not shown up to the Fullers' house this evening with a constable to force her to comply. She had to come of her own volition. I gentled my voice. "You are twenty years old, Thea. You've nearly reached your majority. Does anyone have it within their power to force you to do anything?"

Her round eyes widened, giving her the appearance of a frightened porcelain doll. Had she not considered that point before? It was the very reason she was able to leave school and find employment, and we could do nothing legally to stop her. The only man who held such power over Thea was not in the least inclined to use it. Her uncle hardly cared what she did or where she went, and his power would abate on Thea's twenty-first birthday.

When her expression hardened, I longed for the Thea of before. Before she had gone to school and I to Cambridge. The girl who laughed easily, not the woman who worried over her future. She'd never laughed much with *me*, of course. But that did not stop me from hearing the melodic sound in the halls and corridors of Chelton often, then missing it once it went away.

I wanted to know what had happened, to understand the reasons for this change in her demeanor. Her flour-crusted hairline and raw, dried knuckles were a testament of how deeply she disdained the future that Mother had shaped for her. "Is it really so distasteful for you to attend the Season?"

"The Season? No, it's not distasteful. I enjoy dancing and wearing lovely gowns. Being under Lord Claverley's thumb, however? Yes. That truly is so distasteful."

Something had happened to her. I had speculated on it before, but I knew it now. "What did he do to you?"

"Nothing."

"Thea—"

"Truly, nothing." She shook her head, returning her attention to the dirty soup bowl. I could see how she had to shift her focus when she was hiding something. "I dislike the man. That is all. I am shallow and rude."

Not only was she hiding something, but she was protecting Claverley somehow as well by keeping this secret. Knowing

Thea, she had her reasons, however misguided they were. "You mustn't tell me, then, unless you choose to."

She looked up again, and I fought the urge to wipe her cheek clean where she'd missed a glob of something. "Then we have a deal?"

Never in my life would I have thought I would be in the kitchen of a great country house in Leicestershire, striking a deal with Thea Northcott where I would vow to protect her. She had always seemed the sort capable of protecting herself. But she was wise to force me to her side now, for Mother wanted nothing more than to secure a decent match for Thea, and Lord Claverley was her ticket to do so.

"Yes, we have a deal." I hoped my mother would not be too angry with me.

"Swear it," she said.

I gave an exasperated sigh. "Very well. I swear, Thea, that if you come with me to Chelton, I will make certain you are removed from the agreement regarding Lord Claverley and not required to go to his house in Cumberland, nor his house in London."

"Thank you." She turned her attention away again, her hands red from the heat of the water and the acidity of the soap.

I'd never washed dishes before, but I was tempted to offer my assistance now.

"I'll need time to work out my notice," she said, focusing on her task. "A week, or perhaps a fortnight. It's only fair."

Notice? Yes, of course. Ridiculous as this position was, she could not leave them without help, as she had said. "Then I will leave and return for you in a fortnight. I will write to my mother and tell her when to expect us so she can cease worrying."

Thea nodded softly, but I could see the defeat in her down-turned lips, and it did not give me the satisfaction I'd assumed it would.

She sighed. "You ought to leave before anyone else comes through here. Mr. Fuller's valet has yet to come down."

"Too right you are." I moved to walk away, but Thea stopped me at the bottom of the servants' stairs, calling my name.

"Yes?" I asked.

"You mentioned you will return for me when it is time to go to Chelton. Will you not remain here for the fortnight?"

I couldn't help the smile that flickered on my lips, despite how I tried to suppress it. I knew the Fuller family in passing after having met them in the vicar's house in Brumley a few days ago, which was nothing short of luck. Finagling an invitation to dine had been easy enough after mentioning my shared passion for hunting to Mr. Fuller this afternoon when I had called on him, and he had regaled me with tales of his own. Then, of course, pretending to drink enough during dinner to deem me unfit for riding had done the trick to secure my invitation to remain overnight. But I would not allow Thea to learn how hard I was forced to work for the opportunity to speak to her this openly.

As kind as Mr. and Mrs. Fuller had been, I could not stretch my stay into a week, let alone a fortnight.

None of those explanations would leave my lips. I settled for, "I have other matters to attend to." Like obtaining a carriage and a chaperone to ride the length of the journey from here to Cumberland. "If you have need of me earlier than a fortnight, you may send a note to the Horse and Crown. I will check periodically for any letters."

She nodded.

I left her behind with a basin full of dishes—some I had dirtied myself during dinner—and a pull in my gut to return to Thea's side and ease her burden. Whatever that impulse was, I needed to squash the desire forthwith. It was not something I was used to feeling around Thea, and I would do good to remember that.

She was a devil of a woman sometimes.

A smile curved my lips as I made my way up to my bedchamber. Relief flowed through me like the current of a swift river, warming and soothing my tired body. I'd found her at last.

I remained in Brumley for the following week. Purchasing a carriage proved difficult, but I found a woman in Upper Trumby who was willing to lend me one, provided I had it returned and paid her for the use. She offered her older son to drive it for me for an additional fee, and while the price was exorbitant, it seemed worth the expense.

It would aid me in my attempt to return Thea to Chelton without inciting any rumors, as well. The last thing I needed was to create a situation that would force me to honor Thea's reputation and offer myself up in matrimony. That may have worked well for my older brother, James, and his wife Felicity, but it would never be a favorable option where Thea was concerned. We were more likely to argue one another into the ground before we found an accord in marriage.

The sun highlighted the drooping leaves and changing of the seasons as autumn blended into winter. I left my horse at the livery on High Street and walked down to the Horse and Crown to request any mail that might be waiting for me. I'd spent the last week at various inns in the surrounding towns, hoping one of them would have the carriage I sought, before finding luck in Upper Trumby. Now I needed to find a way to pass another week before Thea would be able to leave.

"Any post for Benedict Bradwell?" I asked the innkeeper, removing my dusty hat and hitting it against my thigh.

"Yes, sir." He left, and I found myself a seat in the taproom.

The innkeeper returned and dropped a letter on the table. "Can I do anything else for you?"

"A meal, please. Anything hearty will do."

"Right away." The portly man left to retrieve my early dinner.

I turned my attention to the letter he set on the table. Despite Thea's easy shift into the appearance of a kitchen maid —complete with floury face and tired eyes—she did not so easily pass as a low-class woman, and I wondered at the intelligence of her employer for not being more suspicious of her. Her walk was too graceful, her neck straight and not stooped in the least, as it should be from years of manual work. Her voice, though she had added some gravelly affect to it, was properly trained in a high-class tongue, a lilt to it that I could only imagine came from her time living in Sweden, or possibly from Vienna after that.

But above all, the loopy, elegant script she'd written my name in possessed all the class and delicacy of a woman of esteem. She could not write to me in this manner and expect anyone to believe that she was a simply-born miss.

The paper was thin and the pencil she wrote with dull, but her words flowed across the page prettily, despite those obstructions.

B.B.—

Notice has been fulfilled. Position has been replaced. I am prepared to leave Monday at the earliest.

—D.N.

While I understood and appreciated her attempts at anonymity, the date she wrote was alarming. It was Wednesday now. Had she been ready to leave two days ago?

The innkeeper set a bowl of steaming stew before me with a chunk of bread and slices of ham and cheese.

"Do you recall when this letter was left for me?" I asked.

He scrunched up his nose and looked to the door as if it held the answers. "Four days ago? Maybe five."

Much earlier than either of us had expected. Perhaps Thea

had not been as difficult to replace as she'd thought. "Thank you."

He left me to eat, and I tried to consume my fill, but I found my nerves warring with my appetite. It wasn't customary to allow a servant to remain when they were no longer employed. I had to hope the Fuller family was different in this regard, or that Thea had enough funds to provide lodging for herself for a few days.

I tossed coins on the table beside the half-eaten meal and strode from the inn.

It took a quarter hour to retrieve my horse and ride out to the Fuller residence. A gentleman knocking on the kitchen door again would prove odd, but what other choice did I have? I strode across the garden, rapped my knuckles on the door, and pulled my hat low over my eyes in case one of the footmen who served me dinner last week or the butler happened to be nearby.

The craggy cook opened the door, scowling at me, with deep set grooves lining her forehead and fanning from her down-turned mouth. "I told you last time, there isn't nobody here by the name of—"

"I hoped to speak to Mary."

"She doesn't work here anymore."

My heart swooped. Had she given me the slip, or merely been told to leave? Surely her note was enough proof that she intended to go with me to Chelton.

She'd promised.

"Where can I find her?"

The cook's face crumpled further. "You can't." She slammed the door, and I bit back a curse. I yanked off my hat and turned away, running a hand through my wild curls. I was in sore need of a haircut, and my hair tangled on my fingers, yanking hard. I winced and slammed the hat back on my head.

"Where the devil are you, Thea?"

"You mean Mary?" a small voice asked.

I spun to face a waif of a girl, hardly out of the schoolroom. She probably had yet to *enter* a schoolroom at all, if I had my guess. She slipped from the kitchen quietly and closed the door behind her.

"Yes. I meant Mary. She is my friend, and I need to find her."

"She's not here," the girl said apologetically. "They made her leave when I arrived. Can't pay two kitchen maids."

"Understandable," I said, hoping to keep her talking. "Where can I find Mary now?"

"Are you her brother?"

Brother? Far from it. But something compelled me to tell this chit that I was. It was clever of Thea to give me such a title so she might avoid any rumors. "Yes, I am her brother."

"She worried you would come for her after she was gone, so she gave me this to give to you." The girl pulled a paper from her apron pocket and handed it to me. It was wet, the ink likely running. I unfolded it, grateful to find it written in pencil.

Brumley Livery.

The livery? Gads. She was bound to make me run all over the county. I looked up, catching the child's hopeful look. I fished a coin from my pocket and placed it in her grubby hand. "Thank you. You've done both Mary and me a great service."

She beamed.

Now to find the dratted waif I'd come here for.

CHAPTER 4

THEA

Sleeping on a bed of straw was not nearly as comfortable as goats and cows made it look. By my second night on the ground in the Brumley livery, I was sore and achy in places I did not realize a body could ache. I was much too dirty to enter the Horse and Crown in search of Benedict, and I did not have enough funds to sleep or eat there.

I had not considered when I went into hiding that I would also be forfeiting my quarterly allowance, but I could not retrieve the money without informing my uncle or his solicitor of my whereabouts. Until Benedict had promised to keep me away from Lord Claverley, I was not willing to risk returning for anything.

Bless little Pippa and her sweet willingness to aid me. The new kitchen maid did not know me, but still she was willing to help. Without her supply of bread and extra vegetables from the Fullers' garden, I would be half-starved by now.

I passed the day yesterday at the stream in the woods behind the livery, watching for Benedict's return, but during the nights I crept inside the warm building to sleep in safety, and I was certain I looked a mess. Life as the daughter of an English ambassador had given me a certain toughness one usually acquired in a less luxurious lifestyle, or from the rigors of living and traveling abroad. While sleeping on a bed of straw was not my first choice, it was far better than the hammock I'd been forced to use in the captain's quarters during my lonely return from Sweden. The captain's wife had tried to make me comfortable, but there was only so much that could be done on a full ship.

I wasn't sure how long I could sleep among the horses before being discovered, either. My fitful sleep had hardly been restful, needless to say.

The clopping of hooves drew my attention to the lane, and I jumped to my feet to see if I could discern the identity of the rider through the trees. Benedict's familiar profile came into view, his posture tall and straight, his command on the horse unmistakable.

I never thought I would be glad to see him, but here we were.

My small valise was not too far away, tucked beneath a half-naked bush on the bank of the small stream. I retrieved it and set forth toward the livery. By the time I reached the door, I reminded myself to stand tall. I was not sneaking this time.

Benedict swung his leg over his horse outside the door and jumped to the ground. I called to him, and he looked up. Relief fell over his face when he spotted me, and my stomach did an odd flip.

He led his horse in my direction. "I wondered if I would find you again."

I stepped back around the side of the building and waited in the shade, Benedict following. "Pippa gave you the note?" I asked.

"The kitchen maid? Yes. I paid her for the trouble."

My chest gave a warm squeeze, and I scolded it. *Not now,*

please. It would not do to humanize the flirt. "Are you prepared to leave?" I asked.

"Nearly. I need to retrieve the carriage and inform our driver that we are ready, which will take a little time." He ran a hand over his jaw, the day's stubble likely bristling against his palm. "I can come for you in the morning."

In the *morning*? I faced another night on the straw-covered, mucky floor?

My nose wrinkled of its own volition. "I will not be able to . . . that is . . ." He watched me expectantly, but it was difficult for me to admit any vulnerabilities to the man. Depending on others did not come easily to me, and neither did asking for help. But in this case, I could not bear to sleep in the stables again. I squared my shoulders. "I do not have a place to sleep tonight."

His eyebrows lifted. "Where did you sleep last night?"

"That is certainly none of your concern." I would rather lie in the ice-cold stream and let it freeze me slowly than admit to Benedict that I slept among the horses and was forced to hide from the man who worked in the livery—*twice.* The rodents squeaking through the night had never made a visual appearance, but it was only a matter of time.

Benedict clenched his jaw. Voices within the livery drew our attention, and I moved further behind the building, Benedict following me with his horse in tow. He stopped far closer to me than he had been a moment before and his familiar spicy scent wafted on the breeze. For such a difficult man, he smelled divine. I knew I looked a mess. I only hoped I didn't smell like horses, too.

He lowered his voice. "Where did you plan to sleep tonight?"

"In the carriage set for Chelton, to be honest."

"That will not work."

"What do you propose we do? It was you who dragged me from my warm bed in the Fullers' house. I had food and a blanket there, though I do not think one could reasonably call the lumpy thing they provided a mattress."

He glanced away, then back to me. "I have an idea, but you will not like it."

"Naturally."

Benedict's mouth bent down in a frown. "Remember that it is me doing you a favor."

"Remember that you begged me to come with you."

We were at odds, and I wasn't sure how we were going to come to an accord on this. I clenched my hands into fists behind me to release some of my pent-up frustration and turned a bland smile on him. "What idea did you have, Benedict?"

"I have been able to find a carriage and a man to drive it for us, but no chaperone has made herself available. I admit that my questioning has been vague, but it is a delicate matter and I'm not sure how women typically go about this, so I am not in a position to easily find one."

"Mrs. Fuller would not do?"

He looked away before settling his deep blue gaze back on me. "No. She would not have been a good option."

"Then what do you propose? We cannot ride alone in a carriage together, not if we plan to keep our reputations intact. We'll need to stop at inns to eat and change the horses, and I do not wish to be taken as a hussy."

The silence sat between us for a few beats, broken only by the clopping of hooves on High Street and the birds calling to each other in the trees behind us.

Benedict's blue gaze pierced me, and he drew in a breath before speaking. "You trust me, do you not?"

"That would depend on your definition of the word *trust*."

He sighed. "That I will not hurt you. That you are safe in my company."

"Of course you will not hurt me." That had never been in question. Though Benedict and I never got along well, I knew he was not a bad man—not where it counted. He and Lord Claverley were different sorts entirely.

"Then consider my plan before you dash it away, yes?" he asked.

"I will."

Benedict paused, then spoke carefully. "You can dress as a servant for the duration of our trip home . . . as *my* servant. No one will question my traveling alone with a servant. In fact, no one would look twice at you."

"Even a servant would wear a dress. What reason do you have to travel alone with a maid?"

"None, of course." He smiled sheepishly. "But I hadn't meant for you to act in the capacity of my maid."

I looked at him in confusion. If he was about to imply that I would play the role of his mistress, he would be sorely disappointed.

"I meant for you"—he swallowed hard—"to act as my servant boy."

It took a moment for the words to form and develop meaning in my head. Benedict wished to cross nearly half of England in a carriage alone with me dressed as a servant boy. It was true that no one would look twice at me then, particularly not when Benedict was so tall and easily commanded the attention of anyone in the room. I would be his shadow, slipping slowly across the countryside in anonymity.

It was utterly ridiculous, but it could work. And it would mean not involving anyone else in our scheme, which would further protect our reputations. We only needed to fool strangers in inns and the man driving our carriage. If no one discovered our ruse, we would never be forced to face the consequences of ruined reputations from being alone together for such a length of time.

I hated to admit that he had come up with a good idea, but it was the truth.

"Fine, I'll do it."

His eyebrows rose. "That was easier than I thought."

"Anything that removes me from this place and deposits me at Chelton without anyone else the wiser about my whereabouts is an acceptable plan to me."

Benedict nodded. "I will take two rooms at the Horse and Crown tonight, and we will set off in the morning. I've taken the liberty of obtaining a set of clothes for you in case you agreed to my plan."

"Does this room at the Horse and Crown include dinner?"

"Yes."

I sighed in relief. It had been a few days since I'd eaten a hot meal, and I was ravenous. Pippa's bread and vegetables, as grateful as I'd been for her charity, were only just enough to sustain a body.

"Shall we, then?" I asked, eager to eat.

He grimaced. "I'd hoped we could wait until dark. I believe it would be easier to sneak you into the room as a woman at night—"

"And then out the following morning as a boy." I nodded. I was impressed with how meticulously he'd thought this through. "We've an hour or so yet before the sun sets. I'll wait near the stream. Come for me when you're ready."

Benedict nodded once in agreement. "I will return soon."

The room at the Horse and Crown wasn't much better than any of the servants' quarters I'd slept in over the previous months since leaving Mrs. Moulton's school, but there was something about the safety of the situation that made me sleep deeper than I'd expected—straw mattress and all. Washing the filth from my body and sliding under the thin blanket had been exactly what

I'd needed to feel like a person again and not a disheveled urchin.

Benedict gave me the clothing he'd procured when he first showed me to the room last night. I stood in the faint glow of my one candle in the darkened early hours of the autumn morning and stared at myself in the small looking glass nailed to the wall. Despite having a maid to attend to me for most of my life, I'd spent the last few years alone, and thus had grown adept at fashioning my own hair. If my maid had opted to travel to England with me when I had left Sweden after my mother died, I would not have gained this skill, but she'd chosen to remain there, and I was glad of the talent I now possessed.

The breeches fit well, if a little too snug, and the shoes and stockings were just a smidge too big, but for the most part, the outfit was comfortable enough. I wrapped a length of linen around my chest in lieu of stays—hoping it would provide a flatter effect—and the shirt Benedict provided was large and loose enough to hide any hint of my feminine curves. If not for my long hair, I think I very much resembled a young lad in the service of his esteemed gentleman.

If only I esteemed Benedict, then I would completely fit the part.

I touched the ring tied to a string around my neck, safely tucked beneath my shirt. It was my mother's and much too flashy to be worn when playing such a role, but neither could I bear to be parted from it. I was her spitting image, but if I kept my voice silent and my face hidden, no one who knew my mother would recognize her in me. She was much too glamorous to be confused with a servant boy.

A soft knock rapped on my door, and I moved quietly near it.

"Thea?" Benedict's voice, familiar and low, was a comfort I had not expected until it reached my ears. I opened the door and ushered him inside quickly. The candle light washed over his plain traveling clothes, his black coat long and thick, his curly hair perfectly mussed—just chaotic enough to give me the desire to straighten it for him.

He stepped back and appraised me slightly.

"We could fool everyone, I think." I lifted a lock of my long dark hair. It trailed over my shoulders and down my back, loose and freshly combed. "If not for this. Do not ask me to cut it, for I won't."

Something flickered in his eyes, evident in the warm light from the candles, but was gone as quickly as it had appeared. "I don't wish for you to cut your hair. I thought you could wear a cap."

"Oh."

"Was it not with your things?"

I went back to the chest set against the window and looked about. The room was so dim I hadn't noticed the dark lump of fabric fall to the floor. I lifted it and grinned. The small, brown wool cap was perfect.

"Can you fasten your hair up?" he asked, suddenly dubious as his gaze trailed the length of my dark locks.

"Yes." I moved to the looking glass and plaited my hair, then coiled it around the crown of my head and pinned it in place. It was as flat as I could make it. I secured the cap over my curl of braid and turned to Benedict with my hands on my hips. "Well, what do you think?"

He was quiet for a moment, sweeping his gaze over me in unabashed perusal. "Perfect." He cleared his throat and swirled his fingers in my direction. "Except for the hands."

"What is wrong with my hands?" They were certainly possessed of enough calluses and cuts to pass as a servant's.

"That position is not servile in the least. No one will believe you to be in my employ if you look so contrary. You oughtn't rest your hands on your hips."

I dropped them to my sides. "Better?"

"Not quite." He circled me slowly, rubbing his fingers pensively along his jaw. "Perhaps behind you?"

I clasped them lightly behind me and bent my head the most delicate way I could.

"That is much better." He paused. "You should stand this way more often. It is pleasantly peaceful."

My hands found their way to my hips once more, and I scowled at him.

Benedict ignored my petulance. "You'll carry your own valise and another of my bags if you can manage. I know you won't like it, but do try to remember you are my servant until we reach Chelton. It will protect both of our reputations."

"So long as you do not take advantage of the situation, I will play my part."

His eyes narrowed. "Try to remember you are male."

"I will play my part," I repeated in a decidedly lower tone.

Benedict turned away, but not before I saw the hint of a smile touch his lips.

Benedict Bradwell found *something I said* funny? Apparently I was still dreaming. Or having a nightmare, rather.

He helped me gather my things, then held my bag toward me. I took it from him and followed him meekly from the room and outside to the awaiting carriage. A man sat atop the driver's perch in a long, dark coat, not much older than me if I had my guess.

Benedict offered me a hand to assist me into the carriage, then immediately stole it away again, as though remembering that I was a servant and not a lady.

I pressed my lips together. If he so easily forgot I was meant to be a boy, was it obvious I was in costume and acting a part? I climbed inside and settled in my seat, waiting for Benedict to join me after speaking to the coachman. He sat across from me and closed the door, then rapped his knuckles on the ceiling and we took off.

"We have four travel days ahead of us. Three, perhaps, if the roads are smooth enough and the horses frequently changed."

I nodded and looked out the window. The sky was still dark, and silence enveloped us. I rocked along with the motion of the carriage and sighed. This was bound to be a long journey. Four days alone with a man who could not abide my company. Four days to pass in his scrutiny and bake in unpleasantly thick silence. My skin prickled with the awareness of eyes upon me, and I lifted my gaze to find Benedict watching me with a dark, troubled look, his face cast in shadows from the early morning dimness.

"What sort of misdeed have you done to deserve such a punishment, Benedict?" I asked, my voice a quiet caress in the sharp silence.

His thick eyebrows knit together. "What punishment is that?"

"To be forced into a carriage with no company but me for the next few days. Surely some misdeed of yours has led to this unsavory point."

"Do not worry on my account, Thea. I'm certain my reward in heaven is growing by the minute."

"Hmm."

"You can practice calling me St. Benedict now. For I'm certain my sainthood is coming."

"Blasphemy."

"Just rewards, rather," he muttered.

For putting up with me. I could not fault his teasing, not when I had been the one to incite it.

Silence weighed on us like a thick quilt until Benedict spoke again. "Most people enjoy my company. Perhaps I am not the issue here."

My chest constricted. He could not know his words touched a tender place in my fears. I shoved them down, not allowing my mind to traverse the path toward misery and unpleasant memories. It would take a magnitude of patience on both of our ends to reach Chelton without accruing a great deal of battle scars, but I was determined, after Benedict's comment, to prove myself. I was not *solely* to blame for our discord.

The little wriggle in the back of my mind, that there might be some truth to his words, that my inflammatory attitude was at fault, gave me pause, but I shoved the thought away and squared my shoulders. By the time we reached Chelton, he would admit his role in our tumultuous relationship. I might be the servant, but in the cause for why we did not get along, he would submit to me.

CHAPTER 5
BENEDICT

It was quickly becoming clear over the course of the day that Charlie Drool, the man I had hired from Upper Trumby, was not a skilled driver, but he *could* drive fast. If given the choice again, I would have hired him to convey us to Chelton, merely because he cut down our time on the road by a decent margin, even if he sent us jolting from one side of the carriage to the other from time to time. Just after nightfall, we reached the inn where we intended to rest the horses and stay the night. Charlie managed the conveyance and found his own lodgings while I went inside and ordered Thea and me two rooms.

"We only have the one," the woman said from behind the counter. She shrugged. "Sorry, I am. I'd give you two rooms if I had them."

Thea stood beside me, her gaze directed at the floor so the woman would only see the top of her cap. It was wise of her to assume that pose, and I was impressed by her quiet deference. But when the woman explained that her inn was full except for the one room, I'd sensed Thea tense, her shoulders betraying her discomfort.

We'd have to share a room. It appeared that hard wooden

planks and a thin blanket were on the menu for my sleeping arrangements tonight.

"We'll take it," I said. "And dinner, too. Do you have a private parlor available?"

"Yes, sir. Straight through that door there." She pointed to the door with her drying towel, then tossed it on the table. "I'll fetch your dinner straight away."

"For my servant, as well," I requested.

She bustled away and a sudden, sharp pain radiated through my ankle.

"Servants!" Thea whispered.

"What?" Had she *kicked* me? I had asked for her blasted dinner, too. My ankle pulsed from the abuse.

"The servants' quarters," Thea said through her teeth, her eyes wide.

Oh. I tried to get the attention of the innkeeper. "Madam?"

She turned.

"Do you have . . . um . . . a place for my boy in your servant's quarters?"

The woman scrunched up her nose, her gaze flicking to Thea and away again. "I could throw him in with Billy, I s'pose, for a fee."

Neither of us had thought this through, and I would not permit anyone to throw Thea into any room with a man. Not unless the man was me.

I was the only man in this inn I trusted not to hurt her.

Thea must have had the same thought. "Private room," she hissed.

I moved my foot away before it could be prodded again. "You do not have a private servant's room available?"

The woman laughed. "I don't know where you come from, sir, but here we make do with what we have."

"The one room will be fine," I said with a tight smile. "My servant and I can share."

Thea wasn't pleased. I could nearly feel the disappointment and irritation sloughing from her in waves. I waited until the woman was gone before speaking again. I leaned in and lowered my voice. "You are much safer with me than—"

"Quite," she said with a degree of skepticism.

My hackles rose from her cynical tone. I took a moment to gather my patience, careful to keep my voice low. "You do not believe you are safe in my care?"

"I know you would not let anything happen to me that might anger or sadden your mother," she said.

It was a rounded answer, as if she slipped about the edges of the truth but refused to jump into the meat of it. My pride stung that she would not have faith in my character, but the mere point that she trusted me—though it was through an extension of my mother's trust, of course—was enough. Our situation was far from ordinary, and the sooner I returned Thea to Chelton and gowns that did not define the shape of her legs like the breeches she now wore, the sooner we would both be able to cease being around one another and return to our blissfully separate lives.

"I will not harm you."

"Glad I am to hear it," she muttered.

"It is I who will be sleeping with one eye open tonight." I leaned down further and lowered my voice. "Do not think I've forgotten the tomatoes." Thea's round eyes widened and her cheeks formed spots of color. It was cruel of me to bring up the particular trick she had played so long ago, but the reference to our childish antics was sure to remind her of our shared history —both the good and bad. I turned for the private parlor and left her behind to receive our key and take the bags to the room.

The inn quieted down long after our dinner had come and gone, and I sat on a threadbare chair near the fireplace, the warmth of the flames making my cheeks hot. I would have backed farther away from the hearth, but from my current vantage point I could perfectly see Thea on her seat against the wall, her attention riveted by a small item in her hand that I had not yet been able to identify.

She was altogether ridiculous in how determined she was to prove herself better than me in every way. It was not a particular skill to sit quietly in a private parlor in a ramshackle inn, but it seemed she was willing herself to outlast me.

Or perhaps the both of us were of equal mind about the discomfort of sharing a bedroom and agreed that it should be put off as long as it was reasonable to do so.

I scrubbed a hand over my face, hoping to ease some of the exhaustion from my tight skin. This was silly. We were both tired, and we had multiple days on the road ahead of us. We should both be asleep already.

When I lowered my hand, Thea was watching me. She closed her fingers around the item in her hand. Blast. I wanted to know what it was.

"If you are worried I'll hide tomatoes in your bed, you needn't fear," she said quietly. "We shan't be here long enough for them to rot."

"In that case, I'm off to sleep."

She rose in quiet acceptance, joining me as we made our way toward the door. "Your carriage, however, is another matter," she said when we moved into the corridor.

I gave a start, but she kept her head bent, walking behind me like an invisible servant boy ought to do. Surely she did not mean to hide tomatoes in the carriage. It did not belong to me, so I would not be the man suffering the stench of rot. She must have been joking.

I hazarded a glance at Thea over my shoulder, her small

frame and bent head much too submissive, irreconcilable with the person I knew her to be. When we reached the top of the stairs, she brandished the key she'd received from the innkeeper, then unlocked the door to let us inside.

The room was narrow and the bed surprisingly wide—likely meant to hold an entire family or more than one guest when the need arose. It certainly would not be holding more than one guest tonight. Our small bags were neatly lined against the wall, and I moved to mine to retrieve my tooth powder. I would have to sleep in my breeches tonight, an altogether uncomfortable prospect.

"There are additional blankets in the trunk," Thea said, her voice matter-of-factly. "Mrs. Heath told me so."

We both looked to the floor. There wasn't room enough for me to lie anywhere on it.

"I will sleep on the floor tonight," she said, taking me by surprise.

"No. I am more of a gentleman than to allow—"

"It is not a matter of you being a gentleman. It is a matter of practicality. The inn tomorrow will likely have more than one room available, and if it does not, we can pray for more available space on the floor."

I shook my head. "My mother would be disgusted to learn I allowed you to sleep on the floor."

"Your mother will be livid to learn that we traveled from Leicestershire to Cumberland without a proper chaperone. She will *never* learn that we also slept in the same room."

Thea was correct. It could never leave either of our lips. But still, the prospect of taking the enormous bed when she slept on the hard wooden planks did not settle comfortably in my chest. I was raised to be a gentleman. Despite my discord with Thea— and her current apparel—she was still a lady.

"If we push the bed up against the door, there will be room

enough," I said, analyzing the shape of the room and the space available to us. It would work, I thought.

Thea bent over the trunk, pulling a musty quilt from it and shaking it out. "I do not intend to sleep on the floor *every* night, Benedict, but I can be the one to begin."

"I don't like it."

She gave a frustrated huff. "Will you accept the situation if I vow to never speak a word of your ungentlemanly behavior tonight? Not only to others, but also to you. I will not tease you about it if it bothers you."

"That is not the point—"

"It is, though, is it not? I can appreciate your deeply ingrained sense of chivalry, but you must admit that practicality overrides it in this circumstance. Your pride requires that you insist on sleeping on the floor, not your sense of right over wrong." She removed her cap and set to unpinning her hair.

"My pride?" I scoffed, frustrated that she could not under-stand me, and doing my best to ignore the long hair she unrav-eled from its coil atop her head and fanned out in luscious waves. Perhaps it was more practical for Thea to sleep on the floor—she was small and could easily fit in the space—but it wasn't my *pride* pressing the issue. It was the discomfort that filled my body at the thought of taking the comfortable bed over the hard floor.

"Yes." She laid out a blanket on the floor and took a pillow from the bed to make a small sleeping nest. I watched her climb into it and pull a quilt over the top. "I am too tired to argue further, Ben. Do hurry and get into bed so we can blow out the candle, please."

"You are sleeping in your clothes?"

She opened her eyes, her hair fanned around her head, making her look like a dark-haired angel. "You likely wouldn't credit it, but this ensemble is one of the most comfortable things I've ever before worn. I could grow used to it."

"It will come in handy when you escape again," I said, moving to the washbasin to clean my teeth. "Perhaps your next position could be in the stables."

"Oh, I'd love that," she said dreamily.

It was one thing I remembered we had in common—an adoration for riding—which was not so uncommon a thing. The only woman of my acquaintance who did not love to ride was my sister-in-law, but that was not typical for gently bred young ladies.

I removed my coat and waistcoat, then worked on untying my cravat, laying each item over the trunk beneath the window. "It would certainly be better than a kitchen maid."

"That was not the only position I held," she said, surprising me. I knew of her original destination after she had left the school, but not where she spent her time between Gallingher and Brumley. More than that, though, I was surprised that she was forthcoming with any information at all.

"I wondered," I said, hoping she would tell me more. "My search originally took me to Gallingher Park, but Mrs. Parker had not been able to help me. She told me you were only at their home for a week."

"Indeed, though not as a guest."

My stomach dropped. "You were a kitchen maid for Mrs. Parker too?" She was a high enough society matron to fuel rumors, were she to learn of it.

"A governess." Thea's voice grew lazy, the slow words leaving her mouth and passing through syrup before reaching my ears. She was halfway asleep, if I had my guess. Warm light from the single candle flame flickered over her face, and in her state of near-sleep, she seemed so small and delicate, I had the unexplainable urge to protect her.

I shook the thought. Ridiculous. This was *Thea*, not a lady in need of rescuing.

And I was no rescuing knight in gleaming armor.

"You, a governess?" That was far better than a kitchen maid, or a maid of any sort, really.

Her lips turned up in a semblance of a smile, though she did not open her eyes. "It did not last."

"Shocking."

"To you, perhaps. Some people actually like me, Ben."

My heart did a strange pulse, and I blew out the candle to avoid looking at her further. No one else called me Ben outside of my family. No one. But somehow, when Thea did it, my body reacted without my mind's consent.

I liked it.

Shaking off the feeling, I pulled off my boots and slipped under the thin blanket. The room was dim and cold, hardly any starlight sneaking through the window to soften the darkness. The fire in the hearth had burned out and the coals were not throwing enough heat to warm us. I was extremely aware of the sound of Thea's breathing growing deep and even, and it was not until I was convinced she was asleep that I felt my body relax.

CHAPTER 6
THEA

I opened my eyes to a large hand dangling directly above my face. I'd always been quick to react, but I suppressed my initial shock and emitted nothing louder than a sharp inhale. Morning light slanted through the cloudy window panes and rested on Benedict's skin, and I took the moment to observe the bend of his fingers and the dark hair covering his knuckles while my heart returned to a normal rhythm. From his hand alone, he appeared strong, the fingers large and capable. Limp with sleep, they also appeared deceptively harmless.

This hand had hardly touched me, but it belonged to a man who was as careless with the female heart as he was with his handkerchiefs. Easily discarded and possessed of little worth.

When I arrived at Chelton as a lonely girl of almost sixteen, I'd been overcome by the enormity of the Bradwell residence. I'd lived a life of relative luxury as the daughter of an English ambassador living abroad, but the constant traveling and living in countries where I failed to speak the languages perfectly had resulted in a lonely existence, and a hole in my heart I'd been eager to fill. Lady Edith had been just as eager to fill it, and she presented me as a member of the family, a surrogate sister to the Bradwell brothers—or one brother in particular. With James a few years older and Henry off in the military, Benedict had been the one nearest my age and available to entertain me.

If only he'd gone to Eton as his brothers had, then I would not have been forced to put up with him. As it stood, he was at Chelton with his tutor until I went off to Mrs. Moulton's finishing school and him to university, and every moment we spent under the same roof was torment for the both of us.

I closed my eyes and pushed away the memory pecking at me like an angry bird. If I had not foolishly allowed my heart to become engaged, to believe the flirtations he spoke, it would not have hurt as deeply when I was forced to watch Benedict flirt with every other girl in the parish. The man was like every other gentleman of power and privilege—a cad.

In those early weeks at Chelton, Benedict ruined what could very well have been a good friendship between us by giving me reason to believe he might hold a *tendre* for me, then swiftly cutting me down. After my experiences in Sweden and Vienna, I was wary of gentlemen. My experience with Benedict was the final straw, and I vowed to never again be taken in by a handsome gentleman with a brilliant smile. It was the smile of a wolf, after all.

He stirred, as though he could feel the vitriol of my thoughts, and his hand dropped lower, nearer to my face. I sucked in a breath and pressed my head further back into the pillow, meeting with the hard surface of the floor. Benedict's fingers curled slightly, swinging from the movement, the backs of his knuckles grazing over my nose. I stared at them. It was too late to roll away from his touch without knocking into his hand, and I didn't want him to know he had me trapped. I could not cede anything to this man.

Quietly, I drew in a breath and let it out slowly, hoping the wind on his fingers would make them pull away. Benedict mumbled something incoherently and shifted, and I blew softly on his fingers again.

They dropped lower, resting against the side of my face, and I followed the trail of his arm, sprinkled with dark hair until it met with the billowy white shirt sleeve, until I reached the edge of his shoulder, which was leaning precariously over the side of the bed.

It was then I noticed the way the rest of his body lined the mattress. It slipped slowly over the edge, and it seemed as though I watched it happen from above and not while lying beneath the man on the floor. He fell over the side of the bed and landed hard on top of me with a heavy thud. The air knocked from my lungs, and I inhaled hard.

Every inch of Benedict Bradwell was lying on top of every inch of me, and I could feel the racing of his heart and the panic in his lungs as though they pulsed in time with my own.

"What in the—"

"You are on top of me," I said, struggling to breathe and ignore the warmth spreading over my skin. The pressure of his weight on me had a surprisingly comforting effect that I had to, at all costs, disregard.

Benedict blinked, his sleepy eyes hovering just above mine. He pushed up on his forearms, and I sucked in a deep breath once my lungs were no longer encumbered by his heavy body.

"Forgive me," he said softly, his gaze falling to my lips.

I pressed my hands against his chest and shoved, needing more space and clear air between us. He smelled faintly of both spice and tang, and I fought the curiosity bubbling to identify the smells further and give them a name, pushing against his sturdy chest. But the man didn't budge. He was constructed of a heavier substance than I'd expected and was difficult to move for such a lanky man. I shoved again, and he lifted an eyebrow.

"You're trying to remove me?" he asked softly—far too quietly for the intimate situation in which we found ourselves.

His voice was hoarse, gravelly with sleep. He rolled to the side and got to his feet. Amusement tipped his mouth into a soft smile, and I forced myself not to notice the perfect symmetry in his bent lips. *Of course* they were perfectly symmetrical. The only thing about Benedict that was not perfect was his personality.

"I assumed you needed assistance, since you'd yet to do it yourself," I said, struggling to speak normally under the weight of his attention.

"You mean to say that you did not appreciate my fall? I could feel the rapid beating of your heart, Thea, so there is no bother denying your true feelings."

A heart that had yet to fully calm itself. "You are mistaken, sir. It was not excitement that sped my pulse, but the fear that your enormity would crush me before I could ever taste Cook's marzipan again."

Uncertainty flashed in his eyes. "Did I hurt you?"

"No."

Benedict regarded me for another long moment before offering me his hand. He stood above me in nothing but his breeches and shirtsleeves, a shadow of growth over his jaw and his curly hair in disarray. My stomach tightened, and I noted how unfair it was that my attraction to him could not die as swiftly as my regard for him had all those years ago.

Ignoring his outstretched hand, I pushed myself up and turned away, busying myself with gathering the blankets from the floor and folding them neatly. I pressed a hand to my chest, ensuring that the ring was still there, still attached to the string around my neck, feeling the warm metal press into my skin with relief.

Benedict and I worked quietly in the tiny room to prepare for our departure, and I studiously avoided watching him shave in the small mirror or dress for the day. Never had a braid taken such concentrated zeal, but I managed to direct all my attention to the task of putting my hair up and tying my ill-fitting shoes.

"We will pass through York today. If there is anything you left behind at your school, we can stop to retrieve it."

"Oh, can we?" I tempered my surprise. I'd left my trunk behind with the request that Mrs. Moulton store it until I returned for my things, but I hadn't yet found a permanent situation and feared that sending for my trunk would also alert the Bradwell family to my location. Now that they knew, I had no reason not to retrieve it. "That would be good."

Benedict held the door open, and I gestured for him to precede me. "After you, gov," I said, lowering my accent as best I could. It was wiser to put myself in a servant's frame of mind now so I would not slip up and reveal myself when we were in front of others.

He shook his head softly but stepped into the corridor, and I followed him, carrying my valise and his bag.

Mrs. Moulton's school had not been a place of unhappy memories. Indeed, I had enjoyed the years I spent there and the woman who directed my learning. When the red brick building came into view, three levels of even windows and a gabled roof above, my heart did a leap.

"I do not think I will have any trouble retrieving your trunk," Benedict said, watching me. "I'm on familiar terms with Mrs. Moulton now, and I will tell her you are en route to Chelton and have requested that your things be directed there."

I tore my gaze from the bedroom window that had belonged to me for three years. "Mrs. Moulton will believe you have traveled to retrieve it out of the goodness of your heart? Is that not rather unlikely?"

He ignored my slight. "No. I will mention I was passing through and sought to save our servants a trip."

"Much more believable."

Benedict's lips flattened. "I will return shortly." He let himself from the carriage, and I sank against the squabs, watching from the shadows as he knocked at the front door and was subsequently let inside. I waited in front of the school for what felt like ages, but was probably closer to a quarter of an hour, before Benedict reappeared behind a pair of servants carrying my trunk. My heart squeezed at the familiar sight of my one constant companion—the leather luggage that had traveled with me while my father was the ambassador in Sweden, to our trips to Vienna, Brussels, and Denmark, then back to England upon my parents' deaths. It had been easier to leave school and seek a position without being forced to lug the thing around, but I was relieved to have it returned to me.

Benedict reentered the carriage a little time later, and we set off toward Cumberland again.

"How does Mrs. Moulton appear to be faring?" I asked, breaking the tense silence.

His blue eyes cut to me. "I was unable to ask after her well-being. She was managing a dispute between two younger girls, so she was a little preoccupied. She requested I send her regards to my mother, but that was the extent of our conversation."

I nodded.

"Oh," he said, as though he remembered something. "Mrs. Moulton had been holding some letters for you. She asked me to tuck them into your trunk, so I held onto them."

"They are likely from your mother," I said. There was no one else who would write to me. I had not formed any relationships with the girls at school deep enough to warrant a correspondence, and both of my parents had died within a year of each other long before I came to school here. I had no siblings, no other family except my uncle. But he'd turned me away when I arrived in England, and his man of business corresponded with me in regard to my finances. There was nothing *he* would wish to write to me about.

I took the stack from Benedict and sifted away the two on top—both from Lady Edith—and a third from Lady Claverley. The final letter puzzled me, for I did not recognize the hand, and there was no direction. I slid my thumb beneath the seal and broke it open, unfolding the thick paper and scanning the words.

Miss Northcott—

I would not typically stoop so low as to write to you, but I am desperate for information about your whereabouts and safety. Those I've spoken to refuse to give me a clear answer about where you are, and I cannot help but feel deep within my heart that you are in great peril. Please, heal a miserable man from his anxiety and tell me where you are and that you are safe. I would like nothing better than to call on you. I remain in London at the house in Mayfair, where you can reach me.

Yours,

P. Seymour

Peter Seymour? The words swam, and I read them again, pressing a finger to my temple to cease the blurring. I looked up and found Benedict watching me closely. I desired at once to tell him what the letter contained and ask for his opinion. He was a wise man. Surely he would know what to do.

Or would telling Benedict of it merely add credence to a situation that should be forgotten, a letter whose fate was in the fire?

"Is it terrible news?" he asked softly.

"I would not classify it as such, no." My words were softer than I wished. Far more intimate than the conversation needed. We bumped along the road, and I lowered the letter in my lap and refolded it to put away with the others. "It is from a man who has no business writing to me."

Benedict looked at me sharply. "In what way?"

"I knew him in Vienna. He was the son of the minister-plenipotentiary and was a dear friend to our hosts there. We never courted, but he would have liked to. I was not yet of age, though."

"He knew where to find you—"

"I saw him in York while I was still in school. Our encounter was completely by chance, but he took to visiting me on occasion when he passed through. He lives in London now, though his father is still on the Continent, I believe."

The lines around Benedict's mouth tightened. "The blackguard. To risk your reputation in this way." He shook his head, disgusted.

"Which is far more appropriate than how you have risked my reputation," I said, reminding him of our current situation.

His surprise was a little rewarding. "I am an honorable man."

"And Peter is not?"

"I would never write to you."

"A pity, that. I think we could have such entertaining correspondence."

He looked out the window, seemingly frustrated. "Will you write back to him?"

Did I detect a hint of obstinance in his tone? It took me by surprise. Benedict could not be jealous of Peter. That was a more absurd notion than the idea of me harboring any feelings for Peter at all. Benedict's gaze swung back toward me, and I leveled my voice. "I would not correspond with a man unless I am engaged to him." Despite the one kiss I shared with Peter when I was fifteen—can a girl be blamed for romantic notions at such an age? I should think not—he had no claim on me. "The trouble does not lie in his wanting to speak to me, though. He has asked about my whereabouts in a suspicious manner. He believes I am not in a safe situation."

"Perhaps it would be good to notify him of your return to Chelton then, if only to subdue the rumors before they can begin in earnest. Though we shall ask my mother to write the letter, perhaps."

"Perhaps." It was what I'd been thinking too, and I regretted, not for the first time, my foolish, rash decision to leave school on my own in such an underhanded manner.

The motion of the conveyance bumped my leg against Benedict's, and I glanced up and caught his eye. Benedict, master flirt and tease extraordinaire, held my gaze with the blandest of expressions, his blue eyes fixed on me and his body still. The man was like a blasted water pump—completely dry until one engaged the handle, and then water spewed out at a great volume. When he engaged, he did so with zeal.

But, for now, I did not want him to engage any further. I turned my head away and watched trees and cows pass by the window. If I was not mistaken, I heard Benedict sigh.

CHAPTER 7
BENEDICT

We had the misfortune of finding ourselves at an inn with only one room available again later that night, and that was only after being turned away completely from the other inn in town.

"You may have the room to yourself," I said, understanding that Thea likely wanted to read the remainder of her correspondence in privacy. "I need to walk and stretch my legs."

Thea nodded. She slipped into the room and disappeared the moment we reached it, taking both of our small bags with her. Finding a spare cot with Charlie in the stables almost sounded more palatable than sharing a room with her again, and I did not remove the idea completely from my mind.

I stood in the corridor and watched the door close behind Thea, listening to the bar falling over the iron holder to keep it locked. I did not fault her eagerness to be alone, especially after sharing a carriage for the last two days, but we had not stopped earlier for dinner, and it was late.

Hesitation nipped at me, but I shoved it away and knocked at the door.

"Yes?" Her voice came muffled through the thick wood.

"I will order dinner. Shall I have a tray brought to you here?"

Silence pressed between us until she finally responded. "No."

No? Hmm. "Do you intend to come down to the taproom?"

"No."

I stared at the wooden door, as if it held the answers I sought. She could not mean to skip the meal entirely? I knew her purse was thin and her stomach empty, for I'd heard the rumble myself a handful of times in the last leg of our journey. Thea had always been slender, but the thinness of her body and hollowness in her cheeks when I had found her in the Fullers' garden had surprised me some. Mother will not be pleased to see Thea so reduced.

"You need to eat," I called.

Footsteps crossed toward the door, and she unbolted it before swinging it open. Her brow furrowed, and she'd removed her cap, revealing the crown of dark plaits that circled her head. "I am not hungry."

"Your stomach has been arguing differently."

"I require privacy, Benedict. You offered it to me only a moment ago."

"Ah, but I do not wish to encroach upon that. I only request that you allow me to order a tray to your room."

She folded her arms over her chest and tilted her head to the side. "It's not like you to care."

"I don't," I said, regretting the words the moment they touched my lips. Why could we not hold one decent conversation? Everything she said was incendiary and gave me the unaccountable urge to fight back. Though I would admit my own part in this—I was not blameless. I said the only thing that might reach her understanding. "My mother would care. She would be horrified to know I allowed you to pass the night without dinner, and I would not be doing my job as a gentleman if I allowed it."

The little line disappeared between her eyebrows when she raised them in challenge. "Your mother will never learn about the majority of what has taken place on this journey, Ben, or she would have an apoplexy. We can also refrain from informing her that I was too ill—" She caught herself and quickly redirected. "That I skipped dinner one time."

"You are ill?"

"No."

"You only just said moments ago—"

"Not *ill* in the way you are thinking." She ran a hand over her brow. "It is nothing."

The letters she received, had one of them contained bad news? Had the note from her admirer bothered her more than she'd let on? Surely the reason she felt unwell had something to do with that. I could grant her a little grace in this instance and drop the matter.

"Besides," she continued. "What would the servant think when he or she is directed to deliver a tray to a servant boy?"

She had a good point. I would need to think of something else. "Very well. I'll leave you in peace, Thea."

"Thank you." Thea closed the door swiftly and left me in the corridor, staring after it. I would never come to count this woman as a friend, but must we be such bitter rivals? It was exhausting.

"I will take the bed tonight," she said through the closed door.

A hint of a smile tugged at my lips, and I was inordinately grateful she could not see it.

"For the sake of my safety," she continued.

I stepped closer and spoke near the door, lowering my voice so the other occupants of the inn did not overhear. "Of course. I wouldn't dream otherwise." Though I could safely promise that I would not fall on her again. I would hug the opposite side of the mattress if it killed me, had I needed to sleep above her again. How I'd managed to hover so close above her in a bed so large last night was a mystery unto itself. It was as though Thea was possessed of a string to my chest that drew me toward her always, without my control or her desire.

I took myself downstairs and ordered dinner to be brought to me at one of the long, wooden tables in the taproom. A large group of travelers appeared to be eating their dinners as well, all of them men, and the smell of roasted meat and yeasty bread filled my senses.

Thea had come to us at Chelton so young and fresh from rejection all those years ago. I had done my best to be the friend I had thought she needed at the time, the friend my mother requested that I be to her goddaughter. But our easy camaraderie had only lasted a few weeks. A shift in our relationship was born after a midsummer's festival, its cause a complete mystery to me, and neither of us had learned how to act differently since. It was as though paint had been poured over our relationship—black in discord and misunderstanding—and we could not find the turpentine to scrub it clean.

A serving girl set a plate before me and I tucked into my dinner, allowing my mind the luxury of wandering over my memories of Thea. One of the things that irked me was how I never knew what had changed her mind about me—what had happened at the festival to take the charming girl with a cherubic smile and fill her eyes with disgust. I had attempted to ask her once, but was met with the resistance of a draft horse and the stubbornness of a mule.

I tore a chunk from the roll and shoved it in my mouth, chewing with more zeal than the bread warranted. Thea made it increasingly difficult to be kind to her, but the more irritating thing was that I knew I would take a plate of food up to her, regardless of her obstinance. She needed to eat, even if she was too fraught with nerves to do so in a crowded dining room. I ate the remainder of my dinner and flagged down the serving girl.

"I need a plate of food for my servant. I will take it up to him."

"Yes, sir." Her gaze ran the length of my torso. I felt her appraisal seep through my layers of clothing and squirm in my stomach, and I fought the urge to haughtily dismiss her.

I spread a small smirk over my lips and kept my gaze on her eyes. "Thank you, lass."

Her cheeks mottled and interest sparkled in her eyes. It was not difficult to flirt, but I would keep my attentions reined in. Hopefully my feigned interest would speed her along in the kitchen.

The serving girl flitted away, her hips swaying dramatically, and I averted my gaze.

"Benedict Bradwell, in the flesh." A man's creamy voice slid under my skin. Frederick Keller. I would recognize his foppish nonchalance anywhere, and I followed the heinous ensemble he wore up to a hooked nose and slanted smile. His half-lidded eyes swept over me. "You're far from home. Did you come for the fight?"

Fight? That certainly explained the magnitude of men in the taproom and the nearly full inn. I gave the present patrons of the taproom another sweep and saw now what my cursory glance failed to see earlier—the men gathered were mostly gentlemen. "Just passing through," I told Keller.

He pouted. "Shame. I always did like to win your money. Can I persuade you to stay one more day?"

I laughed, giving him the cheerful Benedict he expected. The grin on my face felt raw and taut, but I persevered. "I'd hate to deprive you of such joy, but I'm afraid I'm far too eager for the comforts of home to delay another moment."

"There are comforts to be had here," he said, watching the serving girl sashay back toward us, Thea's dinner in her hands.

"Nothing that appeals to me at present," I said, taking the food and giving the woman her coins. I threw in a few extra, hoping she would not need to search for money elsewhere tonight.

"Too bad," Keller said. "You can always change your mind."

I shot him a smile and rose to my feet. "Another time, perhaps."

Keller swaggered away, and I stole from the room before Thea's dinner could grow too cold. When I reached the door to our room, I faltered in my resolve. She would not expect this of me. If I entered with a plate of food, she would be suspicious of my motivations or—given her flair for the dramatic—the plate itself. What reason could I devise so she would not be wary of me? I looked at the plate of unassuming ham and boiled potatoes, the roll teetering over the steaming meat.

I could tell her it was delivered accidentally, that the innkeeper mistook my ordering of one dinner as me ordering two, and that it had been paid for and we ought not to waste it. Surely she would believe such a tale. So long as it did not paint me in a favorable light, Thea would eat it up.

My curled fist pounded on the door, and I only had to wait a minute before Thea unlocked it and peeked out. When she saw me, she released the door and allowed it to swing wide before she turned back into the room and sat on the edge of the bed. Her hair was still plaited but uncoiled from her head, falling limply over her shoulder.

She eyed the plate in my hand. I entered the room, closing the door behind me, and lifted it like an offering.

But the carefully crafted lie lodged in my throat.

"I told you I did not want dinner," she said quietly. Her letters sat folded on her lap, her fingers turning one of them over slowly, absently.

My shoulder lifted in a nonchalant shrug. "Then do not eat it. It is no trial to me if it grows cold. My belly is already full."

"Good."

She could not be in earnest. Of all the ridiculous, stubborn—

Her gaze dropped to the letter in her hands, and I swallowed my irritation. I could not understand the reason for her distress until she chose to bring me into her confidence and explain what awful news the missive entailed. Was her beau worrying her? His ardent pleas too much for her? Did she miss him? That idea sent a nasty discomfort through my gut.

I moved closer and set the plate on the small, rickety table beside the bed and lowered myself onto the spindly chair beside it. "I suppose we shouldn't waste it. If you're in earnest, that is?"

She looked from the food to me, and I saw the light of challenge brighten her previously dull eyes. "I would never lie to you."

"Oh?" I lifted an eyebrow and took the roll, tearing a chunk from it and popping it into my mouth.

Thea swallowed.

It was almost painful to keep chewing, watching her watch me eat. "This is divine."

"Of course."

"And the ham . . ." I reached for the plate and cut a bite of the tough meat, sliding it into my mouth and chewing as though it was moist and delicious and not, in actuality, cold and dry enough to make me wish I'd brought a drink with me.

Thea did not take her gaze off me, and under the scrutiny of her round, blue eyes, I wished I had not begun this game.

But I had begun it, so I would see it finished.

"I'm not a man prone to enjoying vegetables, but these potatoes have been seasoned well." I reached for the fork to spear a potato and Thea slapped my hand away.

"Enough."

Victory swooped through me, but I kept a placid expression on my face. "Enough?"

"Yes. I know what you are trying to do."

"Is it working?"

A flicker of a smile danced on the corner of her mouth, but she suppressed it well. I would likely not have noticed it had I not been searching ardently for any sign that she was breaking. "No. But I will take the plate and eat it if only to make you stop. No one appreciates listening to another person eat with such enthusiasm."

So it *was* working,

"On the contrary," I said lightly, glad to see her lift the roll and take a bite. "I enjoy nothing more when seated at dinner than to listen to others enjoy their food."

She gave me a disbelieving arch of an eyebrow.

"Truly," I said, leaning back in the chair to the sound of an ominous creak and resting my ankle on the opposite knee. "It is even better when the food is described."

"Like this warm, buttery potato?"

"Yes."

"Or this"—she cut a bite of ham and laid it on her tongue—"dry, cold ham."

I fought a smile. "Even better. I do not have to eat anything because I have the pleasure of listening to it described to me. It's lovely."

She shook her head, obviously aware of my jest and equally willing to let the conversation cease here. "It is a wonder you have so many friends when you have such strange table manners."

"The trend of describing your dinner is catching on. You will see."

She went quiet, focusing on eating her meal, and when her plate was cleared, I moved my gaze to rest on the ever-darkening window. "There is to be a fight tomorrow."

"That is why the other inn was full," she said, understanding.

"Yes, and why this one is crawling with gentlemen. You would do best not to leave the room at all."

She nodded. "Is there anyone I would know?"

"Frederick Keller?"

She shook her head.

"Then you are likely safe. I knew no one else." I glanced at her flowy shirt and tight breeches. They were tighter than they ought to be, but a boy would wear them this way. I only noticed the definition of her curves because I knew she was a woman—though I did my utmost *not* to notice them.

"This room has no extra blankets," she said, standing and moving to the window. She looked out over High Street. "I almost went to inquire with the innkeeper, but I didn't want to put my hair up again."

"They'll not have any, I'm sure. Not with the crowd downstairs. More men were arriving when I left the taproom."

Thea nodded, then looked to the bed. "I will take the mattress. You may have the blanket."

If it could even be called such. It was so thin as to be more of a sheet. The hard planked floor beneath my feet was unyielding, and I thought maybe the stables with Charlie did sound like the better option tonight, though it would be freezing. At least in here we had a dying fire.

Thea looked from the bed to the empty plate. "It is such a wide bed," she said, not meeting my gaze. "I'm certain it was designed to hold an entire family."

"More than likely. I would have guessed the same of the bed from the inn last night as well." A family, a group of friends, or a handful of strangers. I had been offered a room with strangers more times than I could count on various journeys, and while others I knew would share beds or rooms with strangers to save a few coins, I could never bring myself to do it, even with the outrageous expense of a private room. I held my breath and her gaze, wondering at the implication of her statement.

Her direction turned back out the window, and she leaned closer to the glass. "No. Surely it is not . . ."

"Not who?"

She looked closer, resting her palm on the glass beside her. "It only looks like someone I once knew. But the glass is thick and difficult to see clearly."

"You are safe, even if you do know this person, for you do not intend to leave the room—"

Thea spun and dropped to the floor, holding my gaze, her blue eyes round. "He saw me. I'm certain of it."

"Who saw you?"

She swallowed. "Peter Seymour."

CHAPTER 8
THEA

"Who is Peter Seymour? And why does his name sound familiar?" Benedict asked, rising from the small, rickety chair and crossing toward the window. I put out my hands to stop him. The last thing we needed now was to draw further attention to our room.

"He's the man who wrote me that letter." My outstretched arms did not halt Benedict, so I reached up and tugged on his hand.

He looked at me. "What the devil are you doing?"

"Move away from the window!" I hissed, releasing his hand. It was rough, the skin calloused in a way I had not expected. Or perhaps that was my own rugged skin.

He scoffed. "It is impossible to see—"

I reached for him again, and he stepped back. "Thea, even if the man had seen you, he was unlikely to make out your identity through the dusk and this thick glass. He would not know it was *you*."

"You cannot know that. He looked up and watched me for a few moments before I ducked away."

Ben scrubbed a hand over his face. "Well, if he had not had

69

any suspicions *prior* to your questionable activity, he certainly has them now."

I had not considered that point. Peter was like a scourge who returned with relentless enthusiasm and refused to depart. Our acquaintance began when Mother and I lived with the Richters for the duration of the year following my father's death. Peter had begun a clandestine flirtation with me that ended promptly when my mother died and I returned to England. Two years later, when I left Chelton to attend school in York, Peter happened to be in town visiting his cousin and came to call on me at school a handful of times.

Benedict was correct, most likely. My sudden drop from the window proved my guilt to any onlookers outside. "I've given myself away," I said. And to a man who, when one considered the contents of his letter, had been looking for me.

"More than likely. So long as your friend does not listen outside our door, however, he will not find a woman here."

A slow grin spread over my lips, and I lifted my smile to Benedict. "Because I am a *boy*. Oh, blessed ruse."

He looked warily at me and sat on the edge of the bed. "Is the man dangerous?"

"No. Only . . . persistent." It could not be helped that I'd allowed him to kiss me in Mrs. Richter's garden. I was barely fifteen then, so I could hardly be blamed for being young, naive, extremely bored from the limited social functions we could participate in while mourning my father, and wondering what all the fuss was about in regard to kissing.

I had to admit, I wasn't impressed.

"He must be here to watch the fight," I said. He'd mentioned in the letter that he was still living in London, and we were a far cry from Town now.

"Then we can content ourselves that he will not rise early and see us making our escape."

I turned around and raised my head to peek over the edge of

the glass. The group of men who had arrived with Peter were all gone now, likely drinking in the taproom below us, and I sank down onto the floor in relief. "It would be precisely my fortune to go to the trouble of such a disguise, only to be caught out by one of the few people in England who might recognize me."

"Do you truly care if you are?" Benedict asked. He sounded interested in my answer, as though he believed I did not care for what Society thought of me. He was mistaken. I was no fool—which was why I was extremely cautious in the positions I had obtained for myself after leaving Mrs. Moulton's school. My parents had done their share of the work in ruining whatever reputation our name carried with their infidelity and reckless behavior. I did not want to make the situation worse for myself.

"I care."

"Yet it was you who disappeared from school and took on a servant's position. If you were to see Mrs. Fuller in London, what would you do? It would be a scandal if the activities of the previous few months were widely known."

My stomach clenched, but I refused to allow him to see he was ruffling my composure. "Mrs. Fuller would not recognize me, so it hardly matters."

"I could toss flour on your face to help her memory along."

I scowled at him dramatically, fighting a smile. "I never met the Fullers. I stayed down in the kitchen. If I was to see them in London, they would not know I used to knead their bread."

Benedict leaned forward and rested his elbows on his knees. "And before that? What did you do?"

"Before kneading their bread? That was actually not something Cook trusted me with often." My cheeks warmed. "I was more often cutting vegetables or washing dishes."

"No," he said, a curious smile on his lips. "Before the Fullers' kitchen, what did you do?"

"I worked for a seamstress at a shop in Upper Trumby. My stitches weren't small or even enough for her, but she gave me a fair chance before sending me to the market to find other employment."

Benedict looked thoughtful, his blue eyes interested but the remainder of his face placid. If this was an effort on his part to gather information to share with his mother, he was wasting his time and efforts at his attempted covertness. I was happy to share all of this with Lady Edith when I arrived at Chelton. I did not wish for her to wonder over the nature of any of my situations.

"But I did not go to the seamstress directly from school."

"No?" His curiosity was again piqued, but I allowed that morsel to dangle a moment longer.

I stretched my legs ahead of me and leaned my head back against the whitewashed wall, waiting for Benedict's curiosity to snap. He was handsome—I could admit as much in the quiet of my own thoughts, of course—with a constant disarray of curls and a rakish smile. His lips were now flat, angled in such a way as to try and make me believe he did not care to learn where I went when I left school.

"How long were you looking for me?" I asked.

Benedict's gaze broke, and he looked to the simmering fire in the hearth. "I took multiple trips."

"More than one? I do not know what I did to warrant such generosity."

"It was not for you," he said to the small fire.

Of course not. I knew that. He would never do anything for my sake alone. My gaze sought the empty plate and discarded utensils on the small table beside the bed—evidence of the lie I had just told myself. I looked away.

Benedict ran a hand through his riotous curls. "It took me a good deal of time to discover that you'd gone to Gallingher Park from the school, but when I questioned the housekeeper, she told you you'd left and they did not know where to. It was difficult to piece together where you went after that."

"Yet you found me in Brumley," I said. How had he made that leap? Gallingher Park was the home of my governess position. It could not have been pure coincidence.

"A little luck, and a great amount of searching." His hand moved as though it meant to fetch something from his pocket, but he stopped himself. He looked to the darkened window. "We ought to go to sleep soon so we can make an early start in the morning."

"Not yet," I said, my gaze riveted by his pocket. Something was in it that he did not allow himself to fetch. "You mean to have me believe that luck landed you on the lane behind the Fullers' garden?"

"Not entirely, no. There was a good deal of searching involved too."

"In what way? Did you knock on every door in Yorkshire? Inquire at every inn?"

He looked up sharply, his expression almost turning sheepish. He could not have knocked on *every* door . . . that was fairly impossible.

"How did you search for me, Ben?" I asked, leveling my voice. It became extremely important for me to know this, though I did not know why I cared so deeply.

Benedict stood. He reached into his pocket and pulled out a small, oval miniature in a gold-painted frame. My breath caught when I recognized the tiny painting. It was me, and it had been done just before my mother died, when we had shed our mourning clothes and were just dipping our toes into Society again. Though I was fifteen when I sat for the portrait, I did not look so very different now. Mother had commissioned it with the intent to send it to my godmother, unknowing that I would arrive myself on her doorstep only months later.

My heart squeezed, and I reached for the painting, the warmth of its frame evidence of how long it had lived in Benedict's pocket.

"I showed that to many innkeepers, and it was a great help in pointing me in the correct direction time and again."

The depth of his efforts was apparent, though his motivations remained less so. He had explained that guilt incited his search, as he felt responsible for my discomfort in going to Chelton. But to remain on the hunt for so long could not have been easy. What had maintained his motivation?

"I sat for this portrait while my mother prepared herself for her first ball after coming out of mourning, and I was so eager to join her. I only had another year or so to wait, and it was with great impatience that I did so." At that time, I had still been able to hope that not all men were like my father. I'd still believed there were a few left who would speak only things they meant, who were honest and true.

Benedict had quickly proven that he was the type of man who doled out compliments and flowery speech to anyone bearing a smile and a skirt, and the reminder of our first few months together at Chelton was made bitter by the way he had seemingly sacrificed in order to find me. My emotions were wavering. The embarrassment of thinking he'd cared for me, only to learn that he was nothing but a flirt, that the way he spoke to me was in no way singular or special, still brought the fire of humiliation to my cheeks, and I ducked my head.

"I should return the miniature to my mother."

"Yes, of course." I placed it back in his hand, and his fingers curled around the painting, skimming mine and leaving behind a trail of blazing heat. My fingers moved to fidget with my mother's ring, but I'd yet to remove it from the string about my neck and found, in the place it usually adorned my finger, nothing but naked skin.

"We'll need an early morning if we want to be gone before the hordes awake."

I looked again at the bed. It was large enough to fit both of us twice over, and there was only one blanket—if the thin item could even be called a blanket. With winter encroaching and a chill in the room the fire had not been able to fully snuff, it was impossible to ask Benedict to sleep on the cold floor without a blanket. I considered again the prospect of offering to share the bed and mattress, but the idea stuttered on my tongue, refusing to come out.

Benedict eyed me. "What are you refraining from saying?"

I swallowed, but tried to sound nonchalant. This was *not* an offer because I was grateful for the dinner or the intensity of Benedict's search for me. It was merely a sensical solution to the dilemma that was our sleeping arrangements. "The only logical solution is to share the bed."

He stood and took a step back. "Absolutely not."

It hurt a little that the prospect was so disgusting to him, and I was tempted to let the matter drop, but this had nothing to do with how we felt toward one another.

"We can line our valises between us, and no one will ever learn of it."

Benedict took another step back, as if he could physically remove himself from the idea I presented.

"Oh, do be reasonable." I stood, fanning my arms. "I would be more than happy to let you suffer on the floor, but the bed is large and we will create a barrier between us."

He tilted his head to the side, not unlike my mother's terrier used to do. "If you are more than happy to watch me suffer, then why did you mention the"—he waved his hand toward the bed as though he could not bring himself to say the word aloud— "sleeping on that."

Why, indeed? It was not because I cared for his comfort. He deserved a cold night on a hard floor after what he put so many women through—all the flirting and the false expectations he'd raised in countless other naive misses. My gaze moved again to the plate he'd brought me for dinner and I tore it away. I could not help the smallest tinge of gratitude in my mostly iron heart for the effort Benedict had made to seek me out. It was a shock to realize that anyone cared so much to find me. Regardless of whether he had done it for his mother or himself, he still did it.

For that, I could share a lumpy, straw mattress sewn for a family of six.

"For your mother's sake," I said.

"My mother?" His dark eyebrows drew together skeptically.

"Yes. For Lady Edith. She would be sad to hear that you'd spent an entire evening on the floor, freezing and uncomfortable. I suggest it because of her."

"Hmm." He looked disbelieving.

"Good heavens, Ben. It is the sensible thing to do," I snapped. "One of us does consider the situation as a whole, you know."

He lifted his eyebrows. "Yes, one of us does. *I* do that often."

I cast my eyes to the ceiling and rose, obtaining my valise. I moved to the bed and set it in the middle, then added Benedict's bag and formed a barrier down the center of the mattress. "If anyone is to ask you about it later, now you can honestly tell them that I did not sleep beside you."

"You do not call that sleeping beside one another?"

"No. I call that sleeping beside a valise."

"Mere details."

"Yes. Important details." I blew out the last candle, and we were left in a dim room with only the orange glow from the small fire. It danced over his cheekbones, shadowing the cut of his jaw and the flexing muscles in his cheeks. "Good night, Benedict. I've given you the option, now the choice is yours."

"Wait." He stepped around me and pulled the drapes over the window to grant us some privacy, then ran a hand over his face. "This does not feel right. I do not wish to do anything that might compromise you—that might compromise *us*."

"At this point in our journey, do you not think we are a little beyond that concern? If we have irrevocably harmed our reputations, surely the damage is already complete."

"Not yet. We could make it all the way to Cumberland, be spotted by a mutual acquaintance while stopping to change horses, and *then* it will be over. We must be diligent to the very end."

I put my arms out to the sides. "I am dressed as a boy, Ben. No one will catch us, and if they do, they will not assume I am a woman."

His gaze followed the length of me, from my outstretched arms to my toes, and I fought the urge to squirm. "Your clothing is correct, but your form is not. If you are not careful, you could be spotted."

I swallowed against a suddenly dry throat. My form? "What do you mean? I have been standing demurely in public like you instructed."

"Not your posture . . . Your eyes are too round for a boy, and much too large. Your cheekbones too pronounced, your nose too dainty." His voice dropped. "And that is only your face of which I speak. You are a feminine specimen, Thea, in every way. I fear now that we have fooled ourselves into believing this ruse was possible."

"So far we have managed to fool everyone."

"Strangers, yes." He shook his head. "James married a woman six months ago because they were found alone at a ball. They were dancing, but that was all, and now they are *married*. I refuse to repeat his mistakes and marry for the sake of a reputation."

I winced and dropped my gaze so he would not notice it. Given the dimness in the room, I believed myself safe from that detection. Drawing my shoulders up, I raised my eyes to meet his. "We will not be like James and his new wife, because I would never require that of you, regardless of what happens. I chose to leave Mrs. Moulton's and strike out on my own. My reputation was never very secure to begin with, Ben. I do hope to keep it intact if I can, but not at the expense of a marriage I do not want."

He was quiet for a few beats before nodding. "Then we proceed as planned, and we are exceedingly careful. We have come too far to give up now. We ought to see this through."

"That would be ideal."

He moved away to ready himself for sleep, and I cleaned my teeth and splashed my face with water before sliding into the bed. Benedict's message could not be clearer: if we were to be discovered and my reputation irreparably damaged, he would not do the proper thing and ask for my hand. If we were discovered, like James and his wife, I would not walk away with a safeguarding marriage proposal. I could not blame the man for not wanting to be shackled to me, not when we had always been so at odds with one another. Indeed, I did not truly expect more from him in that way. But to be told outright I would be left on my own in such a situation created an ache in my chest that tore open like the ripping of a weak seam.

I'd felt before that I did not have anyone, not really. But the reminder, the certainty, was a lonely feeling.

The bed groaned under Benedict's weight, and I turned on my side away from him, despite the fact that I could not see him over the mound of our bags. I was mildly surprised he chose to share the mattress, and knowing he slept on the other side of our bags gave me a strangely victorious feeling.

The false sense of friendship I had begun to feel with Benedict was alarming, and his words had served to remind me of our place with one another. He was too handsome, his smile too beguiling, for me to do anything but continue to hold him in contempt. Otherwise, I was afraid of what I would allow myself to once again feel.

CHAPTER 9
THEA

Morning arrived far too soon, and I slid from the bed and crossed to the small, cracked mirror to pin up my hair. Benedict stretched audibly, his grunts and groans reminiscent of an older man attempting to heave himself out of a deep-cushioned chair.

"Struggling?" I asked, my attention on my hair in the mirror.

He immediately quieted. "I do not know what you mean."

Yes, he most certainly did.

We tiptoed around one another for the next quarter hour, preparing to leave. Once we were ready, he paused at the door. "I will go out first and signal if it is safe to follow."

"What will the signal be? An owl's hoot? Perhaps you can trill like a chicken."

He looked thoughtful. "A patterned knock on the door."

"You are no fun."

"I am extremely fun." He looked at me dismissively. "Everyone else thinks so."

Precisely. Everyone *else*.

He unbolted the door and stepped outside. A moment later, he leaned back in through the door. "Cluck, cluck."

I blinked.

He widened his eyes. "Cluck."

"Yes, I heard."

"Then shall we?" He gestured to the corridor behind him.

"Of course. Only, will you tell me how you believed that to be a *trill* of a chicken?"

"That is precisely how chickens sound."

"That might be how they cluck, but it is certainly not how they trill." I stepped into the corridor and followed him down toward the stairs.

"Are you an expert in chickens, then?"

We took the stairs down to a darkened, quiet taproom. "I happen to have experience with them, yes. Our hostess had chickens in Vienna. It is not much experience, but enough to know the difference between a cluck and a trill."

Benedict came to an abrupt halt at the bottom of the stairs, and I nearly collided with his back. I looked beyond his shoulder and saw two men sitting at a table near the center of the room. I dropped my head immediately, understanding my mistake. I hadn't disguised my voice at all while coming down the stairs. Benedict angled his body to hide me, and I assumed the position of a serving boy, hunching my shoulders slightly to better hide my chest and training my gaze on the floor.

"Good morning, gentlemen," he said, setting his hat on his head.

"Morning," one of them answered.

It wasn't Peter's voice, thank the heavens. I hazarded a quick peek, and neither man looked like Peter. They were watching us with curiosity, though, so Benedict and I left the room directly, though at a slower pace than I desired.

I went to fetch Charlie from the stables, and he set about harnessing the horses straight away. When I returned to inform Benedict, as a good servant ought to do, he leaned down to speak softly near my ear. "I will return inside and order breakfast for the road. We need to be on our way. Stay out of sight until Charlie pulls the carriage around. A gentleman passed you and went into the stables a moment ago, and I do not know if he was your friend or not."

I gave him a curt nod and skirted around the side of the building. Our bags were already stored in the carriage. I could have hidden in there if Benedict hadn't seen the man go into the stables. This was all too much, and I was suddenly wishing we had never attempted this scheme. It was far better to be a boy than to be thought a hussy, though. We'd passed the halfway mark on our journey yesterday, so we were nearly to Chelton. Only two days of travel remained.

I could do this. For another two days, I could do this.

My thin shirt and breeches were no match for the November chill, and a shudder ran over my skin while I paced slowly along the back of the building. Stone row houses lined the opposite street, and smoke billowed from the chimneys punctuating their shared roof. The sky was beginning to lighten, gray mixing with the dark blues. I turned the corner again and stopped short. A handful of men stood in a small group between the inn's door and our carriage, speaking to Benedict. He looked up and caught my gaze, then cleared his throat loudly. "I must be off, men."

"You truly will not remain?" The man who spoke swung an elaborate cane, a clear affectation made obvious by the way he shifted from one foot to the other without use of it. "I had not taken you for a coward, Bradwell."

I looked at Benedict sharply. Would he allow the man to speak to him in such a way?

A smile spread over Benedict's face, wide and lazily. "I'm afraid I will always run when my mother beckons me, Keller. I must balance my absences from her house with some decency."

Some of the men chuckled politely. Benedict bid them farewell and turned to open the carriage door. Once he was inside, I peeked at the handful of men from beneath my cap and found Peter standing among them. Drat. The carriage door sat open, awaiting me, and I scurried over and slipped inside, squeezing against the wall as Benedict reached out and pulled the door closed. He banged his fist against the roof of the carriage and we were off.

"That was a nice leap," he said hesitantly.

"Peter was there. He was among the group speaking to you." My chest heaved, my breath coming quickly.

He looked surprised and leaned forward to look out the window. "Which man?"

"Fair-haired. He stood beside the man with the cane."

"Ah, yes." He analyzed me a bit longer. "You certainly have a habit of giving him reason to find you suspicious in perfectly ordinary situations."

"What do you mean?"

"Ducking from the window last night. Running and leaping into the carriage. A typical servant boy would scurry, perhaps, but he would do his best to not be noticed. You, Thea, were anything but sly."

I wrinkled my nose. "What are the odds that he did not see my face?"

"Referencing wagering, Thea? That is not very ladylike."

"I am not dressed as a lady. That affords me some leniency, does it not?"

He gave a dry laugh. "Nothing about this journey is very ordinary, I suppose."

"The odds?" I pressed, using the word to vex him.

Benedict narrowed his eyes, then looked as though he gave the matter some thought. "High, I believe. I doubt he saw your face. You ran too fast for him to do so."

"And my voice? Do you think he heard me speaking of chickens?"

"I haven't a clue. I did not see him in the taproom, but he could have been nearby. He could have thought you were a very young boy." He rubbed a hand over his chin. "But your voice, though feminine, is too rich to sound much like a young boy either."

Silence pressed on us. I tried not to worry. More and more, I regretted my choice to leave school. It had done nothing for me but cause thick calluses on my hands, eternal purple shadows beneath my eyes, and the threat of scandal. What had I been thinking?

Lord Claverley's face popped into my thoughts, and I gave a revolted shudder.

Escaping an awful fate. *That* was why I had taken such drastic measures. I closed my eyes and swallowed. My hopes were hanging on Benedict's word. *Benedict's.* A man who had no patience for me and cared little for women in general beyond the flirtation and entertainment they could provide.

I was placing my trust in him. I hoped I was not doing so in vain.

Benedict pulled a small parcel from the bench beside him I hadn't noticed before. He unwrapped it and offered it to me. Bread, cheese, and chunks of meat sat on the thick, brown paper. "Breakfast?" he offered.

"That is much more than two people need," I said, surprised by the quantity he presented.

A little smirk fell over his lips. "All kitchen maids might not find me appealing, but the one here seemed to like my smile well enough."

He'd flirted for the abundance of food. Of course. Could I expect anything less? I took a chunk of cheese and a roll, though my stomach soured. "Thank you," I said, the words bitter as they slipped over my tongue. "Should we not offer something to Charlie?"

Benedict snorted. "After the fee he's extorting from us for use of this carriage and driving? The man can fend for himself. He was aware of that requirement before we left Brumley."

I took a bite of my bread and looked out the window. Benedict was in no way required to provide for me, either. The cheese and bread filled my stomach as I tried not to think about that, or wonder why he did.

The final inn we stopped at was blessedly situated in a town that was *not* overrun with young gentlemen attending a fighting match, and Benedict and I were able to obtain two separate rooms. I disappeared into mine once we arrived, too shaken after almost encountering Peter in Fremont to loiter in the dining room. My parents had entertained often in Sweden while my father was the ambassador, and while I didn't know many of my parents' friends personally, nor the Society members who stayed with us while abroad, there were a fair amount of members of the *ton* who might recognize my face if they were to see me.

It has been said I am the exact image of my mother, so I am certain that would not aid me in remaining undetected.

These were valid reasons to hide away in my room and adequately disguised my need to be far from Benedict. Spending so much time together over the previous few days had begun to soften and thaw the anger and resentment I held strong in my iron heart, which I could not allow.

The following morning, we left the inn without any trouble, and the remainder of the day passed in agony, sitting across from Benedict without much pleasant conversation to pass the time.

"We shall arrive at Chelton long after the entire household is asleep," Benedict said. "I've instructed Charlie to drop us at the door and leave the vicinity immediately. He is to go as far as Hartshorne before stopping for the night, so no one in our stables will have the opportunity to question him."

"Wise," I said. "And your mother? What will you tell her when she asks how we came to arrive at Chelton at the same time without a chaperone?"

He cringed. "I am hoping she is astute enough not to ask. I cannot lie to her, and she will not like the truth. If she guesses at our situation, she might very well choose to refrain from inquiring so she is not forced to demand that we face the same consequences as James and Felicity."

I looked at my calloused fingers, smooth and hard in places. "She will not speak of it, and our reputations will remain safe," I said with more hope than confidence. "Can you say the same for James's wife if she is to learn the truth?" I did not know the woman, nor whether she was trustworthy.

Benedict seemed confident. "Completely. Felicity is a gem. You will love her, and you can certainly trust her."

"Given that I cannot entirely trust you, I will certainly be forming my own opinion on the matter."

He drew his chin in, regarding me longer than usual, enough to make me squirm slightly in my seat. "Whatever have I done to earn such censure?"

It was more what he had *not* done. He had not been earnest in his attentions or flirtations with any young women, he had not respected anyone enough to mean what he said. He could not be trusted because he was a flirt, and flirts would say anything which served their purposes—like smile for extra breakfast or give two women identical compliments within minutes of each other. Benedict's innocent gaze flitted over my face. He was so confused. I wanted to reach across the carriage and alter his expression myself.

"Nothing," I said, meaning it.

"Do you not feel that we are old enough now to put aside childish bickering?"

"I certainly am." But it was not childish hurts festering in my heart. It was the ongoing proof that Benedict was nothing if not insincere.

A muscle jumped in his cheek. The night was growing increasingly dark on the other side of the window, and his face was drawn in shadows. "Then can we not cease?"

He implored me, and it rose my hackles, straightening my back as though his words climbed up my spine and corrected it. His implication through this question that I was at fault for our disagreeable relationship was unfair. I was only half of the discord, and he made up the other half with his verbal hits and barbs.

Could I be blamed for my defensive nature around Benedict, when he had given me so many causes for needing defense?

"Is Lady Edith aware of our arrival?" I asked, hoping the alteration in conversation would put an end to his uncomfortable pleading.

He looked as though he meant to argue further, to press the matter of ending our bickering. After a moment, he sighed. "Yes. I wrote to her shortly after making arrangements with you to travel home, though she will not expect us quite yet. If I know my mother, she had your room prepared the moment she received my letter, so do not fear that you will arrive without a place to sleep."

"I did not worry about that. Chelton does not lack for bedchambers." Though I quite understated the matter. Chelton was a grand, palladian house nestled in the rolling hills of Cumberland, just outside of a town called Bakewell. It was deserving of the grandeur and praise it received, and in all my travels, I had not yet met its equal in stately beauty.

"You know," he said quietly. "You are much more pleasant after I provide you with something to eat. Perhaps if I carry about apples or cheese and ply you with them, we can become friends."

My surprise was quickly engulfed by amusement, for he was

correct. I'd offered to share the bed after he brought me dinner, and I was far more polite after he'd brought me breakfast. "You propose to treat me as you would a horse? A few extra treats to entice good behavior?"

"Why not? If it works, then I see no harm in it. You should not either, for it supplies you with extra treats."

"I cannot refuse a plan that provides me with treats, of course. Perhaps if they are delicious enough, I will even neigh for you."

"Like a horse?"

"Do not sound so disbelieving. Unlike your failure with the chicken trill, I can sound exactly like a horse."

Benedict laughed. His eyes glittered in the dark carriage, his white teeth gleaming. His smile had a remarkable effect on my body, and I was glad when he did not continue the conversation, for I did not know how I was meant to continue fortifying my feelings when he so easily disarmed me.

We fell into silence for the remainder of the journey, and it was only a few hours later, in the darkness of the middle of the night, that we rode quietly over the stone bridge and up the gravel drive toward Chelton. Benedict and I were both silent when we climbed from the carriage. I waited for him to pay Charlie the remainder of the money owed to the man and retrieve our bags, then watched him heave my trunk from the boot and set it on the ground.

Benedict looked up at Chelton's pale stone facade, the windows dark and the stone stairs split from the front door and sweeping down two ways. I hefted my valise up and moved to take my trunk as the carriage rolled away.

"It is too heavy," Benedict said quietly. The stillness of night made every sound more pronounced.

"I can manage it."

He folded his arms over his chest and leaned back, his body

speaking the words floating in his mind: *this should be entertaining.*

I leaned down, took the trunk firmly in my hands, and hefted it up. The weight strained against my hold. I could lift it, but I could see how correct Benedict had been—I certainly would not be able to carry it up the stairs and into the house. I'd walked two steps before my arms screamed in protest, and I bent to set it on the ground.

"Allow me," he said with a heavy dose of smugness.

"That certainly sounds like a man hoping to mend our differences."

He growled, low in his throat, and lifted the trunk easily. "You were correct. It was a pointless idea."

Something about the way he so easily gave up on me stung, but I brushed it away. The choice I had made to keep myself distanced from him was wise—safeguarding, even. I took Benedict's valise from the ground and followed him up the stairs. For his plan to work, we needed to wake in our bedchambers, where the servants would find us asleep in the morning. They would assume, we hoped, that our chaperone had left with the hired carriage.

We made it quietly to the front door. Benedict set the trunk down and tried to open it, but it would not budge. He looked from the door to me, and I saw for the first time a bit of worry knit his brows. "It's locked."

CHAPTER 10

BENEDICT

"Did you not expect this?" Thea asked, looking at me with mild alarm.

I tried the door again, but it did not budge. "I've returned home in the middle of the night before and never encountered this particular dilemma." I looked up. "Perhaps the servants' entrance is unlocked."

Thea glanced to her trunk.

"Leave the bags and come with me," I said. I did not want to carry that trunk around the perimeter of the house, only to be forced to climb through a window or something equally ungainly. It was far too heavy, and we could return to retrieve it once we made it inside the house.

"I can wait here," she whispered.

Blasted prideful woman. I turned on my heel, her earlier rejection still stinging with gentle consistency. I had thought we were getting along well after a few days of one another's company, but apparently Thea was too stubborn to put our differences aside and admit that we could very well be friends—if she chose. "As you wish."

I had only made it halfway down the stone stairs when I

heard her following. I shook my head and waited at the bottom for Thea to reach me.

"It's too dark to wait alone," she said.

We made our way around Chelton's massive edifice to the servants' entrance, and I pulled on the door, breathing a sigh of relief when it opened.

"I began to wonder if you would have to wake the servants."

"I began to wonder if I would be climbing up to Henry's window. Thankfully, neither of those are required." Moonlight trailed into the small vestibule with us, and I noticed the butler's door just down the corridor sat open.

Thea opened her mouth to speak, and I clamped my hand over her lips to stop the sound. Her round eyes widened further, and I pointed to the butler's open door to indicate why she needed to be silent, ignoring the velvet of her lips and how the softness seemed to cling to my skin.

"If he hears us, we're done for," I whispered, swallowing hard. I raised my eyebrows and waited for her to nod in understanding before I removed my hand from her mouth and covertly shook my tense fingers loose again.

I reached for her hand and took it, tugging softly and holding her gaze. It wasn't a romantic gesture by any means. I only wished to lead her through the darkened corridors I knew so well, but her warm fingers curled around mine and sent a spark up my arm. We passed the butler's chambers to the blessed sound of low, soft snoring, and down another empty corridor toward the stairs that would lead us to the front door.

"I should have waited by the door," she whispered after we had cleared the stairs and made our way down an innocuous corridor.

I looked over my shoulder. "Why did you not?"

Her eyes cut to me. "I felt exposed, waiting there alone. Standing before the door felt like waiting on a stage."

"Have you any experience standing on a stage?" I whispered. "Was that your occupation prior to being a governess?"

"I will do my best not to take offense at that."

"There is nothing wrong with actresses."

"If you are a member of the *ton* there is, and you know it. My reputation would never recover from such a rumor."

"Then I will refrain from telling anyone of your sordid past with the stage."

She pulled her hand free, and I stopped walking, pivoting to find her outline in the dark corridor. Blanketed in darkness, it was difficult to see her expression, but the emotion wafting from her was taut and burdensome. I had only been joking, but she appeared bothered. The moment stretched on. I badly wanted to know what she was thinking, what she was deciding to say or not say.

But she remained silent.

I attempted to lighten the thickness in the air. "We must make haste or someone will find us and wonder why you are wearing breeches."

"You are impossible, Benedict."

"Most people find me charming."

"I am not most people."

No, she was not. She had the ability to drive herself beneath my skin and fill my belly with the flutter of a bird's wings simultaneously. No one drove me to distraction the way Thea did, and despite the bickering, I *enjoyed* it. I fought the lightness in my stomach and the heaviness in my chest and held out my hand for her. I brushed her arm, unable to see very clearly.

"It isn't necessary for you to lead me. I do know how to find my way around Chelton."

I dropped my hand. "Very well, but please refrain from bumping any of the tables along the wall. Some of them hold very expensive vases."

Thea snatched my hand and warmth shot up to my heart. "Be quick about it," she grumbled.

I tightened my hold and continued through the corridors, rounding corners and slipping quietly across the black and white checkered floor in the large hall and up the carpeted stairs to the family rooms. We reached Thea's old bedchamber, and I opened the door. It was cold and dark, but the bed was empty and the blankets were thick.

"What of my clothing?" she asked when I released her hand. "I cannot go down to breakfast in breeches."

"Why not? It would be a lark."

"Ben."

My stomach flipped. "I intend to return for our valises now. I will leave yours just inside your door. You can expect your trunk in the morning."

She hesitated. Moonlight slipped through the window, and I could see the indecision playing across her features. "Should I come for it now?"

"No. We've made it, Thea. You are in your chamber, the driver is gone with our imaginary chaperone in tow, and if anyone was to find us now, it would all be right and proper because you are sleeping in your own bed, exactly where you should have been for the last six months."

Thea seemed to accept this answer. "And you?"

"After I fetch our bags, I intend to fall into my own bed and sleep until Sunday."

She gave a soft nod. "Good night, Ben."

"Good night."

I closed her door and turned away to find my way downstairs to fetch the bags. A person stood in the center of the corridor, and I startled, jumping back slightly as cold swept through my body.

"Benedict?" she asked.

"Mother," I said, equal parts relieved and hesitant. Her

familiar pink dressing gown was slightly discernible in the dark corridor, and her hair was gathered beneath a cap. I could not make out her features easily, for she bore no candle, but I could see the relief in the fall of her shoulders.

I swallowed. How long had she been standing there, and how much of my conversation with Thea had she overheard? *The driver is gone with our imaginary chaperone in tow.*

"Thea is home?" she asked, her hopeful voice churning my stomach. This was why I had gone on that wretched journey, spending five months in and out of various small towns, questioning innkeepers and shopkeepers about a small, dark-haired woman with a heart-shaped face and round blue eyes. The miniature I had taken with me had been inordinately helpful, slowly directing me along Thea's path thanks to her memorable face. The wretch was too beautiful to not be noticed.

I stepped forward and pulled my mother into a brief hug. "Yes, she is home."

"And well?" she asked into my shoulder. "She is healthy and unharmed?"

I released her. "She is thin, but so far as I can tell, she is unharmed. You will have to question her in the morning. For now, I believe she needs to rest." And to have ample time to change into clothes befitting a woman.

The silence and privacy provided a good opportunity to inform Mother that Thea would not be going to Lord Claverley's house, but her weary face reminded me of the sheer amount of strain Thea's absence had put her under. She deserved a break for a moment. I could not bear to add to her worries just yet.

"Rest is good," she agreed, pulling out a tinderbox from the table set against the wall and lighting a candle. "Then she must answer for her absence."

"Of course."

Mother let out a long, deep sigh. "I am heartened to have

you returned to us again, Benedict. Will you remain for a little while this time?"

I tried for a lighter tone. "Under the same roof as Thea? I am not certain that is a good idea." I considered escaping to our hunting lodge for the foreseeable future, or at least long enough to recover from the last week.

"It could give you the opportunity to mend your differences."

I had hoped the same thing, but it had proved impossible over the journey we took together. Thea did not appear to like me, and I could not stop myself from baiting or arguing with her. We were too volatile toward one another. The weight of my disappointment filled me. "If four days in a carriage could not mend our differences, I am not certain remaining in the same house will be any more powerful."

Mother's lips flattened, and a shadow magnified the line between her eyebrows. I hated causing her grief.

"I will stay," I finally said. I couldn't promise how long I would remain, but I could give Mother a fortnight, surely. "And I will do my best not to . . . bicker . . . with Thea."

"Thank you, darling." Mother reached for my hand and squeezed my fingers. "Now get some sleep. You sound fatigued."

I was tired. To the depths of my bones, fatigue wore at me and slowed my movements. The sheer amount of strain I had been under the last few months revealed itself in the heaviness of my limbs and the weariness of my soul. I was tired, but not just physically. When I had told Thea I planned to sleep until Sunday, I meant it.

"We must be careful, I think," I said cautiously. "Or she could run again."

Mother looked at me with confusion. "Why would she?"

I was too weary to begin the conversation about Thea's refusal to go to Claverley's house, and I feared it would only cause Mother to charge into her room for an explanation. Thea was exhausted, and she was still dressed as a boy. I couldn't risk Mother entering her chamber now. I tried to remain vague. "She had a reason for leaving Mrs. Moulton's, I am sure. If we are not careful, she might think running away is her only option again."

Mother nodded. "We must remind her that she is loved here, that she is part of the family." She sighed. "I loved Thea's mother so dearly. She was more of a sister to me than a friend, and Thea has no one else. Her Northcott uncle is lazy and unkind, and she cannot rely on him. We need to prove to her that she is loved, that she can rely on us."

The steady passion with which Mother spoke hit me with great force, and her motivations for feeling responsible for Thea's wellbeing resonated with me. I pictured Thea how I had first seen her in the garden, thin and tired, and I did not like it. I did not want for her to feel, either, that her only option was to run away—not when she had people who loved her like Mother did. Like we all did.

"Good night, Mother."

After I retrieved the valises, I returned to Thea's chamber and opened the door. It creaked softly, and I reached in and set her bag on the floor exactly as I'd told her I would. Moonlight slanted through the window, highlighting her small, sleeping form on the bed. Her face was raised toward the light, and in sleep she appeared angelic, the soft curve of her cheek and gentle slope of her mouth resting in complete contentedness. She was beautiful. I could admit so in the quiet of night and the safety of my own thoughts. I'd often wondered what it would feel like to hold her, to grasp the wild nature of Thea in my hands and follow her along her untamed joy. She exuded happiness in a way I had always envied. I did not want to contain it, but rather to beg permission to bask in it.

It wasn't to be, though, for the woman hated me. Despised me with the depth that only one of such vivacity and brightness of feeling could. Thea did not *feel* on a gentle level—she was a blast of emotion, whether it be good or bad.

When she had first arrived at Chelton, Thea had at once struck me with the deep need to know her and be adored by her. We had gotten along well, or so I'd thought, until she changed. One night we were dancing along the portrait hall, and the next day she was aloof and distant. I'd never understood what had happened to make her despise me, but my temper had flared beside hers with equal measure, and we had dug ourselves so far into a relationship of turmoil and discord that neither of us could climb our way out, even if we desired it.

Which she clearly did not.

I could not say how I felt, for in the heat of argument I often felt the deepest desire to snap. But now, in the quiet darkness of her chamber, my body outside the door and my hand resting on the brass knob, I allowed the regret that had so long sat dormant to rear its pathetic head.

It was a shame, really. We could have been the best of friends.

CHAPTER 11
THEA

My trunk and valise sat just inside the door when I awoke the next morning, and I felt an achiness in my limbs that could only be fixed with adequate rest and a warm bath. I fished my dressing gown from the trunk, tucked my servant boy clothing and shoes into a wad, and shoved them beneath my bed. Benedict would know best how to dispose of them later.

I pulled on the bell rope and crossed to the window to await the servant I'd summoned, gazing through the wavy glass panes at the sweeping lawn and rolling, tree-studded hills that made up Chelton's park. The folly was located just over the hills in the far distance—too far to walk, of course—and I longed for a bruising ride through the trees and over the hills to that restful place.

A knock preceded the short woman's entrance, and Hannah stood in the opening, her bright eyes happy to see me, or so it seemed.

I wrapped my arms over my chest and smiled at the young maid. She'd blossomed into womanhood since I'd gone away to school, but her fresh smile was just as lovely as it had been before. "Good morning, Hannah. It has been an age. How are you?"

"I'm well, ma'am. But it's good afternoon, I think."

I looked to the window again and noted the location of the sun high overhead. I'd slept far later than I'd believed. Clearing my throat, I grinned at the maid. "Is it too late in the day to order a bath?"

"Of course not. I'll see to it straight away. Would you like something to eat, too?"

"Yes, but don't let Cook go to any extra trouble on my account. Anything will do. I'm famished."

Hannah bobbed a curtsy and let herself from the room. I would be lying if I tried to convince myself I had not missed the comforts of Chelton House. A servant waiting at the end of the rope to boil water for my bath, another in the kitchen making me breakfast sometime after the sun had already reached its zenith. It was a far cry from the limited ablutions possible to a kitchen maid with a pitcher and ewer in a dim attic room, or the simple fare we consumed at the servants' table. I far preferred my situation as both a governess and a seamstress's assistant, my room in both houses plain and the food simple, but it was less laborious and provided me more freedoms.

Was I a failure? Yes, a little. It was strange to consider that I would still be picking peas and kneading dough if Benedict had not found me. I had been stubbornly set on proving I could manage on my own, that I needed no one else.

Perhaps I did not *need* anyone, but that did not mean it wasn't nice to have them. I walked away from that life knowing what I was capable of, and with a determination to make sure that any servants in my particular employ were given adequate candles, blankets, mattresses, and food. I could not return to this life from such an experience with lesser goals.

A soft knock rapped on the door and Lady Edith opened it. Her gray hair was pulled back into a soft knot, her high cheekbones and bright blue eyes highlighting the somewhat faded beauty that still held up remarkably well. She stood regally, awaiting my permission to enter the room, and the relief in her gaze and softness around her mouth was nearly palpable.

"Oh, Thea. You are home."

Home. The word plucked at me like a clashing chord. I could not claim Chelton as my home—not truly.

"It is good to see you," I said, crossing the room toward Lady Edith. "I am afraid I smell of the stables, though, so you will not wish to come any closer."

She smiled. "I hardly care for how you smell." She crossed the remainder of the room and pulled me into a warm embrace as only a mother could. Her arms wrapped around my back and pressed into my shoulder blades, surrounding me with affection, shrouding me with the feeling that I was wholly wanted here. "I am so relieved to find you well." She released me and stepped back, appraising my ratty hair and bare feet beneath my dressing gown. "Though you could use some more meat on your bones. You're too thin."

"I am certainly looking forward to Cook's marzipan."

Lady Edith's eyebrows lifted. "You're in luck. It is on the menu for tonight."

I grinned. "I do not need it so soon. I can wait until Cook has the time for it."

Lady Edith shook her head. "I am not teasing, dear. Benedict requested it this morning."

My stomach flipped, but I ignored the strange sensation. "I was under the impression that he would not be awake until Sunday."

She sat on the edge of my bed, and I sat beside her. "The poor boy cannot be told to remain still. He was up with the sun, out riding with James."

"James," I said, looking at her sharply and grasping onto the change in subject, "is married!"

"Yes." She smiled, but sorrow lurked in the shadows of her eyes. "His bride's name is Felicity, and she is a lovely and gentle soul."

"Is she?" Lady Edith's expression spoke to another emotion, and it did not seem pleasant.

"She's wonderful, and you will like her. I'm sure of it. We did not have the most auspicious beginning. Suffice it to say there were rumors about her I chose to believe, and it nearly ruined all relations between us."

Rumors were poison. I was aware of how those could ruin one's life. "But you have mended things between you now?"

"We have. I love her dearly, and now that I know her, I wonder at how I could have ever believed the things I once thought were true. But she was a stranger when she came to us here. I did not know any better then, and I have learned from my mistake." Lady Edith shot me a wry smile. "I have since promised to not form my opinion of another until I've had adequate time to know their character."

"It is a good rule to live by."

A footman carried in the tin tub, and another followed behind him with a bucket of steaming water. We watched them set up the screen and continue to fill the tub. "Everyone is home and eager to see you. Perhaps, after you've washed and dressed, you will come down to the drawing room? Henry, James, and Felicity will be there."

"Of course." Everyone except Benedict.

"Benedict had business to see to in Bakewell. He should return before dinner."

I nodded, watching Hannah carry in another bucket of water, followed by a footman.

Lady Edith rose to leave. "I noticed you did not arrive with any servants, so I have asked Hannah if she would like to become your lady's maid. If it is agreeable to you, I think she would do the job well."

"I would love that," I said, catching Hannah's smile, trained as it was at the floor.

It was not until Lady Edith left that I found myself wondering how she knew I did not arrive with a maid, and what else she'd discerned from our clandestine arrival.

Benedict

It seemed to me the only way to ensure that Mother would not force Thea onto Cousin Matthew—a name I held onto with bitter force merely because it bothered him so plainly and he preferred to be called by his title, arrogant as he was—and his wife, Lady Claverley, was to discuss the matter with them myself. I rode up to the sprawling house and left my horse at the door to the stables, then crunched along the gravel drive and up to the front door.

The butler opened it before I could so much as knock and led me inside. "Lord Claverley is in his study and awaits you there."

The benefit to a long, winding drive, I supposed, was the ability to foresee visitors and prepare accordingly. I followed the butler into Claverley's study and dropped onto the seat opposite my cousin. He cringed, his wide face and rounded cheeks not bothering to hide his disapproval of my casual behavior.

"You look well, Cousin," I said, using the title to remind him of our familial bond.

He nodded, as though agreeing with me. "Lady Claverley has me on a diet of red meats and potatoes, and it has done wonders for my energy."

"I am glad to hear it."

"You've been away a long while," he said.

"So I have. I can never stay in one place for too long, you know."

Claverley gave a little grunt of recognition.

"You might appreciate to learn your charge is in good health." I tried to sound natural, but it was not very difficult. I was not lying. "I left her just this morning and she was absolutely radiant."

"This morning? You came from York then?"

"No, from Chelton." I was careful to maintain an innocent expression. If I delivered this inadequately, the game would be up. "Has my mother not come to see you yet?"

Claverley frowned. "Not recently, no."

I looked to the ceiling as though considering this. "I suppose she has been overrun with preparation, of course. Perhaps I ought not to have mentioned Thea until my mother came first. You will forget I said anything, of course?"

Claverley did not appear inclined in the least to do so. "Hmm. Whatever would bring your mother here?"

Because Mother did not travel. She grew too ill in the carriage, no matter the distance, and my cousin knew this. He would know that she would not plan to see him without adequate cause.

"Thea, of course. The girl has come home." My chest tightened at the word, but I ignored it, leaving my placid smile in place.

Claverley's eyes brightened with greed. "Ah, I understand. Finally had enough of school, has she? We will ready her chamber."

I shrugged. Mother had complained that it had been a feat to convince Claverley that Thea stayed on to assist Mrs. Moulton and to perfect her accomplishments even greater in preparation for the marriage mart. He could not know that Thea had run off or the entire *ton* would know of it within a fortnight. "She has greatly improved her skills on the pianoforte. You will be mightily impressed, I vow." Or so I hoped. I ought to have questioned Thea a little further before undertaking this conversation.

He nodded. "When can we expect her?"

"Mother is so pleased to have her returned to us that she could hardly allow the chit to leave right away, you understand."

"I suppose."

"Thea has greatly bonded with James's new wife, Felicity, as well. It will be a feat to separate them when the time comes to travel to London. It very well may be impossible," I added with a carefree laugh. Planting each seed one bit at a time and watering them to grow. Before Claverley knew it, he would have an entire garden of understanding as to why Thea would not be living under his roof when January rolled around.

Claverley was silent, and I took his sudden disapproval as a good opportunity to cease my gardening and shift the conversation to something that would leave him satisfied. "But I did not come here to gossip. I am here to ask your advice on a matter of great importance."

That successfully captured his attention. Claverley leaned back in his leather chair and folded his hands together over his ample belly. "What is it?"

"My inheritance." The words slipped from my tongue as though traveling through glue. I ignored the anxious fettering in my stomach and held my pompous cousin's gaze. "I cannot decide if I am better suited to purchasing an estate or settling on an occupation."

Claverley sat up, his interest secured. "You did not think to ask James?"

I scoffed lightly. "James would never press me to do anything. He is happy to have me on at Chelton forever, of course, but I cannot very well bring a wife to live at my brother's house. It would never do."

"A man must have his pride," he said, nodding.

"Precisely."

He seemed to contemplate me for a moment. "Do you have any careers in mind?"

Did I? I had not thought this far ahead on the matter. I only wanted to leave Claverley feeling as though he'd helped his young, directionless cousin, and not analyzing my revelations about Thea too deeply. But he was forcing me to consider things I'd long since tried to avoid.

"I can see the answer from the blank look on your face," Claverley said, rubbing his finger over his greasy chin. "You must think, first, about the careers you would be willing to devote yourself to. Are you opposed to a great deal of travel? There are fortunes to be made overseas, you know."

"Travel is not wholly repugnant to me, but I believe my mother would find it displeasing for me to be so inaccessible."

"Hmm. You've given me much to consider. Shall we reconvene on Wednesday next and discuss the matter further? You can take the time to contemplate occupations or whether you would be successful as a master of a modest estate when you cannot like to remain in one place for very long. I can have my steward look into the available estates in the area, too. If there are any for sale, Jenkins will know of them."

Surprise lifted my eyebrows. "That would be greatly appreciated."

I rode away from Claverley with the distinct impression that while I had gone to my cousin to dupe him, he had started my cogs turning on the planning of my future. It was equal parts frightening and—I had to admit—intriguing. If I ever wanted to marry, which someday I did, I would need to have this sorted. The answer of which profession I should pursue had not come to me in school. I supposed I would begin looking for it now.

CHAPTER 12
THEA

I t was impossible not to notice Benedict's absence at dinner later that evening. I would like to think my special attention to his whereabouts was due to the fact that I had spent the last four days in his company alone, but the truth was that I always sought the man out in a room. It was ridiculous, like some sort of punishment I gave myself, that I always wished to know where Benedict was, despite his clear dislike of me.

James took up the head of the table, with his wife on one side and his mother on the other. Henry had the seat beside Lady Edith, so I sat beside Felicity. Benedict and his mother had both been correct, of course, and I liked Felicity excessively. She was far more reserved than me, but the amusement dancing in her eyes was evidence that she was a jolly soul, and I liked that about her.

"We have a dinner party planned for Monday next," Lady Edith said absently, as though I had not been missing for nearly half a year. "It is too late to add Lord and Lady Claverley, but we can extend an invitation for Friday, perhaps. I am certain they will want to see you, Thea."

I dropped my fork and knife and they clattered to the plate

loudly. Four sets of eyes trained on me. "I do not find that necessary."

A line formed between Lady Edith's faded eyebrows. She opened her mouth to speak when the door opened at the far end of the room and Benedict sauntered inside, effectively stealing the attention of the room.

"Forgive my rudeness, Mother," he said, approaching the head of the table and leaning over to kiss her cheek. "I had not expected my business to take quite so long."

"You will join us," she said, clearly forgiving him.

He looked at me but tore his gaze away. "I am not dressed for it."

"That hardly matters to us," Felicity said.

"Come and eat," James added. "You've been away too long, Ben. Surely you've missed Cook's fowls."

The smile tightened around his eyes, and he looked again at me and then away. Nodding, a slow, wide smile spread over his lips. "As you wish."

James directed the footmen to bring another place setting and they set it beside me, undoubtedly making an attempt to maintain evenness as best they could. It would have been better to ask me to move over and put him between me and Felicity, but the Bradwells were not so formal unless it was a dinner party.

"Perhaps next to Henry is better—" James began.

Benedict answered that by pulling out his own chair and taking the seat beside me. "We are not children," he said, though there was an odd bitterness in his tone. "We can sit through one dinner in perfect harmony."

The eyes around the table looked to me. "Of course we can," I added quickly. I could prove to them I knew how to act in public. I was only half the trouble, after all, and if Benedict was willing to attempt civility, I could do the same.

Lady Edith seemed pleased by this. "I was saying to Thea we

ought to have Lord and Lady Claverley over for dinner next week."

"That won't be necessary." Benedict hesitated only a moment before continuing. "I have just been to see them, actually. I think it would be better to wait."

Lady Edith's smile tightened. "What business did you have with your cousin?"

He took a moment to respond, and my fingers tightened around the fork in my hand. Had he gone to void me of the agreement? To keep to his promise? I looked at him and found him watching me. He tore his gaze away, but not before planting the seed of hope in my chest. "I think it would be better to discuss this later, Mother."

Lady Edith no longer seemed pleased. Her mouth tightened, and her eyebrows knit together in concern. "I put a great deal of effort into forming an agreement with Lord Claverley, and even greater effort in concealing Thea's recent disappearance so as to keep your cousin from quitting the agreement. There is much riding on his willingness to aid her in finding a match during the Season."

"I do not see why. We are perfectly able to sponsor her, and Felicity would make a good chaperone." Benedict looked to his sister-in-law. "You intend to go to London anyway to see your parents, do you not?"

"I do, and"—she took James's hand on the table as though needing to touch him for support—"we would be happy to help in whatever way we can."

"It's settled then," Benedict said, his wide smile impossible not to reciprocate in even the faintest of ways.

Lady Edith looked thunderous. "*Nothing* is settled."

The room fell silent. I was certain my heart was beating louder than the longcase clock at the end of the room.

Benedict cleared his throat. "For Thea's sake, I think this will be better discussed privately."

"So long as you mean to include me in the conversation," I said.

Lady Edith pressed her fingers to her temples. "There is no conversation to have. There is nothing to discuss."

"Perhaps it is better for us to give you privacy," James said, rising from his seat. He would certainly learn later of all that had transpired. I could not imagine this family kept many secrets from one another. But the kindness he showed me in not providing an audience for such an embarrassing conversation was greatly appreciated.

Felicity moved to follow her husband, but Benedict shot up from his chair. "If this must be discussed now, then we can leave. You stay and finish your meal."

Lady Edith appeared to be in agreement and stood from her seat. I had not been invited to join their conversation, but as it centered on me, I felt I had a right to be part of it. I set my napkin on the table and rushed after them. We filed into the parlor and Benedict closed the door behind us.

"I do not like that you spoke to your cousin without consulting me, Ben. You do not know the whole of the situation, and you very well could have jeopardized everything." Lady Edith paced to the fireplace before facing us. Nothing about her sleek coiffure was out of place, but she appeared disheveled still, somehow. "What shall we do if Lord Claverley refuses to sponsor her?"

"It hardly matters now," I said, a little surprised by the ferocity of my godmother's feelings. "I am not going with them to London."

"Of course you are."

"No—" I turned to Benedict. "Tell her."

He looked at me long and hard, then ran a hand over his face and helplessly turned to his mother. "She cannot go to them. I promised she would not."

"Promised who?"

"I promised Thea that if she returned with me to Chelton, we would not force her to go to Cousin Matthew's."

"*Lord Claverley*," Lady Edith corrected. "He has the title because he is an *earl*. We need his status in order to receive the invitations necessary to find Thea a decent match."

"But why?" Benedict asked. "Her parents were perfectly respectable. There is no scandal associated with the Northcott name."

Silence fell over us with the heavy thickness of an impenetrable fog. Lady Edith looked to me, her eyes holding the secrets that I'd hoped had long since faded in her memory to nothing. But of course they hadn't. The Northcott name had not been on wagging tongues in recent years, not with my parents' deaths having occurred five and six years ago, respectively, but that did not mean my appearance in Society would not breathe new life into the stagnant scandals that had faded to a dormant state.

"What is it?" Benedict asked quietly, sensing that there was something he did not know. "What are we facing?"

Something about the quiet resolution of his voice and the way he had said *we*, as though accepting that he was unavoidably embroiled in my future, made my heart skip a beat.

Lady Edith wrecked the pleasant sensation by bringing me back to the matter at hand. When she spoke, her voice was calm and measured, careful, as though she wished to handle the matter delicately. "I loved Thea's mother dearly, but after the Northcotts moved to Sweden, she gained a reputation for her infidelity—both she and Mr. Northcott did. If Thea has any hope of gaining a decent match, it will be through the extension of Lord Claverley's spotless reputation and rank."

"I do not want his help," I said, stepping forward and gaining the attention of both Lady Edith and her son. "I never did. I am happy to make my own way, even with the consequences of my parents' tarnished reputations."

"Your own way? How will you pay for your own way, then,

while your inheritance is tied up with your uncle until you come of age? We are happy to have you here, Thea, but you cannot—" Lady Edith stopped, her gaze seeking the ceiling. She was too kind to say that I could not rely on their charity forever. But I did not need to. I had money . . . just not any access to it yet.

"I have never desired to marry a gentleman, and I certainly would prefer not to live under Lord Claverley's care. I refuse, as Benedict is perfectly aware, and I only agreed to return to Chelton under the stipulation that the agreement with Lord and Lady Claverley would be nullified."

She looked to her son. "Is this true?"

Benedict nodded, but he watched me. "It is. I went to Cousin Matthew's house today to inform him that Thea is now with us, and that she will remain here."

Lady Edith shook her head. "He will not be pleased. He wants our money."

Benedict and I both looked sharply at Lady Edith.

"What do you mean?" I asked.

"You are both aware of how he avoids conflict and scandal, yes? I could find no other way to entice him to help us than to offer a healthy sum in exchange for his assistance."

Benedict sneered. "He deserves to lose it, then. Greedy git."

"You were going to pay Lord and Lady Claverley to be my chaperones?" I pressed my lips together in order to avoid speaking further and angering Lady Edith, but the revelation stung, especially when I had been so vocal about my disdain for the Season and my desire to find a love match. I could not bear to be shackled to a gentleman—not when gentlemen in my life had so far proved their unwillingness to commit to one woman.

"Perhaps not anymore. If Benedict has ruined—"

"I *will not* stay with them," I said. She could not make me go to them, for she was not my mother or my guardian. As Benedict had previously reminded me, I had nearly reached my majority, and was close enough to be entitled to some say in my own life. "I was perfectly content in my last position before Benedict forced me to come home with him."

Lady Edith looked at me as though I was a feral cat and she did not know how to contain my outburst. It was immature of me, I would grant her that.

"Until you are twenty-one, you do not have a choice in the matter. Since I have the fortune of being your godmother, your uncle has seen fit to grant me control over your inheritance. He will not move to grant or deny any of your requests without my approval until you are of age."

Another layer revealed. "You are in communication with Uncle Northcott?" The wretch had not wanted me. He had sent me here the moment I'd landed on his front door. I did not wish to be with my uncle any more than he wished to have me, and the idea that he communicated with anyone about me was a shock, since I had not heard from the man in years. My quarterly allowance had always been sent to me by his man of business, and any notices by that same man.

"I had no other choice," Lady Edith said. "He is your legal guardian."

I turned and sat hard on a wooden chair at the round, empty breakfast table. I could not fault her, for it made perfect sense that she would write to Uncle Northcott. How else was Lady Edith to have paid for my schooling or retrieved funds for new clothing or books I needed? He was irascible and a solitary creature, but until I reached my next birthday, he was legally responsible for me.

Except he had passed all responsibility to Lady Edith, had even given her the authority to manage my income. She watched me now with trepidation, and I couldn't help the flood of compassion and gratitude that swelled within me. As one of my mother's dearest friends, Lady Edith had done all she had for me merely out of the goodness of her heart, and I had repaid her poorly.

My expression was undoubtedly as conflicted as my heart. Benedict looked at me with uncertainty, as though he did not know whether to offer me comfort or leave me in peace.

"It is growing late, and we have much to consider," Lady Edith said as though she had not revealed excruciating truths about my situation. "We need to find a way to mend the situation to our best advantage."

"Without using Claverley's help," Benedict said.

Lady Edith glared at the ceiling. She seemed to draw in a breath for support, then looked at me. "Why do you wish to avoid Lord Claverley's house?"

"Because I do not care for him," I said. My voice had lost some of its ire. Ripples of unease ran down my spine where his pudgy fingers had last left their mark, when he'd played with my dress ribbon. I suppressed a shudder at the memory. I could not voice my fear aloud when I had so little proof to validate my discomfort.

"Yet you are happy to remain here, but you also dislike—" Lady Edith cleared her throat, her gaze shooting to Benedict. She did not speak her son's name, but that did not conceal her intent.

Benedict and I quarreled, but he had never given me cause to question my safety. "It is not the same thing."

Lady Edith dropped her head and pressed her fingers to her temples, massaging them. When she faced me again, it was with quiet resolve. "We shall speak more on this later and develop a plan that leaves everyone satisfied. I need time to think." She marched from the room with the grace and dignity of a woman who was raised in an earl's home, leaving Benedict and me in complete silence.

"What now?" he asked softly.

I shut my eyes, somewhat hoping he would be gone once they opened again and I would no longer have an audience to my misery. I counted to ten and clenched my frustrated hands into fists. When I opened my eyes, Benedict had not moved, and it was more of a relief than I knew what to do with that he stayed.

"I do not know," I said quietly. "I am grateful your mother intends to find a solution where we are both satisfied, but I fear that is an impossible task. I cannot help but think it would be better for everyone if I was to leave."

He looked surprised. "Return to the Fullers' kitchen?"

"I do not have that option." If I was being honest, I no longer desired to do that sort of work. "I think I am better suited to being a companion or a governess to older children."

"You've only just returned. Will you not wait a little longer and give my mother a chance to spend time with you before you leave?" His tone was gentle, surprising me with its softness.

"So long as she does not carry me to Lord Claverley's house, I can. I will need time to find a position." I gave him a wry smile. "There is no need to keep my plan a secret any longer."

"Is the idea of remaining here so disagreeable to you?" He stepped forward and played with the back of the chair beside me, as though deciding whether or not to sit. He remained standing, but looked into my eyes. "Am I truly so disagreeable to you?"

"Is not the feeling mutual?"

I'd said the wrong thing. Hurt, unaccountably, splashed over his face. "No. It is not."

"Oh? You do not hate me anymore? Where has this alteration come from?"

"Nowhere. I've never despised you as you do me, Thea."

Hadn't he, though? I might have become prickly after the embarrassment of learning I'd fallen for him and he was merely an insincere flirt, but since that moment, Benedict had met my quarreling with equal fervor. "You cannot rewrite our history, Ben."

"I am not making that attempt. But you cannot tell me, after witnessing my mother's pain, that you do not want to at least *try* to form some level of civility between us? Would laying down our weapons truly be so disgusting to you?"

"Laying down . . . you mean a truce?"

"Yes. A truce, of sorts." He paced away, then back toward me. "We needn't like one another to pretend we do. If we can prove we can be friends, maybe Mother would not press the issue with Lord Claverley. She could see the value in having our family sponsor you instead."

"It cannot make matters worse, certainly."

His mouth ticked up into a half-smile. "Being my friend? No, that would only brighten your life, surely."

"You think so highly of yourself."

"You are about to do so as well, I think."

I laughed lightly, tearing my gaze from his gleaming, teasing eyes. The way they danced when he spoke, full of mischief, made the blue brighter and his smile more handsome. Blasted Benedict. I did not appreciate the way his proposed plan made me look at him differently.

"You desire a love match, then?" he asked.

"I do."

"Then, if it is in my power, I shall help you achieve it."

I didn't know whether gratitude or surprise was the chief emotion flooding me, but I rose and crossed the few steps between us, bringing me close to his side. I leaned my head back to hold his gaze, searching it for truth, while his spicy, tangy scent overwhelmed my senses. "Why are you doing this?"

He could not seem to keep his gaze still. It flitted from my hair to my jaw to whatever hovered behind me. Finally it rested on my face, and I held my breath from the intensity there. "Guilt? Or perhaps it is the innate desire to best you at something. I can be the better friend, and I will prove it."

"Doubtful," I said softly. "It is I who has a multitude of friends and am loved by all."

"All?"

"Well, loved by everyone except you. I doubt that will change."

He stared at me in a way that made my breath catch. "I suppose we shall see."

CHAPTER 13
BENEDICT

Mother was abed the following day with a headache. It was a common occurrence when she found herself overwhelmed, and I didn't like being the cause of her added stress, but I'd made a promise to Thea and I kept my promises. A devil had somehow come over me in the parlor last night, for there could be no other explanation for the way I had spoken to Thea. I still was unsure what my proposed truce comprised of, but I supposed we would soon find out if it was even possible between the two of us.

My bets were on no. It was impossible. Thea's dislike was too potent, too strong.

Stray sunlight peeked over the edge of the horizon, making the trees glow as though a fire bloomed behind their mass of tangled branches. The morning was unaccountably cold, even for November. Or was it now December? I'd lost track of the days.

Gregory had gone ahead and ordered Jasper to be saddled for me, and I marched down the short hall that led into the courtyard, the brick ceiling curving above my head. A woman in a deep violet riding habit was being helped onto a saddle not far from where Jasper awaited me, and it did not take long to recognize—despite the fact that I could not see her face—that it was Thea being helped onto a horse by a groom.

She turned her elegant neck until her eyes locked on me, and I forced my steps to remain consistent in their journey toward Jasper.

"We agreed to a truce, not a friendship," she said lightly, though I could sense she was nervous. "Now you think we ought to ride together?"

"I am not opposed to beating you in a friendly race." I strode toward my horse and obtained the saddle in a smooth, easy motion. I was quietly, internally relieved that swinging onto the horse had worked as well as I'd imagined in my mind, and that my horse Jasper had not stepped forward and botched my attempts at appearing like a Corinthian. I looked at her. "But I did not expect to find you here this morning."

"Interesting." She looked away when I met her gaze, her cheeks pinking slightly. "You are very confident in your abilities. It was I who won the last race, if I recall correctly."

"You do. But I am trusting that, inevitably, your previous situations did not leave you much time for riding." I turned Jasper toward the archway, the gates having been left wide open, and Thea directed her horse to follow me. Her silent acquiescence and agreement to ride together made victory silently soar through me. "Tell me, when was the last time you've ridden?"

"Too long ago to warrant mentioning."

"As I thought." We weaved out of the stables and toward the rolling hills covered in grass bleached of color in patches, the half-barren trees marking the turning of the seasons, their red and gold leaves fluttering in the wind and littering the ground.

"I can still manage a decent seat, I wager," she said, as though not to be discounted.

"Care to place a bet on it?" I asked. It was Thea, after all, who had mentioned a wager.

"What would we wager? I haven't much to give."

"Mother told you of the assemblies next week in Bakewell?"

Thea nodded.

"The first to reach the folly chooses the other person's partner for the first set." I could see it now, forcing Thea to dance with hook-nosed Ned or fish-breath Timothy. There wasn't a woman in all of Bakewell I would be miserable with or suffer through a set beside.

Regardless, I would surely win.

"Very well," Thea said easily. She reached across the space between our horses, and I guided Jasper closer in order to take her gloved hand in mine. We shook once and released quickly.

I nodded to the brown horse she rode. "James lent you Luna?"

"Evidently Felicity doesn't ride," Thea explained, "so he told me Luna was mine to use whenever I wished."

"That was kind of him." It was true that my sister-in-law wasn't fond of the sport. "Felicity has a mule and cart she uses when she wishes to go out in solitude. She is an adept hand with the contraption, according to James." Though if she used it as often as James made it sound, that was no surprise.

"Ready?" Thea asked.

I nodded. "Go."

We both took off at the same time in the general direction of the folly, but the thick trees made it impossible to stay side by side through the hills. Thea and I weaved between trees and up and over green and yellow swells of grass, avoiding the rocky outcrops and boulders dotting the countryside. A flock of sheep appeared on the downhill in our path and we were both forced to circumvent the animals. For having just suffered such a long break in riding, Thea was deft in her maneuvering. She was a skilled rider, and I should not have had so much confidence in my ability to win.

The domed ceiling of the stone temple came into view, and I

pushed Jasper harder. It was tempting to allow Thea the win, merely to learn whom she would choose as a partner for me if given complete freedom. But she would know the win was not truly hers. Somehow, I knew she would.

So I did the only right thing. I leaned forward, pushed Jasper, and reached the columned Greek folly before her. A grin spread over my lips when I met Thea's disappointment.

"It will take some time to decide on a partner for you," I said, sliding from the saddle, my chest heaving.

Thea unhooked her legs from the pommels and jumped to the ground, her chest rising and falling in time with mine. "You will not choose Alfred, the vicar's son. I forbid it."

"Lucky for Alfred, he has now risen to the top of the list."

She dropped her head back and closed her eyes for patience.

"You should not have revealed your hand—or so they say when playing cards. You will not understand the meaning, I'm sure."

"I've played whist enough times to understand it very well," she said, her mottled cheeks and tip of her nose red from the wind and the cold. "You took advantage of my rustiness in the saddle."

A quiet scoff slipped from my throat. "If that was rusty, you shall be winning before long."

Thea laughed and shook her head. She started walking away, and a strong desire rose in my chest to follow her. She disappeared around the bend, the marble wall to one side and stone columns to the other, the long skirt of her habit trailing behind her on the ground.

I followed her.

Thea

Benedict's laughing eyes and flushed cheeks were too much for me, so I had to leave his presence, if only for a moment to cool my racing heart and retake control of my feelings. His hair had become a mass of curly chaos after the bruising ride, and somehow it managed to appear even more rakish and not at all disheveled.

That he could look so handsome while I was tousled and in a state of rumpled disarray was unfair. Strands of hair had come loose from my dark knot, trailing along my neck and grazing my cheeks in the wind. I looked over my shoulder and found Benedict following me, so I refrained from straightening my coiffure. I could not allow this man to see how his presence affected me.

I continued around the circular building and paused at my favorite place. Hills dipped down into the fog resting on the crisp, wet grass. Inhaling the fresh scent of earth and morning dew, I looked out over the beautiful countryside I had missed so dearly in the dim little kitchen at the Fullers' house.

"When I went to see Claverley yesterday, I did not realize I was dipping my hand into a situation so far beyond my reach," Benedict said quietly at my side.

I shut my eyes. "I was just as unaware as you. Your mother never told me that money changed hands. That certainly complicates things."

"I doubt it has yet, but that does not mean my cousin will not fight for it. They are in a bad way at Claverley. He needs the funds to replace his roof, and his crops haven't thrived in recent years as ours have."

Benedict's knowledge about the situation surprised me, and I turned to face him better. "He told you these things yesterday?"

"No. I have been assisting James with the management of Chelton for some time now, so none of this information is very recent. It is true, all the same."

I nodded. "I feel for his trials, but I will not go to his house, so he must content himself with finding the funds elsewhere. I was pleased when Felicity agreed to chaperone me to London."

"Given the scandal she and James were married under, I'm not sure Mother will deem that sufficient."

This was something I hadn't considered. In order for Felicity and James to lend me their good name, they would need to first have a good reputation of their own. Though I could not see how anyone would believe either of them below reproach.

It was unfair that I had to have a chaperone at all. If Benedict attended the Season with the intent to look for a wife, he would not need anyone's patronage—he could live and be received on his own merit. "What of you, Ben?"

He leaned back a little, his brown eyebrows lifting. "What about me?"

"You are older than me. You have no occupation to speak of, and you are not courting a woman, to my knowledge. Why must I be forced to attend the Season and find a husband, but you are not?"

He held my gaze, his eyes growing a deeper blue as the sun continued its ascent over the edge of the earth.

"Do not say it is because you have an independent income," I said, "because I possess that as well."

He nodded as though he agreed. "Our situations are not so very different—"

"Thank you."

"—but they could not be more different at the same time."

"I am not in the mood for riddles."

"No," he said quietly. "I do not think you would be." Benedict looked out over the expanse of land, the muscle in his jaw jumping as he appeared to be considering something. When he turned his attention back on me, it was with a sense of determination that made my heart rate jump.

"Why do you appear as though you are preparing to run into battle?" I asked.

"I've laid down my battle weapons, remember?"

It seemed to me that in doing so, and lowering his defensive walls, he had somehow only become more of a threat.

He sighed. "Do you . . . do you *want* to be married, Thea? To find a husband?" he asked, his face crumpling slightly to show how difficult of a question it was for him to ask.

I looked at him sharply. "Of course I do." I wanted a husband and children and a home of my own that was not dependent on England's relationship with another country or my father's political aspirations. Only, I wanted all of those things *and* the surety that they would remain mine—that my husband would be mine alone, that my home would be steady and secure. I did not wish for a marriage to a lord who blessed me with a child and then spent his time away from us.

"Then why are you so adamantly opposed to attending the Season?"

"Because I do not think the man who will love me will be attending it."

"The man who will love you?" he choked out. "Gads, Thea. If you already had a beau, you need only to have said so."

"I do not have anyone. I only meant that the type of man who will love me is certainly not a member of the *ton*. So why would I waste time going to balls when he is elsewhere?"

"You have not met this man, but you are assuming he does not dance?"

"I have not met him, and I care not for whether or not he can dance." I was tired of skirting the issue. "I've watched Society's interactions from afar, and I know very well the dance and games played between men and women in the ballrooms. I do not wish to be part of that spectacle, and I'm certain the man who would love me would feel the same."

"Your logic astounds me."

"You do not have to agree with me, Ben. You asked, and I am telling you my opinions."

"Fair enough. I am only trying to help you, but you are making it increasingly difficult. If this mysterious man does not frequent Society functions, where had you hoped to find him?"

In a kitchen when he delivered the grocer order. In a quiet country parish away from London. In the seamstress's shop where I'd hoped to meet customers coming in to purchase items for their mothers or sisters. In the churchyard after Sunday service in Brumley. Anywhere that did not glitter with excess and greed.

I looked up into Benedict's curious gaze and found my heart stalling, my breath abating. I could not allow him admittance into the quiet hopes and dreams I'd scarcely admitted to myself —not this man who played the social games in ballrooms and with women's emotions that I was trying to avoid.

Turning away, I set my gaze on the rising sun and watched the autumnal colors glow like fire in the trees.

"Anywhere else," I finally said. "I want a love match, and that cannot be forced."

"No," he agreed quietly, his voice oddly hoarse. "I do not think it can."

CHAPTER 14

BENEDICT

Nearly a week had passed since Thea and I had returned to Chelton, and after that first morning race to the folly, we had made something of a daily habit of finding one another in the stables at dawn and sharing our morning ride. The conversations had not reached the depth they had that first morning, but I was happy to have a companion to keep me from my thoughts.

It was when I rode alone that I most frequently searched my soul, and at present, that felt a dangerous course to travel.

Instead, I turned my attention on determining the best man to select for Thea's first dance at the Bakewell assemblies. I was tempted to select myself, of course, merely to vex her, but I feared what she would think of that.

"Perhaps Mr. Farnes will be in attendance," I mused, rubbing a hand slowly over Jasper's nose.

Thea stood two stalls down, murmuring softly to Luna and ignoring me.

"He is a nice enough chap, but he certainly does know how to carry a conversation." She looked up at me, and I grinned. "All on his own."

Her mouth flattened in an unamused line. "Splendid. Then nothing will be required of me."

Shadows darkened the entrance to the stables, and Henry and James approached, watching us with mild interest. We had returned from our earlier ride and both remained to care for our horses—*that* was the only reason Thea and I were still in the stables together. I ought to have gone inside at least a half hour ago, perhaps, but I was waiting for Thea so we could walk together.

Now I regretted that impulse.

"Are you returning from a ride or preparing for one?" James asked.

"Returning," Thea said. "I prefer the early mornings when the fog makes it difficult to see."

James laughed. "There is a peace to be found then, I agree."

"I wouldn't know anything about peace," she said lightly. "Benedict accompanied me."

Henry and James both chuckled, and I shot them an irritated look. "*Someone* has to ensure Thea isn't trying to jump hedges on her own."

"Oh, of course, brother. We do not employ enough grooms for that," James said, his grin revealing his amusement.

We were no longer in our youth, so I was not forced to sit through the teasing of my brothers. I gave them a wide grin, patted Jasper on the nose, and pivoted toward the exit. "Enjoy your ride," I called, not bothering to watch their continued schoolgirl chuckles. I made it through the stone archway and toward the back of the house before Thea caught up to me.

"They were only teasing," she said.

I kept my gaze ahead of me. "I am well aware of that. They are older brothers and it is what they are best at."

"Then why are you fleeing?"

"Flee—" I shook my head and looked at her. "I am hardly *fleeing*. You make me sound like a heroine in a gothic novel. I am merely going to prepare for some business I must take care of later today."

Thea nodded sagely. "Of course. Business. The excuse all men use when they seek privacy or an escape."

She was not wrong, so I did not contradict her.

"We are meant to be friends, are we not?"

I laughed. "I believe you specifically mentioned we may have a truce, but we cannot and never will be friends."

"Well, I was probably in a foul mood when I said that. Is a truce not a path toward friendship?"

I stopped on the gravel walkway and turned to face her. Did she want that? Desire my friendship? I could not deny I had long hoped for the same. It was wearing to constantly be at odds with one another. The last week of rides in the mornings and reduced quarreling during meal times had been a pleasant reprieve.

But looking at Thea now, I could not help but note the hesitation in her wide blue eyes, or the emotion that seemed to flutter in the energy about her. She was holding her breath.

Which begged the question: why was this so important to her?

"I would enjoy being your friend, Thea."

Her shoulders relaxed. She sent me a wry grin. "Of course you would. Most people adore me."

"I'm not most people," I quipped, returning a phrase she once said to me. "But I can see why you have hordes of admirers."

"I do not, which you well know. I've had *one* admirer, and it was the product of a short relationship that ended before I came back to England." She frowned. "Well, two, I suppose, if you count the vicar's son and his declaration before I went to school."

My stomach flipped at the words *a short relationship*. I resumed walking to cover my shock. "An admirer in Sweden?"

"No, in Vienna." She looked at me and away again as we neared the entrance to the house. "The man we saw in the inn, remember? Peter Seymour. I did tell you at the time that he was persistent."

"Of course. I forgot." A persistent admirer did not necessarily equate to a relationship, though. This was new information, and the souring of my stomach proved how much I rejected the notion. I held the door open for Thea, and she gathered her skirt and shook out the dirt. "You did not love him, then?"

"No. I thought I did until he kissed me." She made a face. "I quickly learned that my feelings for him were fleeting. In my defense, however, I was rather young."

My body jolted at hearing her words. I was not scandalized—I'd kissed girls before, and I understood that the important thing was to not be caught—but that *Thea* had kissed someone made my blood heat to an unaccountable degree. I looked at her lips, then quickly tore my gaze away. "I assume he is not the man you wish to marry then."

"Of course not. I told you this already. I have not met my future husband yet."

We walked through the great hall toward the wide staircase, over the checkerboard floor. "I can take you into Bakewell tomorrow if you'd like. We can call in at the baker, the butcher, the blacksmith. The vicarage might be a little too grand for you, but I will add that stop to my list if you'd like to try again with Mr. Upshaw's son."

She flattened her lips. "You are making too much of my goals. The only thing you need to concern yourself with is convincing your mother I will be perfectly fine with Felicity's chaperonage. I can manage the rest."

"Felicity's chaperonage?" I questioned, stopping at the top of the stairs. "Does that mean you've decided to attend the Season?"

She gave a flippant shrug, but I could see beneath the expression to the apprehension that flicked over her face. "It will please your mother, and I have always enjoyed dancing. I do not expect to leave London with a husband, though, so temper your amusement."

"You can believe I never imagined you to do what was expected of you, Thea. Certainly not in this or any regard."

We continued down the corridor and into the family wing.

"Yes, well . . . your mother has done much for me since I arrived back on English soil, and this is important to her." Her tone changed, growing lighter. "Only think, Ben. Six more weeks and you will not have to see me ever again." Her smile was wide, amusement shining in her blue eyes.

Ever again? I stumbled but caught myself before she could notice. It was a completely foreign concept that Thea could walk out of my life and never step back into it.

Despite our rocky relationship, I did not like the idea of that at all.

I tried for a light tone to match hers. "The house will certainly be more peaceful."

Thea laughed, the melodic sound bouncing about the long, enclosed corridor. "After your dauntless search for me and the resulting stress it provided you, I am more than certain you will feel immense peace at my departure next month."

"I would not say immense peace," I corrected. "More like a great deal of peace."

She chuckled and shook her head, walking toward her door. She dropped the skirt of her habit, the dark violet fabric trailing on the carpet behind her like a queen. I did not know any other women who allowed their habits to trail in the same way Thea did, but it said so much about her personality. Her vivacity and uncaring nature—not that she did not care about people, but that she did not care for what they thought of her. I was envious of her ease in that way, of the way she was so confident in herself and what she wanted that she was willing to leave school and set off on her own in search of that very thing, despite what others—namely my mother—wanted for her, or what Society expected of her.

She had mentioned in the carriage that she did care what Society thought of her, about her reputation, but her actions and attitude belied that statement. She was a puzzle, one I knew I would never have the chance to piece out.

"I will see you later, I suppose," she said once she reached her door. "There's no helping it in this house."

"I thought we decided to be friends. You should look forward to seeing me again."

"I do," she said, a little too innocently. "Almost as much as I look forward to seeing your cousin at the dinner next week."

Her sweet smile was overdone, and I laughed, walking past her toward my own chamber. "Well, in any case, you shan't see me for the rest of the day. I truly have business to attend to."

She leaned against her door frame and crossed her arms over her chest. "Truly? What about?"

"Well, actually, it's about you."

Her mouth dropped open the slightest bit, and I continued, unhurriedly, into my own room and shut the door behind me, my wide smile reaching from one dimpled cheek to the other.

There was a modicum of shame attached to my visit to Claverley House, and I did not tell anyone where I was going when I left Chelton, except for the delectable tease I had left behind in Thea's ear. The shock and confusion on her face when I mentioned that my business was about her was priceless, and I would carry that moment of sweet victory into the meeting I was about to attend. I was no closer to determining what sort of future I wanted for myself, and I did not think Claverley would know any better than I, but it was a good excuse to meet in his study and further Thea's cause.

Now that I knew more of the situation, a conversation with Claverley would be much easier to navigate.

His butler let me in and directed me to the parlor, where he sat with his young son over their tea. "Care for a cup?" he asked, then sipped from his rose-painted teacup softly.

"I would, thank you."

A maid stepped forward and prepared tea for me before passing it over.

"Run along," Claverley said to his son, and the fire-haired boy put his unfinished tea down on the short table and ran from the room, no doubt grateful to be dismissed from whatever lessons he'd been partaking in.

I took a sip of my hot tea. "He's an obedient lad."

Claverley snorted. "Of course he is. He's my son." He drank the rest of his tea and set the cup down, signaling to the maid to refill it. Most meetings I attended with men were chiefly supported by port, brandy, or the occasional whisky. This tea was a nice change.

"Bumpton Hall is for sale," Claverley said, getting right to the point. "My man inquired, and they've lowered the price by two thousand pounds because it won't sell. Take from that what you will. I've heard the roof needs repairs, but the problems could be far more extensive."

"That is near the Westmorland border, is it not?"

Claverley nodded. "Too far, I take it?"

Was it? It was still relatively close, though I would not consider them neighbors. I hadn't thought deeply about how close I wanted to remain to Bakewell. James and Felicity would stay at Chelton always, and Mother, too, I wagered, but it was impossible to know what Henry would choose to do with his life. The man could be depended upon to either be found on a horse or with his nose stuck in a book, so conversations were few and far between. He'd inherited our hunting box, Sedwick Lodge, after my father's death, but heaven only knew what he intended to do with the place.

"You aren't to repeat this to anyone," Claverley said, lowering his voice. He rubbed his chin and watched me, waiting for a confirmation. I nodded, and he continued. "I have it on good authority that Kellinger Park will be up for sale in the next month or so. They are remaining very quiet about the matter, for Mrs. Browning wants to be removed from the house before buyers are traipsing through it and ruining her peace. Or so she says."

Kellinger was a beautiful house situated on the road between Chelton and Sedwick Lodge. It was closer to the hunting lodge, and we often passed it when traveling from one of our houses to the other. It was difficult to miss, even from the road, as it was set on a hill so its grandeur could be seen and admired from afar. It was a tasteful house, not too large, though perhaps a little bigger than I could afford. The inheritance left to me by my father would be enough to purchase an estate, if I so chose, which I believed to be his intention with the money—but I would have nothing left to invest in the land or animals to make the estate profitable.

If I chose an occupation, though, the money would provide enough to help me set up whatever career I chose.

I tore my mind away from memories of my father before his demise and conversations we'd had about my future. I'd been young then and hadn't wanted to discuss it. Now I wished I had listened better.

"When does the family plan to leave?" I asked.

"As soon as they determine where they are going." Claverley shook his head, his chin wobbling. "It is an utter mess. Mr. Browning's debts are too numerous to count and his creditors have been at his door since March. It's a miracle, really, they haven't carted him off to prison already."

"The Brownings must be doing something to stay out of it,"
I said.

"Selling off the family jewels and the like, naturally. A few
marbles were sold only last month—Roman, or some such thing
—but surely they've nothing left to sell. Whoever buys the
house will receive a veritable shell."

"There is nothing wrong with that. It allows the new owner
to decorate easily to their own tastes." If they possessed the
money to do so, of course. Which, after the purchase of an
estate, I doubted I would.

"Hmm." Claverley drank another cup of tea. "If you've any
interest in the place, I can arrange a meeting. Only to walk
through, mind you, to see the estate. We can see Bumpton, too,
if you've the stomach for repairs."

I certainly had the skill. James and I had fixed all manner of
things on his property, and we had been doing so since we were
lads ourselves. James enjoyed the physical exertion, and I didn't
mind helping him. He liked to joke that it was my way of paying
for the privilege of living in his house, but we both knew I was
happy to be of service and that he considered Chelton our family
home, that he would never expect me to think of it as *his*.

But, it *was* James's house. The longer I considered the idea of
striking out and finding my own estate, the more I felt it held
merit. I wanted to raise a family in my own space, and I was
certain Felicity would desire the same thing once she found
herself in the family way. Henry could move into his hunting
lodge, but I needed somewhere of my own, too.

I raised my head and smiled at my cousin, who now frowned
into his teacup as though wondering where his drink had gone.

"I'm interested," I said, garnering his attention. "If your man
will set up the meetings, I would be grateful to tour both
estates."

"Of course." He gestured for the maid to fill his cup once
more. "Now, when will Miss Northcott be on her way to me?"

Claverley watched me with such expectation, such little artifice, that it occurred to me at once what he was doing. He was making me beholden to him so I would feel obligated to assist him in what he wanted.

"You will have to ask my mother that, my lord." I did my best to sound lazy, as though Thea's location and plans were the least of my concerns. "Last I heard, Miss Northcott was planning to attend the Season under my sister-in-law's care. It is only reasonable, I suppose, for the girl to wish to remain with such a dear friend."

Doing it a little too brown, I thought. I hoped Claverley did not pick up on that. Thea had only met Felicity just over a week ago, but my cousin did not necessarily know this.

"We had a deal," he said tightly, "and I expect Thea to uphold her end of the bargain."

"A deal?" I asked, bunching my eyebrows as though I was unaware of the bargain he'd struck with my mother.

Claverley grew agitated and rubbed his palm over his forehead and then down his pant leg. "I suppose I ought to visit your mother. But—" He looked to the clock on the mantel, then out the door. "We are to set off for my mother-in-law's house for a fortnight. Blasted relations."

"Oh? You will not be attending dinner at Chelton next week?"

"No. My wife sent off the note yesterday, I believe, refusing the invitation to dine. We will come for dinner after we return."

I smiled. "It is no matter, then. Certainly Lady Claverley will enjoy seeing her parents."

"Undoubtedly." His cheeks mottled red, and he looked frustrated. "This business will have to wait the fortnight until my return. I will send news of what my steward can put together for the estates."

That he was still helping me after being denied Thea again came as something of a surprise, but I did not point it out to him. I rose, hoping to leave before I could further ruin Thea's situation. "Until then, my lord," I said, adding the deference to leave him satisfied. It accomplished what it set out to do. Claverley puffed his chest a little and waved me off. I walked to my horse, away from the earl's house, with equal measures of hope for my future and concern for Thea's.

I'd made her a promise, however, and I intended to see it through.

CHAPTER 15

THEA

It had been ages since I attended a ball, and the local assemblies of Bakewell were everything I remembered loving about dances. The drink was sweet, the party lively, and the gentlemen plentiful. Felicity hung back, holding tightly to James's arm, and I waited beside Lady Edith for Benedict to retrieve for me another glass of orgeat.

"The dancing will begin soon," Lady Edith said softly, her eagle eyes sweeping over the room in a slow perusal.

Benedict had won the opportunity of selecting my first dancing partner, but I did not know if it was wise to share that with his mother. She would not find it amusing that we had treated my future marriage prospects so lightly. She was very unwilling to recall that I did not mind if I did not find a husband straight away.

I was no spinster and the shelf was far from reach at present.

"Shall we greet the vicar?" James asked, indicating Mr. Upshaw standing beside his son.

Lady Edith appeared to notice Alfred, the vicar's son, and nodded. "Let's."

We had begun our small procession around the outskirts of

the room when Benedict approached and lightly tapped me on the elbow. I turned to find a tall, narrow man standing just behind him with a shock of nearly white blonde hair and a serious expression on his long face.

"Miss Northcott, may I have the pleasure of introducing Bakewell's newest schoolmaster, Mr. Rufford?"

The man looked perfectly ordinary, if a little solemn. He did not seem to smell bad or appear like a man who was prone to talk without ceasing—so what was the catch?

I dipped in a graceful curtsy and held the man's attention as I rose. Thus far, he seemed infinitely better than Mr. Alfred Upshaw, who had long ago professed his undying love for me after church when I was seventeen. But after only a few weeks of knowing one another, I could not truly trust his profession, of course. He had been a difficult suitor to shake, so I tended to avoid him as best as I could.

"Miss Northcott, allow me to welcome you to the great parish of Bakewell," Mr. Rufford said. "Your presence brings a spot of sunshine to this dreary countryside."

I clamped my mouth closed to avoid arguing directly with this stranger. Calling this countryside *dreary*, though, was akin to sin. This countryside was luscious, even in the ebbing autumn and approach of winter. It was heaven compared to the coal-smoke filled London or the industrious York.

He *had* called me a spot of sunshine, though, so I supposed his blunder could be forgiven.

"I am glad to be here," I said simply.

He cleared his throat and bent regally over my hand. "Would you do me the honor of agreeing to dance the first set with me, Miss Northcott?"

It took a great effort to avoid Benedict's eye. A small part of me had wondered if he would select himself as my partner— merely to vex me, of course—and his procurement of another man, a working man even, settled in my stomach strangely. I pasted a smile on my face to cover my disappointment. "I would be delighted to."

Mr. Rufford sent me a bland smile, then walked away. Once he was out of earshot, I stepped closer to Benedict. "What did I do to deserve such kindness? He seemed completely ordinary."

"Kindness?" Benedict guffawed. "He is a *schoolmaster*."

I waited for further explanation, but he only blinked at me. Evidently he'd not chosen the man for his profession after all.

"Which makes him dependable and even-tempered," I said. "If he devoted a fraction of the effort to learning to dance as he did his lessons, then I will walk away with a decent dance partner and all my toes unharmed."

Benedict's mouth flattened to a thin line. "I had hoped you'd find him boring."

"How little you know me, Ben."

His gaze cut to mine, his blue eyes gleaming like the top of a still lake, and my stomach swooped in response. "I think I know you a little, Thea. Likely better than you realize."

His words curled through me and resonated deep in my gut. A response evaded me, and when I turned to bluster at him he was already walking away, his posture easy and his walk refined, as though he was unaffected.

But I was not. I had been wholly affected by Benedict Bradwell and the way he spoke to me. I tamped those feelings down and shoveled dirt over them as though my thoughts of Benedict consisted of hot coals and I needed to snuff out the heat. I watched him curve through groups of chatting people until he came to a stop beside a group that consisted of a handful of gentlemen and a young woman in a silver gown.

"Come," Felicity said softly, suddenly at my elbow and stealing my attention. "Lady Edith wants you to greet Alfred Upshaw."

"I cannot dance with him," I told her, struggling to tear my gaze from Benedict's easy smile. I succeeded, though with

Herculean effort, and set my wide eyes on my new friend. "He once told me how ardently he loves me after an extremely short acquaintance, and if I dance with him now, even though that was years ago, it might give him false expectations."

"When was that?"

"When I was seventeen."

Felicity looked unsure. "Surely he does not still carry a *tendre* for you, not after all that time."

"I should hope not," I said with feeling. The man was unsuitable as a whole. He clearly believed himself in love too quickly, and if he was to become a vicar like his father, he would be in a position to fall in love with any number of women in his congregation after we married. I would not be a wife who sat for his sermons week after week and watched him appreciate every other woman. "But I did give him a particularly unkind set down at the time, so he might have turned over his love for hatred. I should protect myself from him at all costs."

"No one could hate you," she said easily.

"Except Benedict," I quipped.

Felicity's strawberry-blonde hair was styled simply, with wisps of hair escaping and trailing over her neck. She looked over my shoulder where Benedict now stood with the group of men, chatting with the woman in the silver gown, and watched him analytically.

"He does not hate you," she finally said. I moved to argue, but something in her expression made me pause. "Benedict certainly holds strong feelings where you are concerned, but I would not believe hate to be among them. No one would search for a woman for five months if he hated her. No man would sacrifice so dearly or work so hard, not even for his mother's benefit. Hunting for you for a few weeks in the name of Lady Edith was perhaps reasonable, but not five months."

Five months?

My stomach fell to the waxed wooden floor, and I sought

Benedict in the crowd once more as the master of ceremonies was announcing the first set. His smile was trained down at the woman in the silver gown, his strong arm bent for her to rest her dainty hand on his elbow, and I felt sick. Sincerity shone in his joyfully creased smile, and whatever he said to the woman was enough to bring a pleased blush to her cheeks.

"Miss Northcott?" a voice said to my side. Mr. Rufford stood there, waiting for me. Felicity, it appeared, had gone back to stand beside James.

I placed my hand on Mr. Rufford's arm and allowed him to lead me to the center of the room with the other dancers all lining up. Benedict and the silver goddess stood a few couples down from us, and I snapped my attention to Mr. Rufford so I would not be subjected to watching Benedict flirt any longer.

"Have you enjoyed being the headmaster here in Bakewell?"

"It has been an adjustment from Manchester, I will admit."

"Good heavens, in what way?" He could not mean that he desired to return to such a bumbling city, surely.

He looked about the room briefly as the instruments began to play. "Far too slow here for my liking."

Well, that I could understand, I supposed.

The dance began in earnest, and we moved along the smooth wood floors and kicked up our feet cheerfully. It was impossible not to wear a grin while dancing so happily, and my partner, though somber, knew the steps and executed them well enough. That dance and the next passed in relative joyfulness, but each time I lifted my head and noticed Benedict smiling down at his partner or saying something amusing to her glittering cheeriness, my stomach grew a little tighter.

Benedict had searched for me. For *five months*, the man had looked for me. When he'd explained his part in finding me, he had certainly attempted to make it sound like far less than it was. What would be the purpose of withholding the extent he went to in his search? What was he hiding? I wanted to question him, but first I wanted to tear the silver goddess's hand from his arm.

When the set came to a close, I returned to Lady Edith's side. She no longer stood with the vicar, for which I was grateful.

"You are a talented dancer," Felicity said kindly.

"Thank you. I do enjoy it dearly. You are certain you won't join me?" I looked from her to James, and he smiled lovingly down at his wife.

"We only dance when we are alone," he explained. "Liss is a talented dancer, too."

I would have to take his word for it. I understood she had anxious fits when she was forced to the center of attention, but as I did not suffer from the same malady, I could not entirely understand.

"Miss Northcott."

I turned to find Mr. Beesley, a gentleman I had known when I lived at Chelton before. He'd grown taller since I'd seen him last, and his smile was very handsome. I dipped in a curtsy. "Good evening, Mr. Beesley. You look very well."

"I intended to make the same remark to you. Is your next set spoken for, or might I have the honor of claiming it?"

"You may."

I danced that set with Mr. Beesley, the following with Mr. Knox, and the supper dance with Mr. Davidson. All the while Benedict danced each set with various young ladies, and each of them smiled up at him in revolting admiration until the last, and I had to face away from his blatant flirtations during supper so I did not lose my meal.

"Do you intend to remain at Chelton for long?" Mr. Davidson asked, a local farmer who had recently taken over from his father because of an extreme degradation of the older man's arthritis.

"I have found that it is better for me not to plan too far into the future, for in my case, the future has never been predictable."

His blond eyebrows arched up. "You sound like a gypsy."

I could take great offense at that, but he was correct. "I feel like it, too." I caught Felicity's eye across the table, her curiosity spearing me, and I cleared my throat. "Though I believe we intend to travel to London for the Season, so I will remain at Chelton until then, at least."

"Another month?" he questioned.

Less than a month. The Season felt like it was slipping closer to me at a rate faster than I was prepared for. "I believe it has been discussed that Parliament resumes on the twenty-seventh of January. So it is a safe assumption that we will leave for London before then. Though Lady Edith remarked that the best balls do not take place until a few weeks after Parliament resumes, of course."

He nodded, considering. "Do you enjoy Bakewell, Miss Northcott?"

"Yes, excessively. It is most charming, is it not?" I appeared to have said the correct thing, for Mr. Davidson beamed at me.

When we returned to the hall for more dancing, Mr. Davidson left me to see to his next partner, and Benedict sidled up beside me, so close I could feel his arm brush against the back of my shoulder. "Do you often have a habit of instilling hope into gentlemen who do not stand a chance of winning your affections, or have I entirely misread the situation?"

"Good heavens, Ben." I kept my gaze on the couples forming lines in the middle of the room for the dance. "Whatever are you referring to?"

"Calling Davidson *charming* was unkind if you do not mean anything by it."

My umbrage knew no bounds. "You misheard me. I called Bakewell charming."

"He was not asking about Bakewell."

143

"He certainly sounded like he was when he asked me if I liked *Bakewell*."

"That was an attempt to make out your interest," he said quietly, his deep feeling growing more evident with each word. "After accepting him for the supper dance, it is only expected."

I brushed off his words, though they planted a little unease within me. "Your secret language is not known to all, and I highly doubt Mr. Davidson meant it the way you imply."

"Doubt me all you'd like, but I do know a bit about flirtation, and I can, with confidence, assure you that you have taken his measure wrong if you do not believe that he was hoping to gauge your interest."

"Because you know him so well?"

Benedict was quiet for a moment. He leaned a little closer, lowering his voice. "No. Because I watched the way he looked at you."

I swallowed, my mouth suddenly growing dry against the intensity in his blue eyes, as rich and deep as the ocean I'd crossed to return to England. My words scraped out in a whisper. "How did he look at me, exactly?"

Benedict lowered his voice more, his breath tickling my ear. "Like a man in love."

CHAPTER 16

BENEDICT

"He cannot love me. He does not know me," Thea argued, trying for a light tone despite the evidence that I had unnerved her. I immediately regretted my words. I did not know what madness had forced them out of me, except that the extreme jealousy that had built and mounted during each dance she partook of finally erupted, and I could no longer contain it.

"He does not have to know you to believe himself in love," I countered. If anyone in this room was enraptured with Thea, it was Davidson. Even now, the man stood on the far end of the room, watching her over the shoulder of the woman he was in conversation with.

"You cannot truly believe that you, of all people, have the authority to tell me not to flirt with a gentleman?" Thea turned to face me, her dark eyebrows lifted above her perfectly icy eyes. "You, who have flirted in excess with each woman you've danced with this evening."

I would hardly have called any of that flirting, but a surge of victory rushed through my chest anyway. Thea had been watching me all night, as well.

I straightened to put some space between us. Her scent—a

mixture of citrus and something floral—was clouding my thoughts. "I believe some people call it entertaining your dance partner."

"I believe most would call it giving a woman false ideas of how you feel about her."

I shook my head. It was not the same. "The majority of the women I danced with tonight have known me for years and are under no illusions about my intentions. It is perfectly well known that I am a confirmed bachelor."

She shook her head in disbelief. "That does not stop each of those women from hoping they are special and different. That it will be them who will capture your heart and take you off the marriage mart completely."

I scoffed.

Thea continued. "Besides, there is no rule that knowing a man for many years means you cannot later fall in love with him."

My heart skipped, my chest going warm, and I looked at her sharply to find her attention on the people milling about with deceptive calmness. Was her heart racing as much as mine? Could she possibly be implying what I thought—

"Miss Northcott," Alfred Upshaw said, approaching us with a smile. "I hoped to ask you for the next set."

The son of our vicar—the one man she specifically requested not to dance with. I could not very well throw her into his arms now, could I? It was a poor excuse for what I was about to do, but I could not deny that, at this particular moment, I wanted nothing more than to hold her in my arms and learn for myself whether the feelings running through my veins and heating my skin were mutually reciprocated, or if I was perilously close to joining a long line of unrequited suitors for Dorothea Northcott.

"I am afraid she has already promised this set to me," I said smoothly, hoping Thea would not give me away for the cheat that I was.

Thea looked up at me sharply, a question in her eyes that I imagined was much deeper than wondering what I meant by my actions now. I offered her my elbow, and before Upshaw could beg for the following set, she took my arm and pulled me toward the dance floor.

We took our places, and she looked at me with a plain expression. "I only agreed to go along with your ruse because of our truce."

"Of course. Only for the truce."

The music began, lilting violin strings filling the otherwise quiet air. Where had all the conversation and bustle of chatter disappeared to? It was loud only moments before. Now I only seemed to notice Thea, and it appeared that I only could hear the music of our dance. All else was gone.

"Well," I continued, desperate for her to talk to me. The silence weighed upon us and it felt significant. I needed to fill it. "Not *only* for the truce. Also to save you from a fate you seemed to want to avoid."

Her gaze flicked behind me, where I could only assume Alfred Upshaw now stood. "Yes. That was kind of you to extricate me so smoothly. Thank you."

"Is there a reason you do not wish to dance with him?" I kept my voice low as we moved through the motions of our dance.

Thea's nose wrinkled. "Last I spoke to him, he believed himself in love with me and expressed it passionately."

That was unexpected. I'd rather assumed she was avoiding awful breath or a known toe-cruncher. "Then I am happy to save you from the fawning attentions of a man in love." Or perhaps, in truth, it was Alfred Upshaw and his ill-fated hopes I was saving from further pain.

She shook her head. "He is not a man in love. His declaration came after only a few short weeks of knowing one another. I could never trust him to know his own mind, and certainly not for someone like him to remain in a state he believed to be love forever."

My chest tightened. "All the more reason, I suppose, to protect you from one another."

She relaxed a little. "It is nice to have a bit of a break."

"From your many admirers?"

Thea did not respond to this, and I didn't blame her. Why was I pushing her so hard? Why could I not leave well enough alone? I closed my mouth and submitted myself to the pleasure of dancing with a woman who was graceful and knew the steps well. The din in the room had faded to nothing, and with the music pressing on us and the constant motion of the dance, I felt an odd tightness in my chest that only seemed to heighten as the dance continued.

Thea did not speak again until the dance ended and we lined up together for a country dance. "Was Henry ill?" she asked. "I was surprised when he did not accompany us this evening."

I didn't pretend to mishear her, though I wanted to. He was not ill in a physical sense, but his heart had suffered a blow earlier that year, and while I was fairly certain he did not know that I knew of it, I was just as convinced that he was determined to pretend it had never happened. He had developed a *tendre* for Felicity before she ever met James, and losing her to his brother could not have been easy. He would, of course, never speak a word of it aloud, but I had seen the way he had pulled away when she first came to Chelton while simultaneously acting as though nothing was amiss, and I could see now how deeply he attempted to pretend he had never had feelings for her at all.

It was, of course, necessary. He was the best of men, and I was certain he did not desire Felicity any longer—not beyond appreciating her as a sister-in-law. "Henry does not enjoy balls or parties." There. It was the truth and did not force more information from me than I could reasonably give her.

She frowned. "Pity, that. He would have been fun to tease into a dance."

"He is a decent dancer when he can be persuaded into it."

The music began again, and the liveliness of the dance precluded further conversation. By the time we were finished, I escorted Thea toward my mother, trying not to notice the perfect rosiness in Thea's cheeks and the brilliant sparkle in her round, blue eyes. It was no wonder Thea had a string of admirers wherever she went. She was beautiful, with a sweet heart-shaped face that inspired one to consider poetry or the last time they watched a sunrise.

I had watched the sun rise all week in Thea's presence, and I wasn't sure which of the two—the landscape or the woman— were more breathtaking. It was unfair. She would be much easier to dislike if she had a more sour countenance.

"You look lovely dancing, Thea," Lady Edith said. "I do wish you would have been with us when we hosted Felicity's bridal ball."

"We can have another," I said. Thea would need something to commemorate her entrance into Society.

"Thea will certainly need one in London." Lady Edith looked to Felicity. "If that is something that you think yourself capable of?"

Felicity nodded resolutely, looking at her husband. "We can manage, I think. Must it be a very large ball?"

Lady Edith considered the question. "Mr. Northcott certainly had many friends, Mrs. Northcott as well. I imagine they would all expect invitations—"

"I have no desire to pander to my parents' friends." Thea turned her attention to Felicity. "Whoever you choose to invite will be perfectly acceptable to me. Having no ball at all would be perfectly acceptable as well."

Felicity would undoubtedly prefer that option, too, but it would not be enough for Mother.

A throat cleared, gathering the attention from everyone in our group. Alfred Upshaw stood behind Thea, so I sent her an amused smile before she turned around and faced her suitor.

"I hoped to ask for your company during the next set, Miss Northcott. An injury to my foot prevents me from dancing at present, but I would be glad for a turn about the room, if you would honor me with your company."

Faced with such a plea, Thea could hardly refuse the man.

"If you've injured your foot, would you prefer to rest?" she asked with perfect cordiality.

"Yes, that would be nice," he said. "The supper tables are cleared by now, I am sure." He bent his elbow, offering her his arm, and she took it. Upshaw likely did not identify Thea's attempt to remove herself from obligation to him. Fortunately for Thea, being the daughter of a practiced politician had undoubtedly aided her in the art of careful diplomacy, and she allowed Upshaw to lead her into the adjoining room.

"Is it appropriate for them to go off together alone?" I asked, watching their retreat.

"They're hardly alone," Mother said. "The doors to the dining area are wide open and people have been coming between the rooms for the last few dances. I am certain others have sought their respite at the tables as well."

Still, watching Thea disappear on the arm of a man who'd once professed his love to her made my chest tight.

"Oh, there is Lady Whitstone and Miss Whitstone," Mother said, sighing heavily. "Come, let us greet them."

Thea

Mr. Alfred Upshaw's professed love for me had not dimmed in the time and space that spanned the last few years. His fervent, eager eyes beseeched me to recall our final moments together at the Whitstones' garden party before I set off for school, but I shook my head sorrowfully upon his inquiry, despite being perfectly able to recall that day with alarming clarity.

Mr. Upshaw had, in the relative privacy of the hedge maze, recited a poem to me he had written himself. It was one of the most embarrassing moments of my life, for we left the maze to the sound of others talking about the fool they'd overheard reciting an awful poem, and Mr. Upshaw had flushed a deep enough red to give us away.

I had left him, the garden party, and then Chelton with great eagerness. It had not helped that Benedict had been among the party mocking Mr. Upshaw, and me by extension, his amusement irritating as he had walked past us with a woman on each arm. Nor that later Benedict had not seemed to understand why it had bothered me. His explanation had been something along the belief that I would naturally agree Mr. Upshaw was nothing short of ridiculous.

Of course the man was ridiculous, but I had been embarrassed, too. Foolish man.

"Are you happy to return to Chelton?" Mr. Upshaw asked me now, pulling out a chair for me to sit at one of the banquet tables in the adjoining room. People milled about, mostly older men or women who seemed to need a rest after the hearty meal that had been provided.

I smiled at Mr. Upshaw, careful not to beam too widely. I did not wish to give this man any false ideas about my affections. "I am always happy to be at Chelton. Lady Edith is like a mother to me, there is ample room for riding, and I am finding the new Mrs. Bradwell's company very much to my liking."

He nodded approval. "I am glad to hear that you still enjoy riding. Perhaps you might honor me—"

"Your foot," I said quickly, hoping to avoid an invitation to ride together. I could not give the man any reason to believe his suit would be well received. He might still carry affection for me, but that did not abolish my other fears. A man in his situation, who was so quick to feel deep emotions, was not possessed of a sturdy enough character to be relied upon. "How did you injure it? I do hope it was nothing with lasting damage."

He shook away the apparent surprise from my interruption. "It happened during the country dance. I'm afraid I moved the wrong direction and collided with Mr. Rufford. He stomped on it."

"How dreadful." Mr. Rufford wasn't small by any means, and a collision with the man was sure to hurt. "I hope you are recovered enough to walk home."

"I will manage," he said gallantly.

"Have you chosen to follow your father's career, then? Last we spoke, you had yet to decide, but you were nearly certain you wanted to be a vicar yourself."

Mr. Upshaw straightened his shoulders in preparation to answer my question. "I have. I leave for Cambridge after Twelfth Night, in fact, and I am looking forward to my future as a clergyman."

"You will do a fine job in the role," I agreed. "Perhaps you will take over for your father someday." The man was getting old, but I refrained from adding that last bit aloud.

Mr. Upshaw leaned closer, excitement edging his eager energy. "Yes, exactly. I do hope to return to Bakewell and make a life here."

The way he spoke the words, the undercurrent of his meaning, was too much for me. I scooted back in my chair, the scrape of legs against the hard floor jarring my bones. Mr. Upshaw must have sensed my unease, for he sat up straighter.

"I am envious of your confidence in your future. I am afraid to say I do not have the same certainty for my own." I looked toward the double doors, thrown wide to allow us to see the dancers. "Do you think the set might be coming to a close soon? I would not want Lady Edith to worry."

He was silent for a moment, but gratefully took my hint. He rose, offering me his arm. "I am not sure. Shall we go find her?"

"Yes, thank you."

Mr. Upshaw led me back into the dance hall, and I looked for the Bradwell family. Felicity and James stood against one wall, heads bent together in quiet conversation and their hands intertwined, but Lady Edith was missing, and Benedict was . . . dancing with the silver goddess. Again. But not only dancing, he was also smiling down at her with his blasted handsome grin.

A wave of jealousy roared through me, and I tore my gaze away from them. If there was one thing I would never do, it would be to allow Benedict to win my heart.

CHAPTER 17
THEA

The morning after the assemblies in Bakewell I skipped my early morning ride, not yet able to face the feelings that filled my chest and surged through my body—or, rather, unable to face the man who incited those feelings. I wanted to analyze the way I'd reacted to Benedict so I could decipher what had happened and determine a way to forever extinguish the spark that ignited and smoldered within me whenever he was nearby.

It was possible to accomplish. I merely had to find a way. Developing feelings for my enemy would never do.

Once all reasonable breakfast hours had come and gone and the sun had climbed wearily in the sky, I donned my habit and slipped down to the stables for my ride. Maybe I would jump the northern hedges too, just to spite my growing feelings for Benedict.

The grooms had Luna saddled relatively quickly, and I took my seat, analyzing the horses and glad to see Jasper happily resting in his stall. I couldn't avoid Benedict forever, but I would do my best to avoid him today. I feared I could no longer hide behind the curtain of disdain that had thus far protected me from his charm.

Luna led me from the house and up into the hills, as if she understood innately where I wanted to go. Our ride wasn't bruising, but the slow, methodical walk of a horse taking her time. I enjoyed the steady pace, breathing in the cold December air. Christmas was only a week away, and I was afraid the holiday would bring snow with it, as it often seemed to do. Once the snow fell in earnest, riding would become increasingly more uncomfortable. For now, though, I could manage.

The Grecian temple appeared, and I was surprised to find a cart parked at one of the trees behind it, a mule waiting patiently in its harness. Felicity stepped close to one of the columns and shaded her eyes to see me, and I was relieved to find her there and not a stranger.

"Am I interrupting?" I called, bringing Luna to a stop before the folly. "I can come another time."

"No, not at all." She held a book, her finger tucked in the closed pages to mark the place she was reading. "I would love the company."

I doubted that. She had come out here, apparently, to read in peace. In the near-freezing shade of a faux-Grecian temple. I had enjoyed the odd novel or two, but I would never allow myself to suffer such coldness while reading when there was a perfectly warm house available.

Luna stepped forward, and I slid onto the ground before leading her to a tree apart from Felicity's mule and tying her reins to the low branch. "Do you often come out here to read?" I asked, mounting the stone steps to reach Felicity.

"Yes, though it's nearly becoming too cold for it." She walked around the curved exterior to a stone bench and lifted the wool blanket resting there. She arranged it over the entirety of the bench, then looked at me. "It does help keep out the cold a little. The stone feels much like ice without it."

I sat beside Felicity, and my breath nearly caught at the

glorious view before us. I'd seen it many times before, and it never ceased to awe me. "It's breathtaking."

"Evidently, James's grandmother came here to paint when she was alive. Her husband had it built for her."

"I recall something about that, now that you say so. Can you imagine a man loving you so dearly that he would build a folly for your pleasure?"

She looked at me sideways. "In fact, I can."

Oh, of course. "James would do something of that nature," I said. He loved his wife deeply, was so devoted to her that watching them sometimes made my stomach clench in envy. "Given the way your relationship began, I think you are a lucky woman."

Felicity tilted her head to the side a bit. "I would agree that I was lucky to find him in the library that night, but that is not the whole of it. More than that, I was fortunate that such a good man was found with me. That a man with such good character offered for my hand."

"He loves you very much. It is plain to see."

"Perhaps now, but we were not in love when we married. That came later, after working toward happiness together, making the choice every day to learn about one another and make sacrifices. To not storm away and sleep in separate rooms when we're angry, but communicate our grievances and kiss every night."

My heart jumped at the thought of kissing a man every single night, and my traitorous mind developed an image of Benedict in that role. I shook my head to clear it, replacing it with the image of his easy flirtation at the assemblies with other women. I could never take him seriously. It had been the same way when I first came to Chelton all those years ago. I took his flirtation to mean more than it did, developed feelings for the man, and found him flirting the same way, saying the exact same thing to all the other girls that he had said to me.

Exactly like my father did to all the women in Sweden. Flirt and flirt until they slipped away together. It was repulsive.

"James is a good man," I said. "But not all of them are so wholesome."

"No, I agree, they are not. I have heard tales of rakes and rogues aplenty in London, but I do not think we face many cads here in Bakewell."

"Except for the one living in Chelton, you mean?"

She looked at me sharply. "Who—oh, you mean Benedict, do you not? I would not classify the man as a cad, and certainly not as a rake."

"A rogue, then."

"No, not even that." Her light copper eyebrows screwed together. "Has he done something awful to earn such a low opinion from you? I admit, when I heard the two of you did not get along, I did not realize the extent of your dislike for one another."

She had it wrong. It was not that I disliked the man—I did not *trust* him or believe him to be sincere. "I like Benedict well enough. He is always up for a lark, as vexing as he is. And he makes a perfectly amiable riding partner."

Felicity waited, folding her hands gently over the book in her lap.

"But he is extremely self-concerned," I continued, "and one can never take him at his word. He is a tease, and he flirts with all women the same. Like the woman last night. The one in the silver gown?"

"Miss Dodwell, I believe. She is the Dodwells' niece."

I covered my surprise. I knew her, though not well. I certainly had not recognized her last night. "Yes. Miss Dodwell. He treated her as though . . . as though they had some sort of understanding. Smiling at her all evening, dancing *two sets* together. He must see that the remainder of Society in that room was thinking the same as I."

"Likely so, yes."

"Which is simply—" I turned to face Felicity. She'd agreed with me? "You think he acted inappropriately as well?"

"I would not say so, not exactly. I do not think there is an agreement between the couple yet, but that does not mean his actions were too far outside the bounds of propriety. He cares far too much for his mother's opinion to stain the family name."

Yet? She had said there was no agreement between the couple *yet*. The stone bench seemed to fall out from under me, and I focused on the sheep dotting the far hillside, moving slowly as they grazed, while I pulled apart this thought. Benedict, willing enough to be considered courting a woman to dance with her twice. Benedict, willing to be married? The idea was shocking.

"I assumed Henry would marry next," I said weakly.

"In order to do that he would have to meet a woman, and he cannot meet a woman unless he leaves the house." She looked troubled. "I was hoping to convince him to join us in London for the Season, but thus far he has put off the notion."

"Perhaps if we promise him a multitude of new books, he would agree."

Felicity's eyes danced. "You actually might be onto something. I believe he hasn't visited Town in ages. Shall we discuss the Elgin marbles and the things to behold at the British Museum within his hearing? Surely we can entice him with talk of Hatchards and all the new books he could purchase were he to go, or the history to be admired."

"Or a stop at Cambridge or Oxford for intelligent conversation on the way to Town."

"I think we would lose him there if that was our goal," Felicity said.

"Perhaps the man needs to be lost there for a little while." I pulled my pelisse more firmly around me to ward off the chill a bit longer, but my ears and the tip of my nose were already colder than the stone beneath me. "I want to thank you for agreeing to be my chaperone. I would rather find another position in the kitchens of a grand estate than stay for any length of time under Lord Claverley's care."

Felicity gave a small shiver, her cheeks pinking from the cold. "I've yet to form an opinion of Lord Claverley. He has been polite to me, but a bit intimidating."

"Men like that cannot intimidate me," I said. "I will not allow it. It is their goal, I believe, and nothing brings me more pleasure than to prove how little effect they have on me."

"Surely he must have some effect, or you would not have gone to such extreme measures to avoid him."

I looked at her sharply. "I did not find them extreme. My attempts to make a life of my own were pitiful, I suppose, but they were genuine. I do not expect to find a husband in London's ballrooms, but my foray into servitude did prove how deeply I appreciate a life of relative ease. A feather mattress, for example, or hands that do not crack and bleed."

"I can see the merits of both of those things," Felicity said gently, looking at me with a little awe. "What do you intend to do, then?"

"I intend to keep myself open to the opportunities available to me and to thank my parents, God rest their souls, for leaving me an inheritance that will provide for me and my husband—whoever he will be—with enough of an income to enjoy a life of relative ease." I grinned at Felicity, and she laughed, shaking her head.

"You are too much sometimes."

"Yes, I have been told that before." I stood and shook my skirts out. "I cannot sit in this cold a moment longer. I need a hard ride to warm my blood."

"Enjoy it. I will remain here until I am too cold to turn the pages of my book any longer."

Luna, when given her head, soared across the golden hills,

spread with green and yellow grass plucked at by the herds of sheep. I allowed the wind to blow through my hair, yanking strands from their pins and flapping them in front of my face. My gloved hands gripped the reins, and I bounced in tandem with the beat of Luna's hooves, breathing in the scent of earth and damp grass.

By the time I returned to the house, my cheeks were flushed and my body rejuvenated. I could face the prospect of Benedict and his would-be wife, the silver goddess. I could face Lady Edith and her expectations. I could face—Henry?

He opened the door and helped me inside, his muted smile warm. "You've just had a letter arrive. I believe Forester has it in the antechamber."

"Thank you." I moved to walk away but paused and looked at him with an appraising eye. He was much like Benedict in appearance, though not as tall, his curly brown hair in a state of disarray that added a little flair to his otherwise understated appearance. He had intelligence in his eyes but a quietness about him that was completely at odds with his flirtatious brother. He was handsome. He would be able to find a wife in London easily if he would only look for one.

"I cannot help but wonder if I have something in my teeth," Henry said, breaking through the barrier of my perusal and driving me back to the present.

"Your teeth are perfectly fine. I was only wondering why you will not come to London with us next month."

"I do not find Society all that appealing, to be frank."

"Understandable, of course. But you would not be traveling with Society, or staying with them, or dining with them, unless you wish. You *could*, however, spend that time with us, or in the clubs and shops of London. There is a great deal to do in Town aside from attending balls and parties, you know."

He tilted his head a little to the side, his eyes narrowing in thought. "I suppose I hadn't given it much thought."

"I hope now you will." I gave him an impish grin and left.

Letters did not come my way often, so I couldn't help the curiosity that nipped at me. I was making my way to the antechamber when Benedict stepped into my path. He forced me to pull up short in order to avoid running into him, and one glance at the determination in his gaze proved I should not stop to speak to him now. He would challenge me about why I missed our morning ride, I was certain of it.

"We never made an appointment," I said, stepping around him and continuing down the corridor toward the antechamber. Riding together at the same time every morning for nearly a week did not constitute an agreement. "I've missed no engagements."

He fell into step behind me. "I did not take you for the type of woman who needed to sleep late the morning after a ball."

"I didn't sleep late. Not that there is anything wrong with needing a little more rest after a late evening spent participating in such lively activity."

"So you chose to skip your ride?"

"I chose to postpone my ride until the sun was out and could warm me a little, instead of the early morning, which has begun to feel a little too icy for my taste."

Lies. I had skipped riding to avoid Benedict. I opened the door to the antechamber and found Forester, the butler, standing at an open cabinet full of serving dishes.

Benedict, of course, followed me inside. His spicy, tangy scent hung about me, clouding my determination. I had chosen to avoid him, to avoid a conversation, because . . . why exactly? It had been something to do with the way I felt last night and my deep desire to refrain from facing those feelings. But I could no longer remember the particulars now that he was nearby, meddling with my determination.

"I've been told you have a letter for me," I said to the butler.

He moved to retrieve it and presented it on a silver salver.

"Thank you, Forester," I said, turning away and pretending Benedict was not directly behind me.

"Of course, miss."

I stepped back into the corridor and made my way toward the parlor. It should be empty at this time of day and surely Benedict would leave me in peace now that he knew I intended to read correspondence.

The writing on the direction was mildly familiar, but I could not place it. The edges of the folded letter were particularly worn, as though it had traveled a great distance, and I broke the seal and unfolded it in my curiosity. A small, folded note fell from the creases onto the polished floor. A second letter within the first? I bent to retrieve it, my gaze darting between the crisp, freshly penned words on the letter and the aged missive I'd yet to open.

My eyes glued to the writing on the smaller note, and I found that I could not move. I stood frozen in the center of the corridor, an unfolded letter draped in one hand and the small missive taunting me from the other. It had been six years since my father died, a man who loved me despite how little I respected his habits. Six years that I had grown and developed into a woman bent on not allowing for myself the life he and my mother led. I had conflicting emotions regarding my parents, it was true, but holding now a letter in my grip that was most certainly written in my father's hand made my stomach swoop in equal parts dread and eager fascination.

"What is it?" Benedict asked, stepping around to face me.

I could not tear my eyes from it. "It is a letter from my father."

CHAPTER 18

THEA

Benedict's hands came around my shoulders, and he steered me into the empty parlor and toward the far end of the room where a group of chairs was set against the windows. I dropped into one while he more fully opened the drapes to provide me with better light.

He looked at me until I could tear my gaze from the yellowed paper, and the unexpected compassion in his eyes flooded me with warmth. "I will leave you now."

I wanted to reach forward, to channel strength from his touch, but I could not seem to tear my fingers from the letter. A sealed, folded letter from the grave. "No," I said, my voice a low, hoarse whisper. "Please, do not leave."

It had seemed at first that Benedict had not heard me, but halfway across the room, he stopped. "I will remain here if you have need of me."

It was more than he owed me after my flippant greeting this morning, and far more than I deserved. I sent him a grateful smile and shifted slightly so the light better streamed over my shoulder and onto the paper in my hands. My gaze first sought the name at the end of the letter and found it to be from the woman who Mother and I had lived with in Vienna following my father's death. We had needed a place to rest and grieve, and Mrs. Richter was an old family friend. She'd visited us a handful of times in Sweden and we had gone to her in Vienna while my parents were both alive and happy. Her charity toward Mother and me in that time had meant a great deal to me, and I was sad to leave her following Mother's death, but it could not have been helped. My guardian, Uncle Northcott—Father's older brother—lived in England, so that was where I was sent.

Turning my attention away from my memories, I read through Mrs. Richter's letter, my mind whirling like a windmill in a storm as I devoured the words.

Miss Dorothea Northcott—

You'll forgive me, I hope, in time. I discovered this disparity about one year ago when sorting through a drawer in your mother's old room, but was at a loss for how to proceed. In the year that you lived with us, you and your mother both grew quite dear to me, and it has been a struggle to know how to move forward with this new information. Initially, I attempted to forget that I ever laid eyes upon the paper I found, but it was impossible. My soul could not unlearn something that had been made known to me of this magnitude.

Again, I hope you will understand my reasons for bringing this to your attention. I do wish I could have done so myself instead of through this letter, but my gout has reared its beastly head, and I'm afraid I would not pass an ocean easily now.

There was a note tucked beneath the drawer of your mother's writing desk in a way that could only have been put there if she was attempting to hide it. I retrieved the paper and found it to be your father's final will. Evidently, your father divided your inheritance through the help of a man called Adam Robertson from a firm in Bath, Robertson and Sons. It was legally done. I have looked into the situation extensively, and I'm afraid the will is iron-clad and dated after the one that was read following his demise. You will not be able to dispute it. Write to me if you have any needs. I would be honored to do my best to fill them.

Please know that I am available should you require further explanation. According to the man, you are still entitled to a decent sum. I wish you well, and again, I beseech you to reach out to me if you have any need of assistance or guidance.

Yours, etc.

Sofia Richter

Postscript: I have included a letter I received from the solicitor Adam Robertson when I inquired about the will. It was to be delivered to you upon your father's death, but as it came to pass, the firm was never informed of his demise. They sent it to my address under the misunderstanding that you were still here with me. I'm afraid I led them to that understanding so I might gain information in order to pass on to you. Now that they have been notified of the death and your address, you can expect to hear from Mr. Robertson, or you may write to him at the following location.

I swallowed thickly against a dry throat.

"Is it terrible news?" Benedict asked, his voice soft in a way I had not believed to be possible.

Was it? My inheritance had been divided; that was all I knew thus far. Yet, *how* divided? And why? It was not overly large to begin with, but it was a healthy sum. It was robust enough to allow me to believe I could forge a life with any man I chose, that I could seek a love match and still be able to afford a decent tutor for my children and plenty of shoes or gowns as needed.

Playing the roles of kitchen maid, the seamstress's assistant, even the governess had all been taxing, sometimes grueling work, but I had not intended for servitude or labor to be my life *forever*. The prospect that I could be without the security of my father's modest fortune sliced panic through me like a hot blade. Perhaps more so now that I knew firsthand the difficulty of a life of labor.

"Thea?" Benedict questioned, rising from his seat. He stepped toward me tentatively, and at once I craved my mother's comforting arms in a way I had not wished for in years.

"It is not good news," I said.

He crossed the room faster and lowered himself in the chair beside me. My hands rested limply in my lap, the letters clutched weakly in my grasp. Benedict's voice was low and steady, and I grasped onto it with the same force I wished I could clutch to him. "Whatever it is, remember that you are not alone. You have others to support you and carry you through whatever storm is presenting itself in that letter."

I nodded, my eyelids drifting closed. He was correct. I had Lady Edith, Felicity, James, and Henry. As shocking as it was to admit so, I felt, at present, that I also had Benedict's support as well. I looked to him, losing myself in his soft blue eyes, his dark brow lowered in concern that slipped into my chest and buoyed me up.

"It is from Mrs. Richter," I admitted quietly. "My mother and I stayed at her house in Vienna after my father died, and I would still be there today if she had not seen fit to return me to my guardian. Neither of us knew at the time that my guardian would not want me." That he would immediately put me on a carriage to Chelton with a note for Lady Edith explaining that he wanted no part in his young niece's life, that he'd never asked for such responsibility. I could not fault him, I supposed, for knowing his limitations. But I did not like him for it, either.

"She was good to you, then?"

"Indeed." My fingers sought the ring that now adorned my finger, the one I'd worn around my neck when forced to play the part of a servant boy. I yearned for my mother's wisdom and advice now more than anything. She must have had a reason for hiding the will, and I desperately wanted to question her about it.

"Did she give you this ring?" Benedict asked.

My gaze dropped to the piece of jewelry in question, its small red stones circling a larger, oval ruby, and I shook my head. I must have been obvious in my fidgeting if he was going to make such a connection. "It was my mother's." I lifted my hand and showed it to Benedict. "I find myself fidgeting with it when I think of her."

He picked up my fingers and brought the ring closer to look at it better, his gentle touch tenderly holding my hand.

"It does not carry much value," I explained, "except in its meaning to me."

It was one of the few things I took from Mother's trunks when I left Vienna to return to England. It reminded me of watching her prepare for dinner parties and scheming of when we could do so together, of a mother who adored me, despite the choices she had made that I disagreed with. A mother who told me fanciful fairy stories and brushed my cheeks with rouge when I was sad I could not attend balls with her. A mother who made mistakes but did not love me any less for the way my father treated her.

"I can see why this ring means a great deal to you," he murmured.

"It does. It is one of the last connections I have to my mother." I pushed out a breath and looked to the letter in my lap again. "Mrs. Richter is another connection, of course."

"The news she bears," he said gently, his fingers wrapping more firmly around mine and lowering them onto his knee. "It is terrible? You needn't share it if you don't wish to."

My mind understood the words he spoke, but my heart was focused on my dainty hand wrapped in Benedict's large and capable one, nestled in warmth on his leg as he cradled it with care. It startled me back to the present, banishing memories of Vienna and Sweden and bringing my attention back to the second letter in my hand—the one from my father.

"Mrs. Richter found my father's will secreted away in the writing table my mother used when we lived at her house."

"Did he not have one—"

"It is a more recent will, created after the one that was read

169

to us upon his death. Evidently, he used a different solicitor and supplied him with an explanatory letter to have delivered to me upon the reading of the will. But it was never done, because we wrote to Father's original solicitor when he died, and his first will was carried out."

Benedict bent forward a little, beseeching me to look at him. "It could not be all bad then? Perhaps it is very nearly the same."

"Mrs. Richter read a copy of the will, Ben. My inheritance has been divided, whatever that means."

He swallowed, his hand tightening softly over mine. "Oh, I see." He hesitated. "I can leave you to read your father's letter."

My fingers wrapped more firmly around his, an impulse I did not regret in the moment. "Please stay."

Twice now I had entreated him, lowered my defenses and asked for something from Benedict, and it had not had the adverse effect I'd expected.

Benedict reconfigured his hold on my hand to be more comfortable, lacing our fingers together. I ran my finger beneath my father's seal, unfolded the letter on my lap using my free hand, and read.

Darling daughter—

It brings me sorrow to write this, for if you are reading it, that means I am dead. A bitter thought, that. I do not like the idea of leaving you on this earth without a protector, though I do not doubt your mother's abilities, and I am certain she will remarry swiftly.

I will not leave you in further suspense, for I am certain you will be wondering at the secrecy of my methods, but I had to leave the letter with my solicitor or I feared it would never reach you, dearest. You see, I have a son. He was blessed with your same blue eyes and dark hair, and you will recognize the familial resemblance immediately, I dare say. I loved him the moment I saw him. He will undoubtedly be carried into a scandalous light once he receives his inheritance and my transgressions are revealed, but I know I can count on you to steer him through Society and be the family for him that I cannot be.

I would have liked to do so myself, but if you are reading this, then it has fallen on your capable shoulders.

You cannot know how much I love you, and I hope you will one day come to forgive me. You see, I could not abide the thought of leaving either of my posterity without a piece of my fortune. I do hope that, though it has been halved—

"Halved?" I all but shouted, startling Benedict into tightening his hold on my hand.

"What—"

"Shhh," I admonished him, and continued to read.

—you will find your inheritance to be hefty enough to satisfy future suitors. You are a darling girl, and I am convinced you will not struggle to find a decent match when you come of age.

All my love,

Father

I lowered the paper and looked to Benedict. "I've a brother."

"A brother?" he repeated, appropriately surprised.

"Yes, and my father halved my inheritance so it would go to us in equal parts."

Benedict blinked at me. "Did he say any more on the matter?"

"Only that he hopes I shall orchestrate my brother's entrance into Society and that I will certainly see the familial resemblance straight away."

He placed his other hand over the top of mine, pressing down and offering support in a way that soothed me. "Has he given you any information on . . . the mother? Or how you might contact this brother?"

I shook my head. "Mrs. Richter provided the contact information for the solicitor in Bath. She explained that he should be reaching out to me soon, but I may contact him if I wish."

"What do you think you shall do?"

I tilted my head to the side in consideration and laid both of the letters on the empty seat beside me. "Is it an option to pretend I had not read either of these?"

"It is, of course." He smiled softly, disarming me. His thumb grazed my knuckles absently. "But I am afraid that will not make them go away."

My voice dropped to a whisper. "How do I make them go away?"

"You cannot, Thea. You can only face this new future and decide how you wish to proceed. You shall not be forced to contact this brother unless you wish to. No one will force the acquaintance on you."

"Half brother."

"Pardon?"

"He is my *half* brother. If he was fully my brother, my mother would not have hidden the will that gave half of everything to this man." For surely Mother had to have hidden it as Mrs. Richter assumed, in order to provide me with the full inheritance I'd expected. It was done out of love, most assuredly—but I could not help but agree with Mrs. Richter. It would not have felt right to pretend it had not happened, that this man was not real, that he was not, as my father's son, entitled to some inheritance.

I only wished it wasn't half of mine.

CHAPTER 19
BENEDICT

Thea did not appear disturbed by my continuing to hold her hand, so I did not release it. It was small and fit into mine so well, as though our Maker had seen fit to design my hand with the express purpose of holding Thea's.

At present, it seemed there was nothing she needed more than support. I was glad to be the one present and able to offer it.

"Will you write to the solicitor?"

She looked up again, a small line forming between her brows. "Yes. I would like to know the whole of the situation, and my father was a little sparse on explanations. I can only assume this brother is near my age if he requires an entrance into Society, but he could be a rogue or a blackguard for all I know. In regard to the will, on the other hand, Mrs. Richter looked into the matter extensively and informed me that it is ironclad. I cannot contest it."

"You trust Mrs. Richter?"

The little line did not smooth away between her eyebrows, but she replied without hesitation. "Completely. She has only ever had my best interests at heart."

I still believed it would be good to look into the situation ourselves, but I would mention that to my mother, perhaps later. "Then I suppose we ought to proceed as though it is all true."

"I could not do otherwise." She closed her eyes, and I could not imagine the amount of shock that had coursed through her upon reading a letter from her father, upon seeing his handwriting or hearing his voice in her mind as she read his words. If my own father had written me a letter to be read later and I found it now, I would treasure it above all things.

"There is one benefit of this, though," she said, and I sensed a bit of humor slipping into her words.

"What is that?"

"If Lord Claverley was not convinced to drop the matter of his wife chaperoning me for the Season, he will likely balk the moment he hears of this."

I smiled softly. "You were already safe from his clutches, Thea."

"I know." She slipped her hand from mine and stood, straightening her gown as she did and taking the glowing, warm feeling with her. "I do realize I have you to thank for it. We have made a decent team, I think."

I stood beside her, missing the feeling of her skin on mine. "Yes, in this matter, I think we have."

"It is too bad we are destined to remain enemies, Benedict. You can be pleasant company sometimes."

"Only sometimes?" I asked, a teasing smile crawling up my lips. My hand itched for hers again. I wanted to reach out and pull her against me, to envelop her in a hug and comfort her with my embrace.

Though, since it was Thea, I doubted a hug from me would be very comforting.

"Very occasionally," she said. Sadness crept into her eyes, and she stepped forward, closing the gap between us a little more and resting her hand on my forearm, her floral and citrusy smell wafting up and tickling my nose. "Thank you, Ben. That was difficult to read, and I am grateful to have had your support." She laughed lightly. "Ironic, really, that it is you supporting me as I read about my father's indiscretions—"

"Ironic? In what way?"

She snatched her hand back quickly, her eyes widening. "I forgot. You have—" She swallowed. "Miss Dodwell, was it?"

Thea's ability to jump from one topic to the next with no apparent connection made my brain spin. "What of her?"

"She is very beautiful."

"Yes, she is," I agreed. Though she did not hold a candle to Thea. I could not very well say so aloud, though. Not without frightening Thea into running from the room.

"She will make a very good wife, I think." Thea gave a small nod to punctuate her words.

That was an odd thing to say. "Do you know her well?"

Thea shook her head, and I felt her pull away from me in more than just a physical way, her distance both an emotional and physical force that left me bereft. She gathered her letters and refolded them along their original creases. "We did not speak much before I left for school, so I know of her more than I know the woman herself."

"Then why—"

"*There* you two are," Mother said, sweeping into the room. She came to an abrupt halt near the door and looked between us with suspicion. "Have I interrupted something?"

I gestured for Thea to explain. It was her life that had just been torn apart.

She lifted her chin and faced Mother. "I received a letter from Mrs. Richter, the woman my mother and I lived with in Vienna after my father died." She paused as though her voice would not speak the words that needed to come next. Instead, she lifted her arm, offering the letters to my mother. "Here,

175

Lady Edith. It is better if you read them for yourself. I do not mind."

Mother crossed the room gracefully and took the letters.

Thea paced away while they were silently being read, pulling her bottom lip into her mouth to chew in her concern. It took every ounce of will I possessed to remain where I stood, my hands grasped together tightly behind my back, and not go to her.

"That is quite the development," Mother said quietly. "But it is one we can face together, Thea. You will not be forced to help this half-brother's entrance into Society unless you so choose, and we will write to this"—she looked down and consulted the letter—"Robertson gentleman to ensure that everything was done properly and it is, in fact, a legal will."

"Thank you," Thea said, her eyes suspiciously misty. She crossed toward my mother in a few quick steps and was swallowed into her motherly embrace. Mother's arms went around Thea's back, soothing her, while the deep violet train of Thea's riding habit spread out regally on the carpet behind her. I'd never before been so envious of my mother, but I wanted to be standing where she was now, offering the comfort she was able to give so freely.

I clenched my jaw to fight the impulse to join them, to hold Thea against my chest. I had never before fully understood the power of longing to drive a man mad until I watched Thea embrace someone else and wished it was me instead.

Pulling my gaze from the women, I quietly circled them and left the room. I could see it was time to retreat.

———

Exactly four days later, I received word from Lord Claverley's steward that Bumpton Hall was empty and the groundskeeper would be happy to give me a tour of the place whenever I should find it convenient to visit. The words had a great impact on making my future tangible, and I had the sudden desire to see the house straight away.

I found Henry in the long, narrow library, the dark-paneled walls richly lit from the midday sunlight slanting through the open windows.

"Would you care to go for a ride?" I asked, coming to rest in front of his chair.

Henry put his book face down on his leg and looked up at me. "Did I not see you returning from a ride this morning?"

"You did." I had hoped, in vain, to find Thea waiting for me at the stables at dawn. She had not joined me to ride since before the night of the Bakewell assemblies, and I feared something had happened to alter her opinion of me. It was too similar to last time, when I'd thought we were becoming friends and suddenly everything changed without explanation.

Though, to be fair, I had not yet sought an explanation. I could not be angry with her for failing to provide one until I'd asked her about it.

I pasted an easy smile on my face. "I have some business to see to, and I would like to have your opinion on it, if you think you can be spared."

Henry was slow to answer. His thoughtful, considering gaze felt penetrating at times, and I was nearly positive my brother could see into my thoughts. He nodded and stood, stretching his arms. "I've been sitting for far too long. A ride would do me good."

He marked his place and put the heavy tome on a nearby table, then followed me from the room.

"Meet me at the stables?" I asked, for I was ready to leave, but Henry needed to change into riding attire. He nodded and left.

The wind picked up as I made my way across the gravel drive toward the stables, and I did not feel relief until I passed under the wide archway into the courtyard. I directed a groom to saddle both Jasper and Henry's horse, then waited. For a man so often lost in books or unwilling to attend social functions, Henry was a dab hand at the curricle and a bruising rider. He was also wise, and I was eager for his advice.

We were on the road and heading toward Bumpton Hall not long later. It was only a few miles from Chelton, blessedly situated off the road and neatly pressed against the yellowing hillside. The grass was long, lacking enough sheep to keep it trimmed. But that was something I could rectify eventually. If not with animals, then at least with a scythe.

The sun glared overhead, but not strongly enough to ward off the late December chill. It was only a few days until Christmas, and the air felt like it. Bumpton came into view as we rounded the bend, and I halted Jasper so I could look at the house from this distance.

Henry did the same and waited beside me. "What are we doing here, Ben?" he asked, though the tone of his voice implied he was halfway to guessing the purpose for this trip already.

"I'm considering purchasing an estate."

He nodded softly. "No one has occupied Bumpton in at least a year. They've had to lower the price, or so I've been told, because it won't sell."

How the devil did he know that? "It also needs extensive repairs, so it might not be worth the headache."

Henry lifted one shoulder. "We will not know until we look at it. Is someone meeting us here?"

"The owners have employed a groundskeeper to watch over the place. He will let us into the house."

Silence settled between us, and though the conversation had naturally reached its conclusion, I was hesitant and did not urge Jasper forward.

"What is it that's worrying you?" Henry asked.

He recognized my delay for what it was—fear. This was why

I'd really asked him to accompany me. Henry's quiet nature had the added benefit of making him extremely observant, and his extensive reading made him wise. I was not foolish enough to believe him simple minded, but rather the opposite. A man so well-read, so quiet and unobtrusive, was certainly far more knowledgeable than I could ever hope to be, despite the fact that he'd joined the military instead of attending university. I would trust his opinion on the state of this house implicitly.

I was afraid he would deem it a good buy. This was an enormous step to take in my life, and I was apprehensive about taking it. The responsibility and shackles it would provide me were looming, and without a wife in mind, I feared it was too soon to make this move toward independence and responsibility.

"So many things are worrying me," I said lightly. "From this distance, the house looks well enough, but I am certain it will only be a decrepit mess upon closer inspection."

"We shall not know until we move closer."

I ran a hand over my face and turned toward my brother. "What if I am not ready for this, Hen? What if I botch it all?"

"Then you've squandered your inheritance and will be forced to live with me at Sedwick. Two aging bachelors who spend our days hunting and our nights by the fire."

"That is a terrifying prospect."

"Then let us both hope you do not make the wrong choice." Henry shot me a grin, then urged his horse forward. I chuckled softly and followed him.

The house was not anywhere near as large as Chelton, but it was made out of the same light stone, and with the sun shining on it and the overgrown hedges about, it was a blend of classic architectural beauty and wild landscape.

"It's a lovely house," Henry called as we rode up. "But the roof leaves something to be desired."

The obvious need for repair did not lend itself to any confidence that the attics were not already ruined by rain. We stopped in the small, circular drive and dismounted. A man with overlong hair beneath his cap and a dingy coat stepped out of the far stables and came toward us.

"Mr. Bradwell, is it?" he called.

"Yes," I replied. "Good day, Mr. Tanner. I've brought my brother with me."

"Tanner," he said, implying that he was happy without the added *mister*. "I'll be showing you around."

We followed him to the front door and waited while he produced a key and unlocked it for us. As the door creaked open, the musty smell from inside assaulted us at once.

"Needs a bit of airing out," Tanner said. "But it will come about right enough."

He led us through a small entryway and into each of the rooms on the ground floor before we took the servants' stairs up to the attics. Tin pots and tubs were strategically placed about the dusty floor and sheets covered a good deal more furniture than I had expected to find.

Tanner moved one of the larger pots aside to reveal a wide circle of damaged wood, and my stomach sank. How many other areas were exactly like it?

"There's a fair bit of repair that needs doing up here. The bedroom below will need new plaster on the ceiling, and there's another place down at that far end in bad shape. But we've managed to keep most of the water from reaching the floor."

"We?" Henry asked.

"The missus and me."

"Why have they not repaired the roof before now?"

"Can't afford to, I reckon." He leaned forward a little and lowered his voice. "Between you and me, I think they're so desperate to sell the house they'll take anything for it."

Offering a pittance of the price would be the only way I could afford to buy the estate and also make the necessary repairs.

Tanner led us down to the rest of the servants' rooms, one of which had the ceiling damage he'd warned us about. We continued the tour, and by the time we finished seeing every room in the house and had made our way down to the kitchens, I was reasonably convinced visiting this house had been a waste of time. Tanner led us outside again and left us near our horses.

I stood on the front porch and looked out over the land, overgrown and yellowing with winter. It was a wildland that reached my heart and filled me with a heavy yearning to be part of something solid and secure like this, to put off the bachelor life I'd long since grown weary of. When Frederick Keller had tried to entice me to remain at the fight during my journey with Thea back to Chelton, I had not even been tempted to join him. It did not appeal to me any longer.

What appealed to me now was the idea of tending to my own land, my own animals—not James's, as much as I loved him, but my own. I wanted to fix *my* ceiling and repair *my* roof. It was immature, perhaps, but I wanted to be a master of my own self, and this seemed a possible way to do so.

If only I could talk the owners down to nearly half of what they asked for. It was an insurmountable task, and I was perfectly aware I was hoping for something unrealistic.

"Would you become a hermit, then, if you were to live here?" Henry asked, pulling me from my musings.

"Naturally. It would never do to marry or have a family, of course. I shall grow out my beard and yell at any children who dare to approach my door."

"Do you have the woman in mind?" he asked, clearly knowing me better than I knew myself.

I pictured Thea standing on the porch beside me as the winter wind whipped her hair and the sun began its descent to visit the other side of the world. The long grass blowing would be shorter, of course, and green. I would have my arm around her waist, and she would be cradling a little—

No. That was unhealthy, and I needed to cut that dream off at the pass. It was more of a shock than I'd admit to, realizing my dreams immediately contained Thea at my side in matrimonial bliss. The ensuing warmth in my belly from the mental image I'd created had permeated my body and left a resounding ache for something that would never come to be.

Henry said nothing more, and I did not bother answering him. Speaking aloud the attraction I felt for Thea would only solidify my hazy thoughts and make them too real. We mounted our horses and turned for home, riding in silence over the long road until we reached Chelton.

It was not until we had dismounted and made our way to the door that Henry stopped me with a hand on the shoulder. "You cannot predict what the future will hold, and she will not wait forever."

There was pain in his eyes as he spoke, and I was certain he thought of his own past while giving me advice for my future. But it was pointless.

"She does not feel for me the same way—"

"Nonsense," Henry said, shaking his head. "Listen to me, Ben. She will not wait forever."

He left me standing on the gravel road, staring up at the door, with those words bouncing about in my head.

She will not wait forever.

CHAPTER 20

THEA

I t had been a week since Christmas, an entire fortnight since I received the original letter informing me of the demise of my inheritance, and almost a month since Benedict had brought me back to the warm and welcoming arms of Chelton.

"Part of me wishes I'd stayed in that kitchen where Benedict found me," I said to Lady Edith, sitting on the chaise longue watching her maid put up her hair for the dinner party we were holding at Chelton that evening. "Then I would not know of my half-brother or the expectations my father had for our relationship."

She frowned into the mirror, as she often did when I mentioned my soiled months spent in hiding. "You would do better to forget about any of the time you spent away from Mrs. Moulton's school. If you think of it often, you are more likely to slip and reveal it to the wrong person. Besides, if you had remained in your position in that kitchen, you would still be under the assumption that a fortune waited for you on your birthday."

"True." She had a valid point, for if I had learned of it after marrying, I could only imagine the trouble that would have caused. "My farmer husband would have been distraught to learn of my halved inheritance, at any rate."

"Farmer—" Lady Edith cast her gaze to the ceiling. "You cannot say such things, Thea. Some people will *believe* you."

"As they should. It is not such an outlandish thing. I have not entirely ruled out any man in any position."

"A gentleman farmer? Is that what you are considering for your future?"

I wrinkled my nose and played with the sheer pink overskirt on my dinner gown. "Only if I love him."

"Your mother would never have permitted it," Lady Edith said, her eyebrows lifting.

My stomach clenched in discomfort, for it was true. When I used to sit and watch Mother prepare for dinners or balls in much the same way I was doing now with Lady Edith, Mother would speak of the dukes and earls I would dance with and the lords she planned to introduce me to when we returned to England. My coming out was equally anticipated between Mother and me, and eagerly planned and prepared for. She would sweep rouge across my cheekbones, her eyes glittering over her beautiful smile, and excite my spirit for the day I would enter the marriage mart.

It was strange to feel guilty for allowing that dream to wither and fade, but Mother was no longer here, and despite the future she'd wanted for me, the life she had led was not one I would submit my heart to. If I did not marry for love, to a man who intended to have me fill his heart so full that there was no room for others, then I would not marry at all.

"My mother isn't here to permit it or not, and next year I will be my own mistress."

The maid completed Lady Edith's toilette and stepped back, and my godmother turned on her small, tufted seat to face me. "When you are in London, enjoying the Season, ask yourself if your mother would be satisfied with your choices. Felicity is a good judge of character, and I value her opinion, so I would also beg you to ask *her* if she is satisfied with your choices as well. Sometimes we need another's insight in order to understand if we are making the right decision, and sometimes we need only to listen to the inner workings of our hearts. The wisdom comes in determining which of the two is necessary for you."

I nodded. My instinctual reaction was to brush off her advice, for I knew it aligned with my mother's: find a wealthy, titled husband of good standing. The truth to her words sunk into my understanding, though, and I could not deny the power of listening to my heart or others' sage advice.

"Do not squander this opportunity merely out of spite, Thea," Lady Edith continued, concern edging her words.

I sat straighter in my chair. "Me? Spiteful? Absurd."

She gave a rueful laugh. "Sometimes I do wonder if you are listening, but then you prove me wrong."

"I am always listening," I assured her as I rose and shook out the skirt of my gown. "But whether or not I heed the advice is another matter."

We moved toward the door together, and the impending dinner and guests we were to greet settled on my chest with a dooming heaviness. Lord and Lady Claverley were coming to dine, and I was already preparing to dance delicately between being polite and keeping my distance.

"Lord Claverley will speak to me tonight, and I will secure your official release from the agreement," Lady Edith said. "Though it might be best to inform him of the new development with your inheritance."

"If I do, then news of my brother will spread, even before I have the opportunity to meet him."

She seemed to consider this. "That is something you wish to keep a secret?"

"I hoped to, yes, at least until I make his acquaintance. I do not know if an entrance into Society is something he even requires or desires, and I do not know if he lives in England or in Sweden. There is too much unknown to make him known to such a censorious group as the *ton*."

"I understand. We will do our best to void the agreement without mentioning him."

"Thank you, Lady Edith." I stopped at the door and pulled her into a hug. "Thank you for everything."

She blustered a bit. "Yes, well, I am certain if our situations were reversed, your mother would have done just the same for any of my sons."

I spun the ring on my finger and considered the truth of her words. My mother, indeed, would have done the same.

We went down to wait for our guests in the antechamber, and Felicity and James joined us. They crossed the room to greet us, and Benedict followed shortly after. The energy between us had been tenuous since the assemblies, no doubt due to my discomfort in his presence. I could not see the man without imagining the silver goddess on his arm and the way he'd smiled warmly down at her. He had directed the same warmth at me, and I had been mistaken in thinking it had meant something.

I would not allow my heart to become engaged to a man who would treat it with equal regard to other young ladies. I *could* not. But putting Benedict from my mind was much simpler in theory than in practice.

"It only recently occurred to me," Benedict said, joining us near the blazing fire, "that I set Cousin Matthew up to believe Thea and Felicity are the very best of friends, and *that* is why Thea has chosen to accompany James and Felicity to London for the Season."

"How could that have only recently occurred to you when you must have told Claverley weeks ago?" James asked.

"Well, the part I recently realized is that I forgot to mention it to any of you." He flashed a wide smile. "If we are to keep up the ruse, you need to be aware of it."

"I can do that," I said. "I like Felicity, so it will not be a great trial."

Felicity's cheeks pinked. "I can say the same, of course."

"Splendid." Benedict clapped his hands together. "I hadn't realized at the time I was predicting the future."

"Save your self-congratulations, Ben," James said. "We must still make it through dinner."

"Ah, but in that I have every faith the women will make us proud."

Lady Edith laughed and shook her head as the guests were announced. Lord Claverley stepped into the room, a bit shorter than his wife, with a round face and fair hair. His wife followed, regal and tall, with jewels dangling from her ears and dripping down her chest.

My spine straightened upon the impact of seeing a man in the flesh that I had so long avoided, and I fought the instinct to flee the room. I glanced up and caught Benedict's eye, and the serious blue gaze he had glued to me felt as though it was saying far more than he could speak at present. He turned away to greet his cousin, but angled his body just before mine in a way that caused me to wonder if he realized he'd stood in a protective stance.

"Miss Northcott," Lord Claverley said, resting his greedy gaze on me.

I dipped in a curtsy and greeted both the earl and his wife.

"You are the picture of health," Lord Claverley said.

I turned to Lady Claverley. "How are your children? The littlest one is not yet a year old, yes?"

Her smile blossomed, her eyes lighting with interest. "Oh, yes, they are all such lovely little dears. The babe, Gwendolyn, was blessed with the same fiery hair her oldest brother possesses. It is such a shock, I vow you will be impressed when you lay eyes on her. She is a veritable cherub, and I sometimes wonder if she has been sent to us directly from heaven. Though, are not all babies such sweet spirits? I suppose I had that same consideration when each of my children were born. You know, it is that time between six months and one year when they truly shine with such distinct personalities. It has been an absolute *dream* to discover sweet Gwenny's affection for her siblings, and I do believe she will be blessed with the sweetest disposition, for she already has proven to be of such a sweet nature and only cries *very* occasionally during the night. Her nurse is—"

"Darling," Lord Claverley said, "I believe the present company does not wish to hear about our children's *nurse*."

"On the contrary," I argued. "I am very interested to hear about the woman who cares for such a sweet-tempered babe."

Lady Claverley was interrupted and precluded from expounding on the subject when Forester opened the door and announced dinner was ready. The earl looked at me but was prevented from asking to escort me to the table when Benedict pivoted and held out his arm.

"May I have the honor of your company?" he asked quietly.

Relief flooded me. It did not matter that I had been actively avoiding him over the last few weeks. He was currently my savior, and I could have hugged the man in my gratitude. I placed my hand upon his arm, and we followed the processional. Henry must have slipped into the antechamber at some point during the countess's monologue, for he was now leading Lady Edith into the room just behind Lord Claverley and Felicity, James and Lady Claverely at the lead.

Once we were seated at the table, Benedict leaned over and said quietly, "Now you owe me a favor."

A quiet scoff begged free, and I kept my attention on smoothing my gloves in my lap while I responded. "Is it such a chore to escort me that you require payment?"

"It was certainly a risk. Everything with you is a risk."

His low, velvety voice skittered over my skin, and I did my best to hide how deeply it affected me. "It is a wonder you ever dare speak to me at all."

"I did not say it wasn't worth the risk."

I looked up sharply to find his blue eyes darkening, staring down at me with something lurking deeply behind the plain expression. "What—"

"Miss Northcott, you have been quiet this evening," Lord Claverley said. "That is most unusual. Tell us, do you plan to have a ball?"

"In London," I said, my fingers trembling from the effect of Benedict's expression. "Felicity insists on it."

Felicity looked at me, then seemed to sense what I was up to. "Oh, of course. We must bring her out properly." She turned innocent eyes on Lady Claverley. "I am so looking forward to taking Thea to all the balls and parties in London."

That was a lie, and anyone who knew Felicity well would know it. It was a good thing Lord and Lady Claverley did not seem to know her well.

"But you will not have a ball here at Chelton?" Lord Claverley asked. "That is surprising."

"She will have a greater chance of meeting suitors if her ball takes place in Town than if it is here," Lady Edith said reasonably.

"I suppose we will have to come to London then." His lecherous gaze flicked over me. "I do hope you will promise me a dance."

"But darling, you told me we no longer are needed in Town—"

The earl shot his wife a quelling look. "We cannot very well miss our dear Miss Northcott's come out ball."

"Well, of course we should *like* to be there, but to travel such a great distance only for—"

"We will discuss this at a later time." Lord Claverley dipped his spoon in the soup that had just been set before him and slurped it with satisfaction.

Conversely, I had lost my appetite.

I stared at the white soup in my bowl and recalled the night in the Fullers' kitchen when Benedict had first found me and snuck down to convince me to travel home with him. It had been frustrating to see him, of course, but had it not also been something of a relief? I'd been found, told to return to my regular life and to people who cared about me, and saved from further ruining my callused hands. I lifted my hand a little to better see it in the candlelight, and though my fingers were wrapped around the spoon handle, I could see the callouses and hardened skin. Would I have scars? The soap had been harsh, and my skin had once been so soft.

Pressure beneath the table against my knee stole my attention, and I leaned a little toward Benedict. "Calling in your favor so soon?"

His voice was not teasing as he responded. "I will let nothing happen to you."

I could not joke now, not after hearing the strength that marched along his words. I turned to look at him again, my soup forgotten. "I was only just thinking about the Fullers' kitchen."

His knee pressed again into mine, and he left it there. "You will never have a reason to run away again. Not if I can help it."

It was then, without any thought for what I was doing, that I slid my hand beneath the table and pressed it softly to his arm where it was resting on his lap, before retrieving my napkin to dab at my lips. The action was so quick and smooth, I was positive no one else could possibly have noticed it. But from the way Benedict's forearm muscles had bunched during that brief connection, and from how still he had grown afterward, I was certain it had some effect on him.

Which was a little concerning, because it had certainly had an effect on me.

CHAPTER 21
BENEDICT

L ord Claverley had been doing his utmost to put himself into a position where he could be close to Thea all evening, and I was about ready to take the man by the cravat and throw him from the house. Had he always been this way? If so, why the devil had I not noticed it before now? He was ridiculous in his attempts to sit beside her on the sofa, and I was not positive, but I was nearly certain he pressed his shoe to hers beneath the table while we were playing whist from the way that she startled and looked at me—perhaps questioning if I was the culprit.

But that hadn't been me. The only time I'd dropped all semblance of being a gentleman and touched her tonight was an attempt to gather her attention during dinner. I wanted her to continue to feel safe as she had before coming to Chelton. I was responsible for her being here, but above that, I cared about her.

The second time I'd pressed my knee to hers had not been quite as innocent. It had been a product of the overwhelming urge I had to be near her.

I supposed I could understand why Claverley desired to be near her as well, but the man needed to rein it in. He was married, and his behavior entirely inappropriate. It was no wonder Thea had been adamant about not going to stay at his house. I swallowed hard, fighting the burning rage that filled my body with fury.

Lady Claverley yawned for the fourth time in the last quarter hour, and her husband shot her another irritated glance. "I suppose we ought to be on our way," he said. He looked to James. "Though it is rather dark, and the roads might have ice."

"It did not rain today," I said.

There was only a beat of silence before James cleared his throat. "All the same, if you would like to stay the night, we would be more than happy to accommodate you."

"Yes, I can speak to Mrs. Prescott straight away and have her make up a room," Felicity said.

Panic seized Lady Claverley's face in a way that shocked me. "It did not rain, as Benedict said. I'm certain we would not wish to put anyone out when our ride home is not so very great a distance. We have done it before numerous times."

"It would be safer—"

"But Gwenny," she pleaded. "She will certainly be missing me already. And poor Nurse is always so glad when we arrive home, for I can soothe Gwenny straight away. She will be keeping the entire household awake all night waiting for me if we do not make it home, of course, and we cannot have that when the children become so very ornery when they do not sleep the full night. You must agree that the risk of driving in the dark is not as great as disrupting two households—"

"Very well," Claverley snapped, his round cheeks mottling red.

The countess let out a long breath, unequivocally relieved. She was not the only one to feel that way. Thea's shoulders relaxed in the same manner.

We all gathered while their carriage was brought around and Claverley stepped apart from the group to approach me. I had been watching him closely, and I wondered if he had discerned as much and wanted to question my actions.

"Bumpton, then? How was it?"

He surprised me, and I looked at Henry quickly, who was listening calmly to the countess share a story of their oldest boy's recent success training his pony.

"Dilapidated," I said. "Not worth what they are asking, of course. I considered offering less."

"Worth the effort to inquire, at least," Claverley said with approval. "The family is out this week, and you may walk through Kellinger tomorrow at noon sharp. They are very particular about it, so do not be late."

"Yes, of course. Thank you."

Claverley nodded once and walked away, but I looked up to find James watching me curiously. I sent him a grin and pretended as though I had not just transacted business in the drawing room—business he had no knowledge of.

We saw the earl and countess off, then sighed as a collective group once the door was closed behind their retreating carriage.

"It can be such a chore to host one's family, can it not?" Mother said.

"I was thinking it was a wonder Lady Claverley ever agreed to go to London at all, given the state of poor Gwenny when she is not by her side," Felicity said.

Thea chuckled. "You did not hear? The countess shared with me while we were playing whist that her intention had been to take the entire family to Town, but she was unsure how she was going to manage all the children and all the balls. She is mightily grateful she no longer needs to balance them."

"Do they not have servants?" Felicity asked. "Aside from their nurse."

Lady Edith sighed. "They do. The countess is a very involved mother."

"I think it is sweet," Thea said. "I should like to be just as involved when I am a mother."

I couldn't help but admire her wistful smile then. She would be a loving mother one day. Thea did not do anything by halves.

Felicity nodded as though agreeing. "Which you will have every right to be."

The party soon after broke up, and James cornered me in the drawing room when the women had all left for the night. "Fencing in the morning, after your ride?"

"Absolutely," I said. Fencing was a great way to burn some of the anxious energy that had not left my body since the night of the assemblies. I would work hard enough to overcome all of the residual feelings I was developing for Thea, and then she would no longer have such control over my thoughts.

I would master this. I had no other choice.

James was already waiting in the long gallery by the time I had changed out of my riding attire, the rugs rolled up and the curtains drawn to let in soft mid-morning light.

"I often feel as though our ancestors are watching us when we fence in here," I said, crossing the room and giving my foil a good swipe through the air, testing my wrist.

James lifted his mesh wire mask and affixed it over his face. "They would be disappointed by how infrequently we practice, I think."

I shrugged. "Duels are fought with guns these days. It is not as necessary a sport to learn for us as it was for our father's generation."

"You intend to fight a duel now? Whose honor are you defending?"

"Last night I worried it was to be Thea's." I lowered my sword and lifted my mask to my face, blurring the image of my brother a little. "Did you notice Cousin Matthew's focus on her?"

James lowered his voice. "I did. I wondered if he had always acted in such a way, or if it was new. Given Thea's adamance that she would not go to his house, I am inclined to think it was not the first time he'd paid her such marked attention." He laughed without humor. "I was prepared to move her into Felicity's room for the night so I could keep an eye on her. I was glad when the countess insisted on going home."

"As was I." I finished tying my mask in place. "For a man who despises scandal to such a degree, his behavior was shocking."

We took our positions, and James began. We'd blunted our foils, but still chose to wear masks to protect our faces, though sometimes I felt it put me at a disadvantage.

"Kellinger?" he asked, out of breath from the parries and thrusts.

So, he had been listening last night when Claverley spoke of the house. "They do not want it to be widely known that they must sell."

"The family is kidding themselves if they do not believe most of Bakewell is already aware of it."

I was out of breath and lost my focus. James landed a hit on the right breast of my jacket, and we both dropped our foil points and retook our positions to begin again.

"I am going to look at it today," I admitted.

"Interested in an estate?" James asked. "What brought this on? You know you can stay here as long as you wish. There is room enough at Chelton for all of us." He threw his arms wide to illustrate his point.

"When you start a family, you will not want your little brothers around."

"Of course I will—"

"When *I* start a family, I should like to do so on my own estate as well."

James paused, dropping his arm and directing his foil toward the floor. "That is another point entirely. Have you anyone particular in mind, or is this merely a matter of feeling ready for matrimony?"

I was restless and did not appreciate this pause in our bout. "Mother would like for me to consider Miss Dodwell, but I gave the girl two sets at the assemblies a few weeks ago and knew by the end of the night we would not suit."

"Mother must have shared her opinion with my wife." James chuckled. "Liss was certain you and Miss Dodwell were on your merry way to courting."

"Correct your wife before her hopes are too far engaged. Miss Dodwell and I will never be."

"Pity."

"Is it?" I thrusted forward and James was quick to engage. He always had been the better fencer. We continued on for the better part of an hour before I had to concede defeat. Sweat trailed down my temples and gathered on my back. "I need to leave soon if I am to make it to Kellinger by noon."

James untied his mask and tossed it on the floor before swiping his arm over his forehead to mop the sweat. "You'll take someone with you?"

I looked for my handkerchief in my pocket but did not find it, opting to use my sleeve as well. "Henry agreed to come."

James nodded. "He will advise you well." He crossed the room and clapped me on the back. "I think taking on an estate is a wonderful idea. It's surely what Father had in mind when he left you the money, and I think it would please him to know you chose to settle so close to home."

I blinked away the sudden moisture that threatened my eyes and drew in a shaky breath. "I considered taking up a different occupation, but nothing appealed to me so much as managing land. I am not averse to hard work."

"By the sound of things at Bumpton, you mustn't be."

"You heard of Bumpton, too?"

James smiled, dipping his chin a little. "Henry may have mentioned the state of the roof."

"For a man who is so closed-lipped on matters of his own affairs, he has been remarkably open about mine."

"Do not be angry with him. He was concerned about the roof."

Umbrage filled my belly, and I stepped back a little and picked up my mask. "If I choose to repair the roof, do not fear. You and Henry will both be first on the list of men I recruit."

James clasped my forearm and beseeched me. "You know we will be first to arrive, too. Do not take your anger out on me simply because your brother was worried. We no longer have Father, so we must look out for each other. All three of us, for all three of us." He softened his tone and gently added, "We are not trying to take his place."

Grief sluiced over my skin and infiltrated my chest, widening the ache within. "I know," I said quietly. "I only wish he was here to advise me."

"He would have loved to help you select an estate. Calculating costs and weighing them against benefits was the type of activity he most enjoyed."

"Second to beating us at horse races."

"Or sitting with Mother beside the fire."

We shared a smile, each of us lost in our own memories. James pulled me into a hug, and his embrace was warm and affectionate, passing over our mutual grief and wrapping it in the familial bond we shared. Sometimes we missed our father so acutely, there were no words to do justice to the loss.

I stepped back. "I must really be on my way."

James turned to retrieve his foil and mask and waved me away. "Ben?"

I turned to face him, walking backwards toward my chamber.

"When you are at the estate, just ask yourself what Father would think. I'm certain he'll speak to you then."

I nodded and turned back to see where I was going. James was right. If I asked, I was certain my father would tell me exactly what I needed to hear.

CHAPTER 22
THEA

I lifted the skirt of my habit so it wouldn't drag in the muck and kissed Luna on the nose before leaving her in her stall. Our ride had been cut short today because the January air was too cold for prolonged exposure. Tomorrow I ought to try going out after noon, for the sun would be stronger then. Perhaps I could last a little longer.

Footsteps crunched on the gravel, and I rounded the corner to find Benedict coming toward me. We both stopped halfway through the arched entrance of the stables, the elongated ceiling resembling a tunnel.

"How unfortunate that I should just miss you," I said.

"I am not riding about the estate."

"Oh? You have more business to attend to?" For a gentleman of leisure and means, he certainly had a great deal of business discussions. Unless . . . unless by *business,* he meant a woman. Marriage contracts were business arrangements, after all. My stomach dropped and I tried to cover my sudden dismay with a pert smile.

"I am hopeful that today will be the last of any meetings for a while."

My heart hammered in my chest. "You think it will be wrapped up so soon?"

"It will have to be." He shrugged. "If we are off to London in the next few weeks, I will need to conduct the rest of my business through correspondence."

"If you have reached a point of corresponding with one another, then you must have nearly reached an understanding." For one certainly did not correspond with a person of the opposite sex unless they were engaged, and Benedict was a gentleman. He would never put Miss Dodwell's reputation in jeopardy.

"Nearly." His mouth tipped up into a smile. "Henry and I are off to look at a house today."

My heart fell to my feet. "Goodness, that is a large step."

He sighed. "It is. I do not feel as ready as I should, perhaps."

"Do not engage your heart if you cannot see the matter through."

Benedict's eyebrows pulled together, and he ran a hand over his chin. "I have been very careful not to let my heart guide my choices thus far. This is strictly business. Numbers and cost versus the benefits, that sort of thing."

I tucked my chin, a little disturbed by the cold way he viewed marriage. It was a good thing I had not revealed my growing emotions, for Benedict was no better than Father, and this was proof. "Gracious, that seems rather . . . well, it is none of my concern. I wish you luck today, I suppose." I started to walk away.

"You could be a little happier for me," he said, gathering my attention.

I paused, turning back to face him. His eyes looked dark in the dim tunnel and the muscle jumped as his jaw flexed, made more obvious by the shadows over his face. "Do you wish it? For me to be happy for you?"

He stepped closer, his fingers crossing the space between us to flutter along the back of my gloved hand where I was bunching my gown. I dropped the train onto the muddy floor at once as a shiver raced up my arm. "Yes," he said hoarsely. "I do, above all things."

"Why should my opinion hold any merit?"

"Surely you have seen by now how much I value it?"

I did. He was correct, and he had proved as much by seeking out my companionship and conversation since we returned to Chelton together and agreed on the truce. But I could not allow it. I wanted to lean forward and inhale his spicy, tangy scent. I wanted his fingers to dance lightly over mine again. I wanted his smile to be for me, and me alone.

But it was not. He was on his way to look into an estate to purchase for a family he would have with someone else. He was being, at present, exactly as my father was—the type of man I could *never* be with.

It was unfair that fate chose to put Benedict into my life, to make me love him, then make him wholly wrong for me.

Love? I gasped and stepped back. It was a truth I could no longer refuse to acknowledge, but I knew I could not do so while facing him. I turned away, striding from the stables with little care for my hem. I would help Hannah scrub it later. I had proven that I could scrub well enough in my last position.

Benedict called my name once, but I ignored him, and he did not do so again. I passed Henry halfway back to the house and managed a smile for him but did not so much as slow my pace.

The house was nearing, and its protection was within reach. I tore inside much faster than a lady ought to and ran up the stairs toward my chamber. Hannah was already in my room, laying out my gown and clearing the implements she had used earlier to put up my hair.

"I thought the light green for today—" She stopped upon seeing the tears streaking my cheeks and laid the gown back on the bed. "What can I fetch for you, miss?"

"Nothing." I closed the door and crossed to the window. From this vantage point I could not see the stables, and something in me desired to, greatly. If I hurried, I could make it to the drawing room by the time Benedict's horse was saddled. I wiped my eyes and faced my maid with resolution. "Help me dress quickly."

Hannah had never worked so swiftly as she had now. My hair was not at the standard she would have liked, but I was dressed, my habit taken away, and my slippers on my feet in a mere fraction of the time we usually spent on my toilette. The drawing room was empty when I reached it, save for Felicity, who sat on a plush chair near the fire with a book on her lap.

"Do not mind me," I said absently, crossing to the window and looking out at the empty landscape. The road away from Chelton was devoid of riders, and the winter sun shone happily down on the empty scene.

"Is there something of interest outside?" she asked.

"No. Which I am glad for."

My behavior must have been odd—no, I *know* it was strange. Felicity seemed to sense the same thing, for she placed her book down and crossed the room to stand beside me. We waited at the window, watching the empty road and serene river feeding under the bridge and out of sight.

"What are we waiting for?" she asked.

"Well . . ." It was so silly I did not think I could speak the words aloud. I waited for the opportunity to watch Benedict without reservation. The hope that he would not leave, that speaking to me had halted his plans to further his future with the silver goddess. Anything that would imply his words had a deeper weight, that he meant it when he told me I was worth the risk, that my opinion held merit, that he cared what I thought. He could not say such things and not mean them, surely. But if he meant them as I'd longed for, then he would not leave for *business* regarding Miss Dodwell, and this road would remain empty.

The longer we waited in silence, watching the river and the empty road, the more I felt my shoulders relax. Had I changed his mind? Surely he could not have left before I reached the window, as Jasper had not yet been pulled from his stall when I walked away from Benedict.

"I cannot help but feel that I am missing an important aspect of this activity."

I laughed. "You will think me mad."

"As a mad woman myself, according to many of my acquaintances, I am the last person to throw that particular stone."

"Because you are shy?"

"Yes, my quietness and my anxious fits. It has given me cause to be teased and judged." She waved a hand as though pushing aside her words. "But we are not speaking of me now."

Movement in the far corner of the window caught my eye, and I noticed Henry ride toward the bridge. I sucked in a breath, waiting and hoping, until Benedict appeared behind his brother and the air blew from my lips in a gust of disappointment.

"Oh, were you hoping to speak with them?" Felicity asked. "They are off to see an estate for Benedict. He fancies the life of a gentleman farmer."

A gentleman farmer. It was not lost on me that I had joked to his mother only last night about marrying a farmer. "It is good to have an estate prior to marrying. I think that will make his suit more attractive to the woman's father."

That certainly was how he had made it sound when he had discussed the business transactions he was undertaking. Perhaps Mr. Dodwell was providing enough funds to make the purchase of the estate possible, or some such thing.

"Who is the woman?" Felicity asked.

I looked at her shrewdly. "The silver—" I cleared my throat.

"Miss Dodwell, of course. It was you who told me of their understanding."

"Oh, that." She cringed. "I was mistakenly informed about the supposed understanding. They did not have anything of the sort; Lady Edith merely wished it to be so. I believe Benedict paid Miss Dodwell special attention to show his mother that he'd given it his best effort so she would no longer press the matter."

I leaned against the window frame, resting my shoulder partially on the cold glass panes, and faced Felicity. I had somehow lost the ability to stand upright and think simultaneously. Benedict was not purchasing an estate in order to form a marriage contract with Miss Dodwell? He was doing so for himself?

This new information spread a different light over the conversation I'd had with Benedict in the stables. He must have thought me the oddest creature when I was disturbed by his wish that I should be happy for him. I had thought he wanted me to find joy in his union with the silver goddess, and he had only asked me to be pleased that he was taking a large step toward his future.

"What purpose does he have in buying an estate if he does not yet wish to marry?" I asked. "James must appreciate his company here, and Henry hasn't a notion of settling at Sedwick yet."

"Perhaps he does have a woman in mind." Felicity shrugged. "Or he is merely ready for a wife and a family. When their father died, he left Chelton to James and Sedwick Lodge to Henry, but Benedict only received funds. He has the most flexibility of the brothers, but he also must make a choice that will alter the rest of his future. It is no small undertaking."

And here I had told the man not to let his heart guide his choices. *This is strictly business. Numbers and cost versus the benefits, that sort of thing.* But it should not be strictly business, not when it was his future at stake. I shook my head, wishing I could return to this morning's sunrise and have a second chance at our conversation with this new information. I would have spoken so differently had I known.

A throat cleared at the doorway and a footman approached with a salver. I took the letter he proffered and thanked him.

"It is from the solicitor," I said quietly, staring at the name and wondering what about my future was next to implode.

Felicity rested a hand on my arm. "I will return to my book and give you some privacy."

I nodded, sitting against the window sill and breaking the wafer. My letter to Mr. Robertson had been a request for particulars about the inheritance and how I might be put in touch with my half-brother. It had been an introductory letter, of sorts, for he had yet to reach out to me.

Miss Northcott—

I sent my last letter to the school you were last known to be attending, and I assume it will be some time until it finds its way to you. Thank you for notifying me of your new address and your plans to go to London. I had hoped that this business could be conducted in person. If it would be convenient to come to Bath, and you would be so good as to come to my office, I would be happy to coordinate a meeting with the other beneficiary, Archibald Danvers.

If that is out of the question, I will inquire about arranging a meeting in London. Though, given his circumstances, that could be difficult to accomplish for some time.

As your uncle has taken control of your inheritance since your father's death, he has been informed of the change in funds and will act accordingly in regard to your quarterly allowance. Nothing in that regard should change, but it is up to your uncle to make that decision.

Do not hesitate to write to me with any additional questions. I eagerly await your reply.

Adam Robertson, solicitor

Given his circumstances? What could that possibly mean?

With half of my inheritance, Archibald Danvers was certainly not struggling financially. Was he caught up in a debtor's prison? Again . . . he now had the funds to free himself. Or could he be caring for an aging or ill relation?

No. I would not allow myself sympathy for a man I knew nothing about beyond the fact that we shared a father.

And what of his mother? I had hoped Mr. Robertson would at least provide a little insight into that.

I looked up, more frustrated than before I'd read the letter, and found Felicity watching me with concern. She was sweet to care, and I had grown to value her company over the last month. I was glad she was coming with me to London so I would not have to face this alone. We were set to leave in just a fortnight, though.

"Do you fancy a trip to Bath?" I asked, making my tone light despite the warring emotions plaguing me.

"Whatever for?"

I drew in a breath. "So I can meet my brother."

CHAPTER 23
BENEDICT

Kellinger Park was a beautiful estate, set on a hill with the express intent of being admired from all around. It had a prestigious history, and though the butler who provided us with a tour would not permit us into the main bedchambers, it was very apparent the house was nothing more than a beautiful architectural shell—and I was certain the main bedchambers were no different. Most of the furniture had been removed, along with the wide rugs, paintings, and tables. The chandelier was missing from the ballroom, and that alone would be costly to replace, to say nothing for the empty walls that begged to be adorned with gilt framed mirrors and family portraits.

It was very clear, upon walking the corridors, how the family had been able to put off their creditors for so long.

"Somehow, Bumpton felt a little more like a home, would you not agree?" I asked Henry when we walked back to the stables to retrieve our horses.

Henry nodded. "Less funds would be needed to bring Bumpton up to snuff."

"This house is in a much better state."

"And utterly empty. It will cost far more to furnish Kellinger than it will to repair Bumpton's roof."

We retrieved our horses and rode down the hill, pausing at the base of the road and turning back to look at the house. James had told me to ask myself what my father would think, and I knew from this vantage point that he would appreciate the grandeur and prestige of such a house. He would find it befitting a Bradwell man, and he would say that I had time enough to fill the rooms, that it would not need to be done all at once, surely.

"Perhaps I will make an offer," I said, looking up at the pinkish stone from the waning sunlight.

"You needn't make a decision now," Henry reminded me. "You can inquire further about both houses and submit prices you are willing to pay and decide later if the arrangement will suit your purposes."

"Did you favor one estate over the other?"

Henry's mouth tipped down in a bit of a frown. "Bumpton's land appeared fertile and rich. There is much you can do with good land."

"True." I ran my fingers through my hair and placed my hat on my head. "One only needs to look between the flourishing of Chelton and the decline of Claverley's finances to see how land makes all the difference."

"Have you put any thought into a land steward?"

"Not yet." I tugged at my cravat, loosening it. "I wouldn't know where to begin."

"Ask James. He might have a local man in mind. Or perhaps take the consideration to London and ask around your old school friends. Maybe someone is looking for work."

"Not a bad idea." We kicked our horses into a canter so we might make it home before dark. "If you come to Town, you can help me find someone."

"Why is it so important to everyone that I attend the Season? You are the fourth person to mention it to me."

The fourth? Which person in our household had not yet mentioned it? "I cannot speak for anyone else, but I think you need to leave Chelton if you have hope of finding a bride."

Henry's mouth flattened to a thin line. "You feeling ready to be shackled to a woman does not mean I want that fate for myself."

"Shackled?" I lifted my eyebrow to him. "You do not truly see marriage in that way."

"No, I don't. But I will not concern myself with finding a wife until I am ready."

"And until then? You will mope around Chelton and pretend you are perfectly content to do nothing but read all day except for the occasional riding break?"

Henry looked away, unable to meet my gaze. "I considered coming to London, but not to attend the Season. Thea reminded me of the other things Town has to offer."

"Like women of good reputation and marriageable age?"

"Like museums and bookstores."

"You are such a bore."

"And you, brother, are in love."

He shocked me into silence.

We rode a bit further, then Henry shrugged. "If you can be blunt, so can I."

That was fair. "I should not speak of your life so plainly. It is not mine to judge."

"No, it is not. But apologizing for your words does not remove mine. You are in love, are you not?"

I slowed Jasper, dropped the reins, and scrubbed both hands over my face. When I removed them, Henry had turned around and come back to me, slowing his horse to walk beside mine.

"Love is a strong word, and I am not certain it is applicable here." I swallowed thickly, fearing the repercussions for speaking the quiet thoughts of my heart aloud. But I could trust Henry. "I care for her. I . . . I wish we were not always so at odds with one another, that she would see me and not immediately put up her defensive walls. But I do not know how to take them down."

"Have you spoken to her about it?"

"We formed a truce, but that has not seemed to open her heart to me as much as I'd hoped."

"Then you must do more. Because she will not wait forever, Benedict, and if you are going to Town for the Season, the competition for her affections will only grow more robust at an exponential rate."

"We leave in three weeks, I believe. I have three weeks, then, to win her over?"

Henry shrugged. "At least it will give you a greater start."

"But how do I win over a woman who will not allow me to win anything?"

"Isn't it obvious?" Henry asked. "You let her win."

By the time we reached Chelton, the sun had long since slipped away. We'd stopped in Bakewell for dinner to avoid joining the meal at home when it was already half over. We rode into the stable courtyard and jumped from our horses in the orange light of the lanterns swinging from hooks on the wall.

"You go on ahead," I said, helping the groom remove Jasper's saddle and blanket. I planned to brush him down and see that he was fed, for it was a good way to delay entering the house.

"You must come inside eventually," Henry said, as though he could read my thoughts.

"I will be in soon." Now that I'd admitted my developing feelings aloud, they were real. Tangible. Something I could no longer deny.

I worried for how I would act around Thea. I only had three weeks to prove to her that I was worth taking a chance on, and it didn't seem like nearly enough time. She was so vibrant, so bold and full of passion, that she would undoubtedly take the *ton* by storm. She would sweep in and have a string of admirers begging for dances and sending her flowers before the first week was over.

I lowered Jasper's brush and slumped against the wall. I was doomed. Thea did not look at me that way, and three weeks would make no difference in her affections. Just this morning, when we'd talked before I left to see Kellinger, I had asked her to be happy for me and she had been shocked, as if I'd requested the most ludicrous thing in the world. Did I need to accept that she and I were never going to be?

Or . . . or I could talk to her. Ask her why she turned away from me after the assemblies. Ask her why she thought it absurd that I would want her support. *Ask her* if I have a chance. It would certainly speed my suit along—or kill it at once.

Determination rose in my breast, and I hung the brush on a hook with the other implements and turned for the house. A brisk walk across the lawn in the cold refreshed me, though I still smelled of horses and sweat, so I would not seek her out now, despite how I wanted to. I stripped off my gloves and tucked them in my pocket, then shrugged from my coat and laid it over my arm. I would sneak through the side door, take the night to develop my plan, and then—

I stopped in the doorway of the house when I came face to face with Thea. Her wide eyes displayed her surprise at my sudden entrance, and I closed the door much more softly than I'd opened it.

"Dinner is over," she said, looking from my disheveled hair to my dusty boots. "You've missed it entirely."

"We ate in town."

She nodded, her hand resting on the wall beside her. "I was heading to bed."

"Through the servants' corridor?"

213

"It is much faster," she defended. One sconce on the wall behind me threw its light over Thea, and I could discern the soft blush warming her cheeks.

"I often use this route when I wish to avoid someone." I tossed my coat on the table set against the wall and crossed my arms over my chest. "Do *you* wish to avoid someone?"

"It didn't work very well, now, did it?"

A playful scoff left my throat. "Whyever should you wish to avoid me? I thought we had a truce between us."

"We did, but I'm not certain it's done any good."

"I would like to argue the opposite. It has been quite pleasant being your friend, Thea."

She mimicked my pose, crossing her arms over her chest. "If there is anyone in this house who finds my friendship pleasant, it is most certainly everyone except you."

"You wound me. I have done my utmost to prove the opposite." I lowered my voice and took a step closer, hoping I would not scare her away. "In fact, I thought you appreciated my efforts."

"If you are referring to the dinner with your awful cousin, then yes, I did appreciate that very much. Tell me . . ." She paused, looking to the side. I saw a flicker of uncertainty and my chest swelled with the desire to comfort her. "Was it you pressing your leg against mine during the whist game? The second round."

Blasted Claverley. I wanted to take my clenched fists to his jaw without reservation, but I swallowed that violent reaction and breathed softly through my nose. "No. That was not me."

She looked away. "I thought as much. Only, I had hoped—"

"That I had flirted with you?"

Her gaze hardened. I had said the wrong thing. "Not exactly. It is that I know you are harmless. Lord Claverley does not feel harmless."

My entire playful smile slipped from my lips. "Has he hurt you?"

"No."

I believed her, and it shot relief through my veins. "Not *yet*, you feared?"

She swallowed, her round blue eyes trusting me. "That is what I feared. His hands have a tendency to stray where they are not wanted."

Fire swept through me in a swift rage. It was a good thing my cousin was not within reasonable distance, or I would not be able to control my anger. "You are so strong, Thea. Why did you not tell him to cease?"

Thea gave a low, throaty scoff. "I'm not as brave as I look, I suppose. I feared no one would believe me if I admitted to being wary of the potential of being hurt. That he had merely touched my ribbon and it gave me a sickening feeling. There was nothing to share except my fears, and I suppose those fears kept my lips closed."

I did my best to temper my anger, but my voice was hoarse and raw. "I would never allow anything to happen to you, Thea."

She looked up, her round eyes watching me carefully. This woman had been hurt before, and I would not allow her to be hurt again—not if I could help it. It was time. I needed to fight for her. I only had three weeks, and every second counted.

"Earlier, when I asked you in the stables to be happy for me—"

"Oh, please do not mention that." Thea dropped her face into her hands. "It is the very reason I was trying to avoid you tonight. I am so embarrassed."

I reached for her wrists and gently pulled to remove them from her face. I was aware that I smelled awful, that my hands were dirty, so I only touched her lightly. "Embarrassed for what reason?"

"I misunderstood . . . oh, I cannot tell *you*." She twisted her wrists in my hold and pressed her fingers into my arms, clutching them. "You will find all sorts of meaning where none exists."

"Now you have no choice, I fear. My curiosity will not allow this to rest until you've satiated it."

She shook her head. "It's too ridiculous. You will laugh at me."

"If I swear not to crack even a smile, will you tell me?"

"Not even a little smile."

"I swear it."

Thea let out a long sigh. "Very well." She closed her eyes, then spoke. "I was under the misinformed impression that you and Miss Dodwell had an understanding, and when you spoke of business transactions this morning, I believed you to be working on the marriage contract and finding an estate for your soon-to-be bride."

My mouth dropped open. "What the devil gave you that impression?"

"Felicity, because of something your mother said to her."

My stomach tightened in anticipation. Her emotions had been a mess because she thought I was interested in marrying someone else. It was a sign that she held *some* regard for me. "You women are nothing but a bunch of gossips."

Her hold on my forearms tightened. "You should not allow your mother to think you are considering a woman you are not truly considering."

"You should ask *me* if I am considering a woman instead of listening to my sister-in-law."

"You should not dance *two sets* with a woman unless you want all of Bakewell to be under the same misunderstanding."

"You should not tell other men that you find Bakewell charming when in actuality they are asking—"

"Oh, not that again." She dropped her head back and let out an irritated sigh.

I pulled on her arms, and she looked at me, stepping a little closer. I lowered my voice. "You should stop avoiding me."

"How am I avoiding you?" she whispered, matching me tone for tone.

"You haven't ridden with me in weeks."

"But the cold—"

"I do not buy that excuse for one minute. You said tonight that you chose this corridor to avoid me. If we have a truce, Thea, then we are friends, and we should not avoid one another."

"Because it is natural for friends to hold onto one another in dark, quiet corridors and whisper?"

"It is. It is also natural for friends to be upset when they believe the other has already engaged their heart to Miss Dodwell."

She froze beneath my touch, her hands tightening just the slightest bit. "Well, I would have lost you, Benedict. And then who would I bicker with?"

"No one." My chest surged with yearning, her words echoing in the vast chambers of my heart. She hadn't wanted to lose me, and her warm gaze filled me with satisfaction. "You are not allowed to bicker with anyone but me. It is only natural, as we are friends."

"That excuse will not work for everything." I could hear the smile in her voice as her lips curved gracefully up. "That did not make any logical sense."

"It can work if I want it to." I released her arms and her hands dropped to her sides. A moment of hesitation swept over me, but I blasted through it. *Three weeks.* Sliding my hand gently, delicately over her waist, I pulled her a little closer. Her scent, delightfully citrus and floral, met my nose, and I inhaled quietly.

Thea did not pull away, so I slid my free hand over her jaw, losing my fingers in the base of her hair. Her round eyes did not move from mine, and her breathing seemed to shallow in rhythm with my own.

"It is certainly natural for friends," I said quietly, "to kiss."

She gave a sharp intake of breath, and I stilled, my heart racing.

"But only if it is equally desired by both parties," I whispered.

Thea ran her hands up the front of my waistcoat and gathered my lapels in her hands, pulling me closer. "It is equally desired."

My hand tightened on her waist, my other hand sliding to the back of her neck, and I leaned forward, my lips just a breath away from hers, when loud, clicking footsteps sounded at the far end of the corridor.

Thea sprang back, and I turned away, heat slicing through my body and making my hands shake. I picked up my discarded coat and flung it over my arm. "Go that way," I whispered.

Thea did not question me. She hurried down the short corridor and turned the corner just in time to avoid being seen by Forester entering at the opposite end.

"Good evening," I said to the butler, commanding my pulse to slow. I walked toward him.

He bowed. "Good evening, sir. You will not be wanting dinner, correct?"

"Correct. We ate in town." I paused, hoping to give Thea a little more time to get away. "If you see Robbins, will you send him up?"

"He should already be upstairs, sir. We are in a mighty upheaval, preparing to leave with such little notice."

I stopped. "Who is preparing to leave?"

"Most everyone. Robbins believed you intended to go to Town with Mr. and Mrs. Bradwell."

"I do, but that is not for three weeks."

"It has been moved up, sir. We now leave in a sennight."

Only a week? "Whatever for?"

"You will have to ask Miss Northcott that, sir."

"Of course." It stood to reason that Thea was at the root of this change. Though . . . why? How was I to win her over in only a week? A small smile slipped over my lips. If her attitude minutes ago was any clue, then perhaps it would not be as difficult as I had imagined.

CHAPTER 24

THEA

I had gone mad. My brain had been addled and was now scrambled like an egg. There was no other explanation for the way I had allowed Benedict Bradwell to nearly *kiss* me.

I'd been interested to learn if kissing Benedict would be any better than kissing Peter Seymour had been. I had a feeling there would be a large difference between the two experiences, but now I would never know. I'd allowed myself to be carried away last night in the romance of the moment, but the new morning brought a fresh clearness to my mind and a reminder of why I could never be with a man like Benedict.

He was too much like my father—his tendencies too similar for comfort. His flagrant disregard for Miss Dodwell's feelings when he treated her with such distinction and no intention of continuing their relationship was further proof. He lacked a basic respect for women's expectations, exactly like Father had.

My logic did not stop me from wanting to see him again, however.

The passing of night and the appearance of the sun had given me pause to consider meeting Benedict at the stables at dawn, but I could not leave while my room was in such upheaval.

The servants were forced to prepare our departure much faster than expected, and it was because of me.

Hannah was sorting through my gowns, selecting the ones she thought would best work for different uses in London, and organizing them on my bed in different piles. Most of them had been sitting in my clothes press for at least a year, left behind here while I'd visited on school breaks. I did not mind wearing gowns that were not at the peak of fashion, but I was uncertain whether or not most of them would fit me anymore.

A light knock at the door preceded Lady Edith's entrance, and I welcomed her. "I think this is all a little too much," I said, indicating the gowns.

"That is what I hoped to talk to you about. I've given Felicity the name and direction of my favorite dressmaker on Bond Street, and she has agreed to take you there once you arrive in London. You can trust that anything you purchase there will be at the height of fashion."

"I'm not overly concerned with fashion, but I would not be opposed to new gowns."

She nodded, then faced Hannah. "She still must take her habit and whatever dresses are passable for Society. The pink gown and the sage green ones, certainly. Maybe the plum, too?"

"Of course, ma'am."

I crossed to the window in time to see Benedict pass over the lawn. My view was not of the stables, but the back of the house, and his direction appeared to be that of the folly. My heart ticked up in speed watching him ride away, his seat steady and smooth, his posture straight.

Those hands which now so firmly gripped the reins had held me last night as gently as though I was porcelain. I shut my eyes to remove the image. It was never to be.

Spinning on my heel, I said, "If you do not have any need of me now, I think I shall go for a ride."

Lady Edith raised her eyebrows and looked to the window behind me. "Is it not too cold?"

"My habit is warm, and I will wear my pelisse over it."

"Of course." She looked suspicious but backed from the room. "I'll leave you to change then."

Hannah set about pulling my habit from beneath the pile of gowns. By the time it was free and I was dressed, I was nearly certain I would miss Benedict completely. It was a fair distance from my room to the stables, and Luna did not stand idle for her saddle this morning, making it take a little more time. My body was anxious with the need to be on her back and riding through the wind, anxious to talk to Benedict.

We needed to have this conversation where we were certain we would not be overheard. I needed to tell him that he could never kiss me.

Once I was seated, I took Luna's reins and directed her toward the hills with fervor. I swept my gaze along the grassy knolls, through the trees in search of a rider, but did not see him. When I reached the folly, I circled the structure, but again, it was vacant. There was nowhere else I'd thought to look, nowhere else I knew of where he would go.

I was convinced I had missed him somehow, that I had waited too long to join him and he'd passed me on his return to the house over a different hill. Disappointment swept through me, and the cold shook my arms, my gloved fingers struggling to maintain their hold on the reins. Winter approached with ferocity, and the chill in the air penetrated all my layers, slowly driving me angry.

"Thea?"

I turned Luna toward the sound and found Benedict approaching on the other side of the folly, as though he'd gone even further north and was now returning to the house. I had not missed him entirely.

"Benedict," I said.

"You are alone?"

"Yes, and forget any ideas of chivalry or gallantry. I will not come down from this horse to be swept into your arms again."

He directed Jasper closer until his knee nearly grazed mine. I could reach for him, if I wished to.

I wished to.

"You are not required to come down from the horse," he said. "I will never make you do anything you do not want to do. Though, in defense of my honor, you seemed a perfectly willing participant last night before we were interrupted. If I am incorrect in my assumption, please tell me so straight away."

I swallowed. Dratted Benedict, forcing me to reveal bits of my fragmented heart. "You are not incorrect."

His blazing smile had a remarkable effect on my stomach, making it swirl in anticipation. I wanted to scold it. There would be no anticipating, because there was to be no kissing.

"But," I continued, "it is not to happen again."

His smile dimmed somewhat. "Care to explain why it should not happen again when it was entirely enjoyable and something we each wanted?"

Benedict wanted to kiss me. I knew it from the gentle way he approached me last night and the way he flirted now. It made my rejection even harder to deliver, for how badly I wanted to be kissed by him.

"You are a flirt, Ben."

He seemed taken aback by this response and tucked his chin a little. "You say the word *flirt* as though it is the lowest of setdowns."

"Perhaps because I feel that it is."

"You seem to enjoy it when I flirt with you."

This was going to be harder than I imagined. "Yes . . . but that is the problem. It has always been the problem."

"Will you please come down from that horse and talk to me about this?"

"That is not a good idea."

"Because you need the distance between us to maintain your resolve?" He lifted his hat and ran a hand through his hair. "Gads, Thea. I would never press my attentions on you when you do not want them. If nothing else, at least trust that."

"I do." He was a good man, if a bit misguided. He could abuse hearts, but he would never hurt me if I did not marry him and we remained only friends. I knew it as surely as I knew the sun would fall and the stars would shine.

"Then talk to me."

"I am trying to."

We stared at one another, and the torment in his gaze was too much for me. I grasped the saddle with two hands, unhooked my legs from the pommels, and slid to the ground. I crossed to the faux Grecian temple and climbed the stairs before Benedict caught up with me.

"I want to know what turned you away from me after the assemblies," he said, "and I want to know what turned you away from me all those years ago when you first came to Chelton. I cannot fight the demon I do not know, and whatever it is that is forcing you away from me, I want to know what it is."

I stopped and faced him, my breaths heaving and my pulse racing. I no longer felt the cold biting my exposed skin or the warning bell telling me not to look too deeply into his darkening blue eyes. "You are a flirt, Benedict. I cannot take anything you say as truth. You speak flowery, beautiful things to me, then turn about and say them to the next pretty girl. It is impossible to know whether you mean anything you say, and I will not live a life where I am constantly questioning how you feel about me."

He stood silent, shocked. "The assemblies . . ."

"You smiled at Miss Dodwell and every other woman who partnered you with the same warm affection you gave me."

His eyebrows shot up, a quiet scoff tearing from his throat.

"And shortly after you arrived at Chelton? I thought we had gotten along smashingly, and then one morning . . ."

"You told a girl at the fete that she had eyes the color of the purest sapphires and no other gems could compare."

His eyes widened. "How the devil do you remember that?"

"Because you had told me the very same thing only the day before." I closed my eyes and shook my head. "I cannot trust your affections, Benedict. Do you not see that?"

"I certainly understand why you previously came to that conclusion, but I was young then, hardly out of the schoolroom. I was wetting my feet in social activities and with girls. I had not yet understood what it felt to love someone, and I liked making pretty girls smile."

"At the expense of a disingenuous compliment?"

"Just because I delivered the same compliment to another girl, that does not make it disingenuous."

"You cannot tell two separate girls that *no other gems* compare to their eyes. You are lying to at least one of them."

"Well, I was a fool then. You will hold my faults from my youth against me now?"

"No," I said quietly. "That would be unfair."

"Thank you—"

"I hold your faults from *now* against you."

He scoffed. "The ball? Oh, come now. Because I smiled warmly?"

I shook my head. "I sound mad. I know I do. But it was not that you smiled, Ben . . . it was how you made me feel special with that smile, and then I saw you handing it out without reservation to every woman on your arm that evening. You flirt so easily, with little regard to how it is received or even cherished by the woman."

He removed his hat and tossed it onto the stone bench, raking his hand through his hair in agitation. "I do not know how I might defend myself in this situation. How am I to convince you that it is not the same? That I might smile and laugh and call a woman beautiful, but that does not mean she has any place within my heart?"

How, indeed? My heart cracked, my chest jolting from the impact, and I questioned my choices. The longing to step forward and into his embrace surged within me, but I could not survive a heartache of the same volume my mother had endured. I could not live with a man who lavished attention so fully on others that he slowly drifted away from me. And I could not find a way to feel secure about the truths Benedict now shared.

It was unfair, but I did not have an adequate answer, and I hated myself—and my father, by extension—for doing this.

"It is not possible," I said weakly.

That only appeared to harden Benedict's resolve. He appeared as though he wanted to step closer to me but refrained, and I admired his control. "You do not have any feelings for me? Tell me right this moment that you do not feel anything for me at all, and I will walk away from you."

How could I speak such a falsehood? When I invited his kiss last night, I'd given myself away. "That is irrelevant to the point—"

"Tell me, Thea," he said, his voice lowering to a dangerous degree. "Tell me you feel *nothing* for me, that your heart does not beat for mine."

I stood mutely before him, unable to lie in the way he needed to hear. How could I tell this man, this infuriatingly handsome blockhead, that my heart did not beat for him, when in all actuality it pulsed to the cadence of his voice, the rhythm of his laugh? My heart had long ago been lost to him, but I'd fought it for so long, so desperate to protect myself from the eventuality of a broken heart.

Could a heart break worse than this, though? Could it break more? I imagined myself in my mother's place, Benedict as my father, and the way he hurt her time and again until fidelity in their marriage was nothing but a wistful past. Yes, it could. It could break again and again until it became a shattered, pieced-together mess.

I would prefer to only break my heart *once*.

Raising my gaze to meet his, I drew in a calming breath. "I will not submit myself to a relationship with a man unless I have complete faith in his ability to stay true to me."

Shock rippled over Benedict's face, opening his mouth and widening his eyes. "You cannot possibly believe I would ever betray your trust—"

Shaking my head, I lifted a hand to stop him. "I watched my father break my mother's heart for years. He had a *child* with one of his paramours, for heaven's sake. I will never submit myself to the life my mother had. I refuse to turn into the spiteful woman she was, to fall as she did. No." I shook my head again. "I refuse to submit myself to that."

Benedict watched me, swallowing hard, and lowered his voice. "But, Thea, I am not your father."

CHAPTER 25
BENEDICT

It was a near impossible feat to refrain from stepping forward and pulling Thea into my arms, to comfort away the pain that lay in her eyes—pain from her parents' past mistakes, from the present, from *me*. But if I moved toward her now, she would only flee. It was a delicate balance, to fight for my chance to be hers, to convince her I was worth taking a chance on, that we were worth it together.

"I am not your father," I repeated when she failed to speak. "I will never be that man."

"He was faithful in the beginning," she said quietly. "I found their behavior repulsive, and when I spoke of it once, my mother told me it was not always that way. In the beginning of their marriage, he had merely been a flirt, but he had loved my mother and stayed true to her."

I did not know whether to be victorious or concerned that the fight seemed to have leached from Thea's voice. If she was unwilling to fight, did that mean she had given up already?

Her round blue eyes flicked up to me. "He was exactly like you. Charismatic, charming, a favorite of everyone. He was not an awful man, but he lost his way. I refuse to love a man who already exhibits such similarities as to make him frighteningly like my father."

"Your concerns are valid, but you do me harm by placing blame so wholly at my feet. Your expectations for the worst of me are not indicative of happiness, either." My blood heated, and I ran a hand through my curly hair, snagging and yanking it free. "Do you think I am pleased to love a woman who has no faith in me? Who cannot see the difference between the affection and longing I hold for her and the polite chatter I carry on with others?"

"But that is where our problem lies," she crowed, seemingly able to ignore my accidental profession of love. "I *cannot* see the difference."

"Then give me the opportunity to show it to you. Allow me to prove I am different, that my affection for you is real and lasting." That she thought I was similar to her father hurt. I wanted to prove I was not that man—I never would be. But more than that, I wanted Thea to see it for herself.

She gave a small, resigned huff. "Do you not see how much worse that would be? How much more that would hurt us both?"

"Your refusal to give me a chance is hurting enough."

"Then you agree," she said. "We are to end things here. No more flirtations, no more warm smiles, no more touching."

I clenched my jaw. "If I do not agree?"

"Perhaps the distance will do us well."

"Distance?"

She flicked her hand impatiently. "Surely you no longer intend to come to London."

"And watch you be courted by donkeys of the *ton*? That does sound miserable."

Surprise flicked in her eyes. "Well, exactly. So you will remain at Chelton when we leave? You can continue the business of purchasing your estate."

The hunt for a home and soil of my own had suddenly lost appeal, growing dry on my tongue. My stomach soured from the realization that she expected me to so easily walk away. "I will still come to London."

"But—"

"I will not leave you now, Thea, just because things have become difficult."

She stared at me, and I willed her to see through my chest into the recesses of my heart, how it beat for her, how I longed for her.

"We are to go to Bath first, to meet my half-brother."

"I will be there to support you, as a friend."

"A friend."

"I would be happy to be more than that, but you will not permit it. I must settle for friendship." As much as I felt it would hurt to remain near her, I could not leave her now. Not when she was about to face her fears personified.

"Friendship," she repeated, as though wondering what deception I was preparing.

"Yes. It is natural for friends to travel to London together and attend all manner of balls, dinners, and card parties."

Thea shook her head, but a smile tipped her lips. "Is it also natural to confess your feelings to your friend, then pretend it did not occur?"

"I have no intention of pretending anything," I said, keeping my voice steady despite the warring emotions within me. "I do have every intention of continuing to fight for you."

Thea turned away and looked over the rolling golden hills.

I had every intention of being there to support her when it was time to meet her half-brother, of being at the balls when she was presented to suitors, of watching out for my awful cousin and keeping reprobates like him away from her. I could prove to this woman, over time, that I meant what I said.

"You are being ridiculous."

"No, Thea." Forget what my brother said about allowing Thea to win. In this, I never could, for it meant not having the opportunity to be with her. "I am going to *win*."

My renewed determination to become a fixture in Thea's life played a role in the ache I again felt to own land. Now, more than ever, I felt the growing desire to put my name on a deed and sink my roots deep into the ground, to create a home I could bring her to. When Thea and I returned from our ride, I located James playing chess with his wife in the parlor. He agreed to meet with me later in the afternoon to draft offer letters for each of the two houses, and I set off in search of Henry. I found him at a table in the library with a quill and paper before him.

"Will you be coming to London or remaining here?"

He looked up, his confusion quickly clearing as his mind returned to the present. Whatever letter he was writing, it was taking him out of this room and into an entirely different world.

"Sorry. What did you ask?"

I pulled out a chair opposite my brother, and he shifted a bit to hide the letter he was writing. "Are you coming to London, or did you choose to remain here with Mother?"

"Should I remain with Mother?" he asked. "I had decided to come, but it did not occur to me that we would all be leaving her. I would hate for her to grow lonely."

"Yes, and you are such scintillating company."

He flattened his lips into a wry smile. "I am certainly better than nothing. I might not be spirited, but I can carry a conversation."

"Yes you can, with the very best of them. You should showcase that skill in Town."

"I'd planned on coming, but not attending—"

"Yes, yes. I do know." I rose from my chair. Henry was clearly in the middle of something, and I did not wish to further disrupt him.

"What is it you needed?" he asked, his voice level.

"Nothing. I would much prefer you to come with us to Town."

"Is there a service I can provide you if I remain at Chelton?"

"No. I . . ." I lowered myself in the seat again. "It is only that I am going to write to Bumpton and Kellinger both with offers. If you were to remain here, I wanted you to forward me any replies, but I will make sure to inform them of our London address so they might correspond with me directly."

Henry nodded. "It is wise to consider both estates. Gather all information before making your decision."

"My decision has been made, but it will depend upon the owners, of course."

Henry gave a faint smile. "I did wonder about that. I think Bumpton will suit you, if all goes according to plan."

"Yes. We shall see what the owners say." I hid my surprise and walked away from my brother, leaving him to return to his private correspondence. There was a quirk in my brow, though, when I left him. For the house I had settled on hadn't been Bumpton at all.

Dinner that evening was taken up with chatter about the impending Season, now closer than any of us had originally planned. With the extra stop on the way to Town to see to Thea's business in Bath, we would be later to London than we had thought, but because of that same stop, we were now leaving Chelton sooner than Mother felt prepared for. Mother feared sending us off before she could bestow every bit of advice on Felicity that she believed the young chaperone needed, and she took charge of the conversation at dinner to continue her teaching.

"As much as you will hate to do so, it is best to listen to a bit of the gossip, for then you will know which gentlemen to avoid producing introductions for."

Felicity nodded. "I am certain I can call upon my mother's expertise to keep me informed regarding who is fit and who is not for Thea's company."

"And me?" Thea asked, lowering her knife and fork. "Can I be depended upon to make the same decisions?"

"This is why you have a chaperone, dear," Mother said lightly, "to help you make these decisions."

It was not lost on the majority of the occupants at the table that Felicity and Thea were very nearly the same age. The nearly two years that separated them did not make Felicity aged with wisdom in this regard, which she clearly agreed on, if her raised eyebrows at James were any clue.

"Men might seek introductions with you, Felicity," Mother continued. "But you needn't present any of them to Thea if they do not appear fitting acquaintances."

Felicity nodded dutifully. Her hand crossed over the top of the table and took James's.

"We will do everything in our power to find Thea a decent match," James said. "She will have me, Henry, and Benedict watching out for her."

Mother looked to me. "Is that so?"

"Of course. I want nothing more than to see Thea happily settled." With me, of course, in a lovely estate set on a hill. But I left that off for now.

"And Henry?" Mother asked, looking to her middle son.

"Will be far too busy browsing Hatchards and admiring the Elgin marbles to be of much use to us, I think," Thea finished.

Henry smiled, a rare one that stretched from one side of his face to the other. "If that comes to be, then I will not be sad in the least."

Dinner ended and we all filed into the drawing room for a bit of music. Thea took to the piano, playing perfectly as Mother crossed the room to stop by my side. "You might take a look while you are in London as well, Benedict."

I watched Thea play softly, the sweet melody filling the room. "I will marry when I am ready."

"But you will attend the dances and the parties?"

"I plan to."

"Good." She seemed to hesitate. "I worried about you and Thea bickering all the while, making it impossible for anyone to feel any peace, but you have both acted very reserved in regard to one another. I appreciate the maturity you've shown."

My jaw tightened. "We agreed to put our ill feelings behind us and be cordial with one another. A truce, of sorts."

"It has served us all well," Mother said, placing her hand on my arm and squeezing it affectionately.

I nodded to her and returned my attention to the music. Once she'd left me alone, I crossed the room with marked slowness, hoping not to gather too much attention. Felicity and James sat at the card table, a game of draughts between them, and Henry sat on the sofa beside Mother with a book that he likely could not see very well in the waning light.

Thea did not cease playing, even as I approached. I leaned my back against the pianoforte, facing her slightly, my arms crossed lazily over my chest. "You know, it has come to my attention recently that we are impressing the members of my family with our good natures and lack of bickering."

"Was no one at breakfast yesterday when we argued over the merits of jam or honey on toast?"

Mother certainly was not. That was beside the point. "But that was good natured bickering, Thea. It does not distress either of us."

"Speak for yourself. I was extremely distressed when my honey was so viciously slandered."

I fought a smile. For all of her concentration on the keys beneath her fingers, she was speaking in the most ridiculous manner. "It will never be superior to jam, so it ought to grow used to the disappointment."

A chuckle escaped Thea's perfect lips, and my attention was drawn to them immediately. I wanted to kiss those lips. Being as close as I had been the other night, only to have the opportunity stolen from me by my butler's clomping footsteps, was torture.

"What is it?" she asked, the smile sliding from her face.

"I was just thinking about how you are going to kiss me by the end of the Season."

Thea's fingers hit a wrong note, but she played on. I did not tear my gaze away from her face to see if we'd gathered attention from anyone else in the family. She looked at them quickly, then settled her pert smile on me with the smugness of a tiny pug advancing on a boarhound.

She played the song till the end, folded her hands in her lap, turned her face up, and said, "The only thing you will be kissing, Benedict, is my hand."

"The challenge, my dear, is accepted."

CHAPTER 26
THEA

W e arrived in Bath precisely twelve days after the wretched conversation with Benedict at the folly had taken place. The yellow stone and winding, narrow roads were calm and comforting, welcoming us into the aged Roman town. Our hotel was situated in the center of a steep hill, and I sent round a note to Mr. Robertson as soon as we found ourselves settled to inform him I was in town and would be grateful if he could arrange a meeting. I gave him my direction and hoped to hear back quickly.

Felicity was glad to be in Bath. She had always enjoyed the town, she said, and James hadn't spent enough time here to have a strong opinion either way, but I felt the burden of being the reason we were all biding our time in this cold town all the same. Benedict disappeared almost as soon as we'd arrived, and I forbade myself from looking out the window every few minutes to see if he was to return soon. By the time night had fallen, it was clear that he had no intention of joining us for dinner.

"Should we wait for Benedict to dine?" Felicity asked, straightening her glove.

"He likely found himself caught up with old friends," James assured her. "It would not be the first time."

"It is a miracle he has remained with us as long as he has," Henry chimed in. He looked at me. "He's not left us much since returning with you. I wonder if Mother asked it of him."

"To remain?" I asked.

Henry nodded. "She misses him a great deal when he's away. Her worrying can become tiresome."

We dined in a private parlor on the first floor of the hotel, a smaller room than we were used to at Chelton, but well turned out. James left us to see what sort of entertainment could be had for the week while we waited, and Henry retired near the fire with a book.

"I think James has gone to look for ways to fill our time for my benefit," I said to Felicity while we lingered over our tea at the round table. "I know you would not appreciate attending assemblies if you could help it."

She smiled into her cup. "No, but I do like a good musicale."

"I can abide a night of music, so long as it is not opera."

"We are in agreement, then." Felicity covered a yawn with her palm. "I'm afraid traveling has made me weary."

"Shall we go up? Henry doesn't need us to remain here for his benefit."

"You are perfectly welcome to leave me to my own devices," Henry said without lifting his head from the book.

We bade him good night and slipped from the room. I leaned close to Felicity and whispered. "I did hope he would put his books down occasionally and go out with us to meet people."

"Do not despair." Felicity matched my whisper as we made our way into the narrow stairwell. "I think we will find a wife for him yet. It will take a little careful planning, but I've already decided it will not be very hard if we put our heads together."

"Or"—I put up one finger while I shared my brilliant idea—

"we merely lead him to a library at each ball and hope a lady seeking refuge enjoys books as much as he."

Felicity shot me an unamused glance. "Let us make proper plans only, please. You will not benefit from a chaperone who employs such untoward methods." She started up the stairs and added under her breath, "Especially not with the way James and I met. Tongues are bound to wag enough as it is."

I couldn't contain my smile.

The front door opened and closed with a decided bang down on the ground floor, and I looked over my shoulder, hoping it would be Benedict. I slowed my steps in case he arrived—because I was a glutton for punishment, evidently—and was rewarded by catching his eye just before I rounded the steps out of sight. He was coming up to the first floor, his hat hanging in his hands, his head bent.

I paused at the top of the staircase far above him. "I trust you already had your dinner."

Benedict looked up, surprised to find me waiting there.

I noticed Felicity's steps halt, and she said, "Who are you speaking to?"

"Benedict," I answered.

The man in question paused on the landing in front of the private parlor. "I have, thank you. Are my brothers in there? I was told you were all dining together."

Felicity appeared over my shoulder in the narrow, dim stairwell. "James has gone out, but Henry is inside. We are retiring for the night."

"I will see you to your rooms, then," he said, starting toward us.

My heart fluttered at his nearness and the impending scent I knew he would still carry.

"Did you have an eventful evening?" I asked, keeping my steps slow while Felicity went on ahead of us, turning out of sight with the stairs. If Benedict could tell I had missed him for the last few hours and was glad to see him again, he made no comment on it.

"Not as eventful as I had hoped."

My fingers tightened around the skirt I had lifted to avoid tripping. "Is the entertainment in Bath unworthy of your sophisticated taste?"

"Not in the least." He took my arm and stopped me. I looked over my shoulder at him, though he was still beneath me, and I had to look down to hold his gaze. "What did you think I was out doing, Thea?"

"Finding . . . entertainment?"

His thick eyebrows bunched together and grooves lined between them. I dropped the hem of my skirt and pressed my thumb over the grooves on his forehead until they cleared. I had never been tall enough to do that before, though I'd wanted to a handful of times.

His eyes were glued to me, and he swallowed. "I went out to gather what information I could about your half-brother, and the firm that represented your father, so we would be prepared when we meet them."

My hand dropped to my side. He had done that for me? "What did you find?"

"Nothing. That is the odd thing. Given the letters, it stands to reason that Archibald Danvers lives in Bath, but no one has heard of him. Robertson and Sons, on the other hand, has an immaculate reputation. No one I spoke with who knew of the firm could say anything but the best about them. They are widely known and reputed, I'm afraid."

"You'd hoped they were crooks?"

"If either of them were, then you'd have a chance of keeping the entirety of your inheritance. As it stands, I'm afraid—"

"Thea?" Felicity asked from the top of the stairs.

"Coming," I said. I turned away from Benedict and continued to climb the steps, then paused and looked at him over my shoulder. He remained where I had left him. "Thank you."

"You needn't—"

"Thank you, Ben."

He nodded once. "You're very welcome."

Felicity stood at the top of the stairs and watched me approach, a furrow on her brow. "Everything is well, I hope?"

"Oh, yes," I said lightly, passing her and continuing on toward our rooms. Hannah and Fanny, Felicity's maid, were to share a trundle in my room and awaited us there. "Benedict heard this evening that Robertson and Sons has a good reputation."

"At least we know we are doing business with good, honest people then."

Though we knew nothing of my half-brother or if he was the trustworthy sort. "Yes, at least we know that."

The following morning I could not eat my breakfast, instead devouring the note sent over by Mr. Robertson until I had memorized every inky black loop and flourish made by his quill pen. Felicity reached over my arm and rested a hand over the paper. "If you do not eat, you will not have the strength to face him."

"She is correct," James said kindly. "You ought to have something to sustain you."

I nodded and reached for the scones and jam. Felicity selected some bacon and put it on my plate with a smile. "For *strength*," she reminded me.

I ate to the sound of their chatter, filling my stomach with sandy crumbs. I would meet my half-brother today, if all went according to plan, and I was equally nervous and impatient to see it done.

"We will not go to his office until two o'clock," Felicity said, apparently answering a question put to her by James I had not heard.

"Shall we go to the Pump Room? There are always the waters if anyone has a malady in need of curing," James said sardonically.

The parlor door opened to admit Henry and Benedict.

I cleared my throat, eager for the distraction they could provide. "Benedict ought to try taking them, though I doubt it will work."

He sat across from me and filled his plate from the dishes sitting in the center of the round table. "I have a feeling you want me to ask what you are referring to, so I am inclined to do nothing of the sort."

"Suit yourself," I said, popping a bite of scone in my mouth and washing it down with tea.

Henry silently filled his plate beside his brother, and I turned toward him. "What plans do you have for your time in Bath—"

"Oh, very well," Benedict said, as though I'd greatly inconvenienced him. "Whatever were you speaking of, Thea? What is it that I should try but will not work for me?"

"I do not think I want to tell you now."

"That is unkind."

"No, it is a matter of little importance. We've begun to move onto a different topic already. Really, you needn't be so self-centered that you cannot allow poor Henry the opportunity to participate in the conversation as well."

Henry looked up at this, his eyebrows lifted as though they could speak for him and declare how perfectly happy he was *not* to be dragged into any conversations.

"I think my brother will be happier if we leave him to his bacon."

"I second that notion," James said, slathering a slice of toast with jam. "Leave poor Henry to his breakfast."

Henry put down his fork. "I am not a child."

"No, of course you are not," I said in perfect agreement.

His gaze slid to me. "But my brothers are not wrong, and I will be glad not to be placed in the center of your and Benedict's games."

I puffed up my cheeks. "You are no fun."

He grinned. "Exactly."

"I think you are perfectly fun," Felicity said. "No one else is willing to discourse at length on the nuances in *Taming of the Shrew*."

"I would be happy to," James said, grinning, "if you would tell me what the nuances are."

Felicity laughed and leaned over to kiss him on the cheek. "Or we can stick to our gothic novels, since we both enjoy those."

"Only when you are reading them to me," James countered.

Benedict cleared his throat loudly. "Please marry someone you can only mildly tolerate, Hen. I can only take so much of this affectionate bantering with my breakfast."

"Do not fear on my account," Henry said softly.

James lifted one dark eyebrow. "If anyone is to banter affectionately with a spouse, Ben, it will one day be you."

Benedict made a sound of disgust in his throat I believed was mostly for show. "Unlikely."

"Yes, unlikely," I agreed. "First, he would have to find a woman willing to put up with him during breakfast."

There were a few polite chuckles, and Benedict's gaze shot to mine. "Do not throw challenges at my feet, Thea, unless you want me to accept them heartily."

I was reminded of the moment he told me of his goal: to kiss me in London. I would need to remember his strong affinity for winning things when I spoke, but the desire to put my mind to anything except the looming meeting with my half-brother had allowed my tongue to run away from me.

"Shall we walk to the Pump Room, then?" Felicity asked, eager to put breakfast behind us. She appeared to see more vitriol in Benedict's and my bickering than we truly felt. Sometimes I wondered if our teasing was lost on her.

James pushed back his chair. "A brisk walk outside sounds lovely."

Felicity and I left to gather our hats, coats, and gloves and met Benedict and James outside. The road curved down at a steeper pace than I'd expected, and when Benedict offered me his bent arm, I took it.

Yellow stone made up the buildings curving along the road and disappearing into the hazy morning fog. We followed behind James and Felicity, their heads bent toward one another while they were lost in their own conversation.

"I would ask if you are nervous about your meeting today, but I feel that the answer is quite obvious."

I looked at Benedict. "Because I am so distracted?"

"No, because you've been looking for a fight since I walked into the parlor this morning. You do realize there are other ways to distract yourself than bickering with me?"

My neck heated. How did the man know me so well? "But bickering with you is such a pleasant pastime."

"And pursuing you is pleasant for me, but I don't intend to do it forever."

"You don't?" My pulse thrummed, and it was not just from trying to walk down the hill without slipping. "What will make you cease then?"

"When I've well and truly caught you, of course."

I laughed, though my chest constricted and I rather felt like crying. "Good luck, Benedict."

"Thank you," he said, entirely seriously. "I need it."

My steps slowed a little. "What if my brother is awful? What if he desires an entrance into Society that I cannot give? I must be wary of how my own name will be received among the *ton*.

Or . . ." I swallowed, voicing aloud the concern that had vaguely nipped at me. "What will I do if his mother is present at our meeting?"

Benedict stopped walking and faced me, pulling me to stop just beside him. "I had not considered that. Do you have any desire to meet her?"

"I do not have a terribly great desire to meet *him*, but I will do so because my father wished it. His letter mentioned nothing about the mother, though, so I do not feel compelled, exactly, to make her acquaintance." Indeed, loyalty to my own mother made the very idea repugnant.

"You do not have to meet her if you do not desire to." Benedict spoke with such power and authority that I believed him at once. He smiled. "I will come, if you wish. I can step first into the room and give a signal to prepare you for who you will find waiting for you."

"You mean to say that if the mother is there, you will trill like a chicken?"

"We've established already that I have no skill for trilling, but I would be happy to cluck."

A smile warmed my face, and I took his arm, drawing a little closer to him. Did he notice the shift in proximity? It was comfortable to have him so close, despite how I knew I should be putting more distance between us instead. "I can teach you to trill. It would be less obvious."

"Or I could bark. I'm certain I could manage that."

"That might frighten the solicitor. A cat's meow would be much more the thing." I tightened my hold on his arm. "Shall we practice now?"

Benedict cleared his throat. "*Meow.*"

I *tsked*. "Do you wish to sound as though you are begging for milk or warning your friend?"

"Begging, of course. I am so very good at it."

"Then you've achieved the sound perfectly."

Felicity looked at us over her shoulder from where she and James now waited at the entrance of the Pump Room. Bath Abbey loomed behind her, its gothic architecture stunning and filling the sky beyond. I marveled at its grandeur and wished at once to step inside.

"We can visit it later today, perhaps?" Benedict murmured, following my gaze to the building. "It might be the very thing you need after your meeting."

I nodded and followed the Bradwells into the Pump Room. Somehow, again, Benedict had known precisely what I had needed to hear. It was becoming increasingly difficult to recall all the reasons I could not allow his flirtation to develop into something real.

CHAPTER 27

THEA

The office of Robertson and Sons was located on a quiet street, at the top of an inclining hill. The morning's fog had drifted away, melting in the sun, and though it was cold outside, my palms were sweating. I longed to remove my gloves, but I would not have this half-brother thinking me a country rustic lacking in basic manners.

For all I knew, he was a fop or a status climber.

Felicity stopped outside the door. "We will come in with you to make certain everything is right and proper, but then we can leave if you wish."

I looked from her to Benedict. James had opted to remain home with Henry and had asked Benedict if he wanted to do the same—he did not believe I wanted an audience for such an emotional meeting. But my stalwart companion was proving himself and now accompanied us to the door, lending the support I needed from him.

"Thank you," I said, following Felicity and Benedict inside.

Benedict leaned over and whispered quietly. "I will not leave your side unless you ask me to."

His quiet, steady assurance filled me with the strength to

face the embodiment of my father's infidelity—the reason I could never trust Benedict as a husband. The irony was not lost on me, fleeting though the recognition was.

Mr. Robertson greeted us, his long, narrow face much more pleasant than I'd expected from a man who had stripped me of half my inheritance. He paused after the introductions were made and smiled down at me. "Your father spoke so well of you. I can see he did not exaggerate your beauty."

My cheeks warmed, and I nodded my thanks.

"I suppose we oughtn't wait any longer. Mr. Danvers arrived a little early and is eager to meet you."

Mr. Robertson crossed the small room to a door at the end of a narrow corridor and turned back to smile affectionately at me again. His behavior was strange, settling misgivings in my stomach. Something about this situation was off, and I worried about what it could be.

Benedict assumed a defensive position ahead of me and followed Felicity into the room. I hung back, waiting for a signal from him that the mother was present and I would flee, but it never came. The office was decidedly lacking in trills, clucks, and meows.

"Miss Northcott?" the solicitor called.

I stepped forward hesitantly as Benedict leaned out of the doorway. His eyebrows lifted, and a soft smile warmed his face. He still emitted no feline or birdlike sounds, so I took that as an affirmative that my brother was in there alone.

The room was quiet, the three people who had preceded me into it silently awaiting me. I stepped forward, into the surprisingly bright room, sunlight streaming through the window and onto . . . a young boy.

The room was otherwise empty except for the people I had arrived with, the solicitor, and this child. I shook my head a little. I wanted to believe there had been some sort of misunderstanding, but I knew at once that I was looking at my brother, for it nearly felt as though I was looking into a mirror from a decade before.

He stood up immediately when I came into the room, evidence of whatever good manners were being pressed into him. His dark hair was combed and pomaded, the part at the back stuck up a little—though not for his evident lack of trying to slick it down. His round, wide blue eyes and heart-shaped face were my own, and I could see my father in him at once.

"Good day, Miss Northcott," he said, his little voice crossing the room, followed by a polite bow.

I curtsied, for I did not know how else to reply to this small gentleman-child. I'd come wholly unprepared for such a young brother and felt my father should have warned me better. Though, in his defense, I suppose he must have written the letter when Archibald was quite young and did not anticipate how old the boy would be when I met him.

"Good day," I said.

"We will leave you to get acquainted now," Mr. Robertson said, leading Felicity and a wide-eyed Benedict from the room. I gave a small nod, and Benedict closed the door behind himself.

"Would you care to be seated?" Archibald asked, again with polite calmness. He had evidently known of me for a good while if he could be so utterly unruffled.

"I would, thank you." I shook my shock away and took the seat beside him. He was a child, and children—from my limited experience—did not mince words. Despite feeling as though he acted a decade older than he appeared, I decided to speak to him like he was little. "It does not seem as though you are as surprised by my existence as I am by yours."

"How could I be? I've known of you my whole life."

That was unexpected. "How unfair. I only learned of you a few weeks ago."

His little nose scrunched up in thought. "It must have been strange to learn you had a brother."

249

"Strange, yes."

His eyes brightened. "But surely you must have been happy, too."

"Of course." I could not bear to dim his smile now, not when he was so guileless. "Tell me, Archibald—"

"You can call me Archie. Everyone does."

A smile tugged at my lips. "Very well, Archie. Tell me . . . does your mother live in Bath?"

"No, I'm only here for school. Mama lives in London. But she fetches me for every holiday and sometimes pops over for a visit."

I could not imagine anyone *popping* over to Bath from London, not with the distance and time spent in a carriage, but I wondered if that meant his mother did not make visiting him sound like a difficulty. I begrudgingly respected that about her, if it was the case.

"Do you have any other brothers or sisters, Archie?"

"No, only you."

My heart swelled with unexpected affection for his gap-toothed smile. There was a wash of freckles over his nose, darker than mine, and a nervous energy in his fidgeting fingers. "Will you tell me about yourself?"

He straightened in his seat. "I am nine years old, I attend the Goddard school, and my greatest dream is to one day have my own horse."

"I love horses, too," I said.

Archie leaned forward a little to impart his secret, reverently whispering. "I've never ridden one. But Mama says we can afford one now."

"That is wonderful news. You will have to write to me and tell me all about what kind of horse you choose."

His dark little eyebrows drew together. "You do not plan to stay here?"

"I am traveling to London for the Season, but I would like to visit you again when I leave Town, if that is agreeable to you. Perhaps we can even become regular correspondents."

Archie grimaced. "I am not very good at writing letters, but I can try to be better."

"Do you want to know a secret?"

"Yes."

"I'm not very good at corresponding, either. But I think I will be good at writing letters to you."

He tilted his head to the side. "Why would I be any different?"

"Because I will actually *want* to read letters from you, Archie, which will give me more motivation to write them as well."

He smiled, an impish grin stealing over his handsome little face. "Mr. Rothschild, my teacher, told me you might not be happy to see me. But I think he was wrong. You look really happy to me."

My heart swelled again with love for this little boy, and I realized he was correct. Before learning of Archie, I hadn't had any family left on earth, not really. I did not consider my uncle *family* because of the way he had dismissed and ignored me. But I did have family to claim. Now I had a brother, and a little bit of the hole that had been left behind when my parents made me an orphan was filled. A few of the cracks their deaths had caused were now mended.

The Bradwells did their best to be my family, and I loved them for it. They were brothers and a mother to me. But this was different, and it lifted my spirits and warmed my soul.

"Will you leave Bath very soon?" he asked.

"I am at the mercy of my friends, Archie. I cannot stay forever, for they are expecting to continue on to London. But I do think we can spare a day or two, and if your headmaster approves, I would very much like to take you out."

His blue eyes widened, and I wondered if I looked just as eager as him when I was excited about something. "Can we walk down Great Pulteney Street? All the best horses pass there."

I suppressed my chuckle. "Yes, but you will have to wear all of your warmest things or you might catch a chill."

He presented me with the most serious of expressions. "I have a very strong constitution, so you needn't worry about me catching my death."

"How very glad I am to hear that."

The door opened to admit Mr. Robertson, followed by a portly gentleman with spectacles and curious eyes. "Mr. Rothschild has come to take Mr. Danvers back to school, if you could now say your farewells."

Archie stood at once, and I did so beside him. I asked the teacher about taking Archie out for an hour or so the following day, and we set the appointment, provided I came to the school to collect him.

"Until tomorrow, Archie," I said, curtsying.

He replied with another gallant bow, and we bade one another farewell. Once Archie was off down the street with his teacher, I turned back toward the solicitor. "If I wanted to write to Archie's mother, would you be able to provide me with her direction?"

"Oh," Mr. Robertson said, apparently surprised by my request. Felicity and Benedict stood a little behind the man and watched me curiously. "I suppose I could do that. If you will just give me a moment, I will copy it down for you."

He bustled away, and I crossed the polished wood floors toward my friends.

"You plan to write to the woman?" Felicity asked quietly. "The meeting with Mr. Danvers must have gone over well."

"He's asked me to call him Archie."

Felicity grinned. "He certainly looks like an Archie. He has your mischievous little smile, you know."

I startled and looked from Felicity to Benedict for confirmation of that fact. "He certainly does," Ben agreed, a teasing glint in his eye. "Heaven help us all."

The musicale we attended later that evening was held in one of the smaller assembly rooms, lit by fires in the hearths that punctuated the walls and candles in the chandelier. I wore the pink gown that Lady Edith favored and thought she would have liked to be with us, had her health permitted it. It was a sad thing when such an able-bodied woman was forced to remain home because of such violent carriage sickness. Though I could not imagine even a well turned out musicale or a few months of social activities in London were worth a week or longer of sickness in a carriage.

"How did you convince Henry to come?" I whispered, leaning close to Felicity and drawing my arm around hers.

"He enjoys music, evidently. I spoke briefly of the harpist on the program for this evening, and the next thing I knew he was meeting us downstairs in his evening clothes."

"Now that we've found another of his weaknesses, we must exploit it," I said, grinning.

"We're no better than a pair of matchmaking mothers."

"When it comes to Henry, is that such an awful thing?"

Felicity nodded, but the mischief dancing in her eyes proved she was on my side. I liked Henry excessively, and I only wanted to see him happy. What was so wrong with that?

We selected seats in the stuffy room, and I found myself sandwiched between Benedict and Henry, leaning toward the latter so my leg would not accidentally brush the former.

"Do you enjoy harp music, Henry?"

He looked at me with mild suspicion. "I do. It is hard not to appreciate it."

"When your schoolmate is a novice and cannot quite master

the chords, then I do think it becomes difficult to appreciate. One must admire her perseverance, however. She kept at it, and by my last year of school I was dreaming about choppy music and broken chords."

Henry gave me an amused smile. "I have every confidence the woman on the program this evening will not assault our ears with clashing strings."

When the room had filled and the music began, I was immediately swept up in the lilting melody. My posture relaxed into the music until I felt the pressure of Benedict's leg resting lightly against mine, and despite the knowledge that I ought to shift away, I could not bring myself to. We spent the duration of the musical program in this faint contact, the warmth of his leg seeping through the layers of my gown. When the final applause rang out, he leaned over further and whispered in my ear, his warm breath driving shivers down my neck.

"The fop we saw in Fremont, that little market town with the boxing match, is here. Do not panic, for I'm certain he will not recognize you."

"I did not know him," I whispered back, though my heart had begun to gallop.

"No, but I recall your friend was with him last time, so it stands to reason that there is a chance they are together again."

My friend? I did not know if I would count Peter Seymour as a friend. "Peter is in London."

"He was not in London when you saw him in Fremont."

"Drat." Benedict was correct. If Peter had traveled to the fight with the fop, then perhaps they'd also stayed in Bath together.

"Has he written to you again?" Benedict asked.

I shook my head. "Not since the last letter, and I never asked your mother to write to him either." I swallowed. "I did not think it wise when I would prefer the acquaintance to end. I have no desire to further it, at least. I would not wish to give the man false hope."

Benedict paused, his gaze roaming my face. A softness fell over his blue eyes that poured heat into my chest. When he spoke, his voice was muted, delicate. "Keep an eye out for your friend, and I will do the same."

We rose and greeted the couple who was speaking to James. Henry hung back, content to wait for his brothers to finish socializing. I slipped closer to Felicity, looking around James as he spoke to the couple and scanning the room for Peter. I knew seeing him in Town was an eventuality, but I had intended to avoid him as long as I could. He'd had a first-hand view of my parents' infidelity and the unfavorable reputation they were garnering. It had been even worse that my father worked for England, that he was representing our country.

"I do not see him," I said quietly, and Benedict nodded.

The woman who was speaking to James turned her attention on me. Her eyes were dark, a slant to them that looked exotic, and she was breathtakingly beautiful.

"Forgive me," James said at once. "I've been rude. Mr. and Mrs. Rossi, allow me to introduce Miss Dorothea Northcott. We are taking her to London for the Season."

Mrs. Rossi swept her gaze over me and clung tightly to the man on her arm, his dark, coarse hair in disarray.

"Mrs. Rossi is an incredible singer," James said. "I had the opportunity to hear her a few years ago in London."

"What do you sing?" I asked.

"Opera."

"And your husband, does he sing as well?"

She squeezed the man's arm she held onto and laughed. "No. He is a conductor."

I could see how they would have an advantageous marriage. "I hope to hear you sing someday."

"You must come to my show in London. We are to put on a

new opera very soon. The chorus has been practicing for months."

I looked at Felicity and hoped she would not reveal my dislike of this particular type of music, but aside from her amused smile, she did nothing to give me away. "I am at the mercy of my hosts."

Mr. Rossi narrowed his eyes at me. "Northcott. I knew a man by the name, though it was years ago."

"Charles Northcott?" I asked. "He was the ambassador in Sweden most recently and traveled in the Continent a great deal. Though he died six years ago."

His eyes lit up. "Yes. It is the same. Your mother, she was very beautiful. You look like her."

I waited, my shoulders tense, for him to dismiss me out of hand for being a child of two people with so little regard to fidelity or their reputations, but he did not. He merely looked away, bored already by the conversation.

Mrs. Rossi cooed. "I remember your parents, too. They came to the opera in Vienna. Now you really *must* come hear me sing." She dropped her husband's arm and leaned closer to Benedict, wrapping her long, slender fingers around his sleeve and slipping up next to him in an entirely too familiar way.

My stomach sank clear to my slippers, and I watched him, waiting for him to disengage the woman's claws.

"Mr. Bradwell would never miss my show," she said with every confidence, her voice like a paring knife to my soul.

He smiled widely at her. "When I am in Town, you know I will never miss it."

I wanted to run away, but that was a childish response, so I looked away from them, unable to stomach the way her hand stroked his arm or the half lidded way her eyelashes fluttered.

My gaze caught Henry speaking to a man not far behind us, and then it landed on the familiar fair-headed love of my younger years: Peter Seymour. He had seen me, and it was too late to look away, so I whispered in Felicity's ear. "I've seen an old friend, but I will remain within sight."

She nodded, then continued listening politely to the sloppy opera singer and her bored husband.

"Heaven be praised," Peter said when he approached me.

I dropped into a curtsy and smiled up at him. I did not want to pursue an acquaintanceship with him, but I could not very well ignore the man either. "It has been a few years, Mr. Seymour. How are you?"

"I assume you have not received my letter, then?" he asked in a quiet voice.

My smile faltered, but I pinned it in place. "I do not know what you mean. I've been in Cumberland of late, and we are traveling down to London now for the Season."

"Cumberland?" His fair eyebrows screwed together. "You know, it is the oddest thing. I was in Fremont to watch a fight not too long ago, and I could have sworn I heard your voice in my inn. I looked for you the rest of the day, but I never saw you."

I quirked an eyebrow, hoping I was doing an adequate job of covering my trembling. "Do you really think I would be found in a town hosting a fight?"

"Not at first, but your voice is unique, and I could *swear*—"

"Good evening," Benedict said, his low voice cutting in at the worst possible time. "I believe we met recently."

"Ah, yes . . ." Peter looked from Benedict to me. "At the inn in Fremont, actually. It is funny, for we were just speaking of it."

"Speaking of Fremont?"

"Well, I'd thought I heard Miss Northcott in my inn, but I never saw her." He shook his head a little, but the line between his brows did not leave. "Do you know one another?"

"Mr. Bradwell's mother is my godmother," I said. "His sister-in-law and brother are my chaperones for the Season."

Peter's gaze lit up. "I will also be on my way to London

shortly. I do hope to see you again soon. Will you grant me the pleasure of calling on you?"

"Certainly," I said with a smile, for what else could I do? I would have to let him down gently, if he showed a preference for my company, of course. I gave Peter my direction for where he could find me in London, and he left us to return to his party. My smile still in place, I leaned a bit so Benedict alone would hear me. "That was ridiculous. Did you think approaching the man was the best course of action?"

"You looked as though you needed saving."

"Saving? From Peter? Good heavens, Ben. He is an old family friend."

"A friend you ducked from a window to avoid seeing, so I know precisely how trustworthy you find him."

I swallowed my scoff before it could bring attention to us.

"What was that ridiculous bit at the end, giving him your address?" he demanded.

I met his gaze. "What else was I meant to do? I did not hang from his sleeve or send him loving glances. I was merely being a friend."

"Why the devil do you want him to be your friend?"

"I do not. But neither will I be rude. So long as he does not believe I have interest in a relationship with him, I've done nothing wrong." I lightened my voice. "Besides, he could bring a friend with him. One never knows where one will meet gentlemen."

Benedict's blue eyes rounded. "You cannot be serious. I was under the impression you could not marry a gentleman."

"No, I will not marry a *flirt*. I will not marry without love. But I must find a husband somewhere." I lifted one shoulder in the daintiest of shrugs. I did not intend to court Peter, but I was not opposed to all gentlemen anymore. "Felicity found her husband at a ball, and they are perfect for one another." And James, possessed of excellent character, was a Bradwell man . . .

though I did not allow my mind to traverse that path. "Who is to say I will not have the same luck?"

Benedict looked like a fair mix between outraged and disgusted. "I am of half a mind to toss you in the carriage and drive you directly back to Chelton this instant."

"Well, you cannot do that for two reasons," I said, my voice deceptively calm. In reality, the image Benedict created in my head, the idea of him carrying me anywhere, sent a wave of longing through me. After the scene I had witnessed between him and the rapacious opera singer, I was perhaps more ill-tempered than the situation warranted. "I have an appointment with Archie tomorrow I refuse to miss."

"The second reason?"

"If you take me back to Chelton, how will I find a husband in London?"

He looked like a dragon from my childhood storybooks, preparing to blow fire over the village. Only, I was the village.

Benedict leaned forward again to whisper in my ear, and I kept perfectly still so his lips would not touch my skin. "The only husband you will be collecting in London, Thea, is me."

With that he straightened, adjusted the sleeve of his jacket, and walked away, leaving me completely without any memory of how to breathe.

CHAPTER 28
BENEDICT

Thea had spent the duration of the afternoon with her brother sitting on a bench in Sydney Gardens and admiring the many horses that trotted by pulling various conveyances or carrying riders, while James, Felicity, and I walked among the garden paths and allowed the siblings their privacy.

It was cold, but my layers of warm wool kept the chills at bay while my thoughts were wrapped in the image of Thea's brilliant smile. We seemed to have fallen into a rhythm of friendship again, our teasing what it once was, but far less hostile. I wondered, when it came to Thea, if that was all she knew how to do with me: tease.

"That woman last night," Felicity said, her tone full of mild curiosity. "The opera singer? She seemed awfully familiar with you."

"I've known her for a few years," I said.

"As have I, but she did not act the same with me. Bold of her to approach you with her husband," James said.

I whipped my head around to stare at my older brother.

261

"Gads, is that what you think? We were never familiar in that way."

Felicity's copper eyebrows rose on her forehead.

James shrugged. "From the way she hung onto you, it certainly seemed like she had a reason for being so possessive."

"She's a woman. It is what they do." I scrubbed a hand down my face. If James and Felicity believed Mrs. Rossi to be a past paramour of mine, did Thea believe it as well? She had been cold to me last night, but I had wondered if that was due to excessive weariness.

Felicity stopped on the path and tilted her head to look at me, the confusion growing stronger on her expression. "Benedict, you cannot mean that the way Mrs. Rossi acted, groping your arm in such a familiar way, is such a common occurrence that you believed it to be ordinary behavior?"

"Or do you mean," James put in, "that it is such familiar behavior for Mrs. Rossi that it seemed ordinary from her?"

I looked between them, trying to make sense of what they were asking me. Were not all women the same? Ingratiating themselves as best they could in hopes of a compliment or a request to call later or send some flowers?

"This is how most women treat you, is it not?" Felicity asked.

"Well, of course." I gestured to my brother. "I am certain you understand."

James laughed. "I contended with my share of flirtatious women, but no, it was not the same for me. It was laughable, the way she hung on your arm. Most women of good breeding would not dare touch you in such a familiar manner."

"Perhaps my problem is that I ought to surround myself with more women of good breeding."

"I think you already do," Felicity said with a wry smile. "Thea and I are perfectly acceptable."

"And neither of them hang on your arm as though mistaking it for a hat rack," James added.

"No, it is safe to say they do not." I flashed Felicity a grin, but my stomach was in turmoil. I had owed that to the fact that Thea never seemed to want anything to do with me and Felicity was my sister-in-law. Running my mind over the last interactions I'd had with women who were not in my family, though, I recalled them all being of similar behavior. Miss Dodwell, at the Bakewell assemblies, had acted in much the same manner, and the same could be said for each of the other women I'd partnered with that night.

Thea's misinterpretation of my intentions with Miss Dodwell and the way I had treated my other partners could not be dismissed any longer as a flair of dramatics, not when Felicity and James saw things the very same way. I had always known I was a bit of a flirt, but I had believed it was typical behavior, that I was not acting differently than any other man in my position would.

"Tell me," I asked, gathering their attention once more, "do you both believe me to be above reproach in the way I treat women, or am I perhaps . . ."

"Perhaps what, exactly?" James asked.

"Am I too much of a flirt?"

Felicity laughed. "Is that a bad thing? You have never, in my company, done anything which might make you a rake or a cad. Flirting, on the other hand, is harmless, as long as both parties are fully aware of the boundaries."

"Mrs. Rossi was standing beside her husband. She certainly saw nothing wrong in the way she acted." James shrugged. "I would not lose sleep over it if I were you."

"I am not overly concerned with that moment in particular," I reassured him. "But I do not want to give the wrong woman a reason to believe I am interested in pursuing her." Or, perhaps, give the *right* woman a reason to believe I am pursuing others.

"It is something to consider," James agreed. He looked up and lifted his hand in greeting. "Here come Thea and Archie. Gads, but they look similar."

I followed his line of sight until I found them walking toward us, and I had to agree. The serious little boy, with his dark hair and vibrant blue eyes, could have been Thea's son. Their father had certainly influenced their appearance greatly, it seemed. Thea's smile was radiant, her body veritably pulsing with joy, and it was impossible not to return her happiness to a degree.

Would it be difficult for her to leave Bath? Perhaps she would desire to remain here a little longer. I was certainly prepared to delay our foray into London. I worried that once we got there, she would become lost to me forever. For how could a woman, who looked as she did, who exuded such joy in a ballroom, not have a wave of suitors knocking down her door and filling her drawing room within the first week?

"We need to return Archie to school now," Thea explained with some sadness when they came upon us. We walked down the path leading to his school and stood before the building while Thea led Archie back inside. When she returned to us, we remained in front of the yellow stone school Archie Danvers had just disappeared into and waited while Thea seemed to be attempting to memorize everything in sight. I looked at James over the top of her head, and he gave a small shrug.

Thea touched the ring that adorned her third finger, the one that had belonged to her mother, then smiled at Felicity. "I am ready to leave."

We walked back along the Sydney Gardens, slowly making our way toward our inn and the carriage that would take us on to London in the morning.

I asked her how the conversation with her brother had gone, and she only smiled and nodded, as though that was enough.

Perhaps, for her, it was.

"Do you need to remain in Bath any longer?" I hoped my preference for this option was not evident in my tone.

"No," she said. "We gained a good foundation, and I think we can now proceed to know one another better through writing."

"I am glad things have turned out so well."

She shot me a wry smile. "Better than I expected, at any rate. I think knowing Archie has led to only more questions, but I cannot find fault in discovering I have a brother who is such a sweet little soul and desires my acquaintance. I was certain the man awaiting me in Mr. Robertson's office was going to be nearer my age, with an insecure background and a great desire to be introduced to the top echelons of the *ton*."

"That was certainly a valid concern, given your father's request that you help your brother's entrance into Society."

"Yes, well, it seems that won't be necessary for a good long time, and it might not be something Archie ever requires of me. I am certain the boy cares for nothing as much as he does horses."

"Is that not most little boys?"

"I guess I would not know," she said pleasantly.

After making a wide generalization about the way women acted, which was thoroughly discredited, perhaps I ought not to make any generalizations at all. I considered how I'd been wrong and in what light it had made Thea see me. With the discovery that I misunderstood the way women had treated me, I wanted to ask Thea to explain her opinions one more time, to try to see myself the way she saw me.

It was not lost on me now that she could be correct in her concerns about my behavior, and that stung. I had thus far operated under the belief that she was being unfair in her declaration that I was similar to her father, but she had seen me exhibit traits that were not typical, accepting flirtations that were not as innocent as I'd believed them to be. She had a valid reason for being concerned.

"Can I ask you something that is of a more delicate nature?" I asked, leaning closer to her. James and Felicity were a bit ahead of us on the walking path, but I knew my voice could easily carry to them if they cared to listen. Felicity was speaking now, so I trusted that they weren't paying me any mind.

"You can always ask, though I will not agree to answer until I know the question."

"Fair enough." I clasped my hands loosely behind my back to still their fidgeting. "Last night at the musicale when Mrs. Rossi was . . . speaking to me . . . you walked away. What was it that bothered you?"

Her eyebrows shot up. "I was not *bothered* by anything. I simply did not feel the need to watch the woman drape herself over you as though she'd suddenly lost all recollection of how to stand on her own two feet."

A victorious smile widened my lips. Thea had been *jealous*. I might have a great distance to go to become good enough for her, but that was certainly a sign that she had not entirely lost interest. "Of course, there is one way to stop the ladies from draping themselves over me."

"Removing them from your arm?"

She was correct, and that was at the base of why Thea did not have enough faith in me. "Never mind. There are two ways."

"The second?" she asked.

"For you to be draped over my arm instead."

She shook her head, her steps gaining speed. It had been the wrong thing to say.

"Thea, wait," I asked, desperate for another chance to prove myself better than she expected—though not, I hoped, better than she believed possible.

"What, Ben?" The tired way in which she said my name worried me.

I swallowed. "I should not have made light of something that bothers you. But now that I am aware of the issue, I will take better note of it and make an effort to change." I took her arm and tugged her to a stop, heedless of what my brother or Felicity might think. "I want a chance, Thea. A real chance."

"And I need to protect myself. I will not live a lifetime of wondering where you are every night or whom you are with. I will not stand beside my husband while he allows opera singers to drape themselves over his arm. I watched my parents ruin one another's happiness, and I will not have that." She shook her head and stole her arm from my grasp. "We will always be friends, Benedict, but nothing more."

Thea turned away from me and hurried toward James and Felicity, who were still walking on the path and heedless of what had happened just behind them—of Thea breaking my heart.

CHAPTER 29
THEA

The Season in London had already begun. Parliament was in full swing, and debutantes were preparing to make their bows to the queen. There was a sense of urgency and expectancy on Bond Street when Felicity took me to order a few gowns, and despite my broad attempts at not finding the social Season to be fun, I found myself growing excited for the balls. The dancing, at least, would be enjoyable. Perhaps I would find a gentleman who was kind, would fall in love with me, and did not find it necessary to flirt with every woman in a dress. Which was *every* woman.

Oh, who was I trying to fool? I would not be falling in love yet. Not until I found a way to remove Benedict from my heart.

Before that, though, I had a mission I wanted to accomplish, and I could not do so without Felicity's help.

We walked down Bond Street after our appointment with the dressmaker, looking at the beautiful hats and fans in the windows and admiring the general splendor for sale.

"Someday I plan to bring Archie here and spoil him rotten," I said, looking at an adorable little pair of boy's trousers.

Felicity looked at the tiny baby's sleeping gown with acute

longing, then tore her gaze away. "He is such a gentle boy. I am glad I was able to meet him as well."

"I was hoping to invite him to visit for a few weeks over the summer."

"To Chelton?" Felicity asked, her copper eyebrows rising. "What if you marry?"

The idea of meeting a man, falling in love, and marrying him all before summer was preposterous. "That seems outrageously unrealistic. But I suppose if I am not at Chelton for any reason, I would invite Archie to visit me where I am."

She looked conflicted. "For your sake, I do hope you find a good match, but for my sake, I will be sorry to see you go."

The smile that came to my lips was not forced in the least. Felicity had become a dear friend of mine over the previous month, and I valued her companionship immensely. "We will remain friends, regardless of where I am."

"Good."

I strung my arm through hers and moved on to the next shop to examine the array of painted fans awaiting our judgment. "You know, in regard to Archie, I did have a project I was hoping you would help me with."

She looked at me with suspicion. I must do something about my tone. "What is it?" she asked.

"I want to visit his mother."

Felicity tore her arm from mine. "That cannot be a good idea."

"We do not know whether or not it is a good idea until I know who she is."

"But what if . . ." Felicity lowered her voice and leaned in, watching to make certain no one passing by would hear her. "What if the woman is a . . . not respectable."

"A mistress? She clearly was *that*."

Felicity looked to the heavens as though seeking help from above. "I do not think it is a good idea."

"You sound like Lady Edith."

Felicity scoffed and pressed her lips together. "I am not an old woman, but I do have enough sense to be wary of visiting your father's old mistress when you have no notion of the type of person she is, or whether you will be well received."

"I am wary as well. But that does not mean I will not do it. I asked for your chaperonage and your blessing, but neither of them are required." I let the challenge dangle between us. Father had admired this woman enough to love her son and leave him half of my inheritance, so it stood to reason that she was not wholly unacceptable.

Felicity drew in a breath and narrowed her eyes. "Fine. I will go with you, but only because I know that if I do not, you will go alone, and that would send my mother-in-law to her grave if she was to learn of it."

A grin flashed over my lips.

"But," she continued, "you will go on my terms, and you will be mindful of your reputation."

"Of course."

We left the beautiful storefronts behind to return to our carriage. "Please recall that while you are under my care, my reputation is also on the line."

I paused and waited while Felicity climbed into the conveyance. I hadn't considered the point before, but now I could not help but think of it. "I will try not to do anything that will reflect poorly on you."

She did not look entirely convinced but smiled anyway. "Thank you, Thea."

"Can we go this afternoon?"

"Tonight we have the Huttons' ball. We can go tomorrow."

"Tomorrow," I repeated. I would meet my father's paramour and finally receive some answers.

The first ball of the Season was upon us, and Hannah had gone to great lengths to ensure I looked worthy of my first London social event. She had curled my hair and arranged it against a rose pink ribbon that perfectly matched my gown. I had witnessed many balls and parties and had attended a great deal of assemblies since I turned seventeen, but I had been assured time and again that balls in Town were different. They were special.

I was eager to see how they compared to the lavish balls I'd snuck from my room to watch through the banister slats in Sweden. I had a hunch they would not be quite the same.

Hannah placed my pearl ear drops in my hand and left me to put them on in silence. They were my mother's, and it was with a pang that I slipped them on and admired my reflection in the mirror. My eyes closed to block the image of my hair up and the pink dress on. Mother had always loved me in pink, and she would have chosen it herself were she here.

We were so alike that it frightened me.

I shook the feelings away and wiped the moisture from my eyes. I intended to make the most of my time in London, with or without a love match by the end of it. Though it was plainly obvious I wouldn't find a husband. I spun Mother's ring on my finger and shoved away the memories of her alone, waiting for Father, then giving up and finding company else-where. It was a history I refused to repeat. I wanted to marry for love, and until I found a way to scrape every last remnant of Benedict from my heart, it would not be open to another man.

Until then, though, I could still take pleasure in the dancing.

The house Felicity and James had rented for the Season was comfortable but small. I left my room to the sound of another door closing at the end of the short corridor. Benedict paused, his hand on the knob. His inky black coat was stark against his bronze waistcoat and ivory cravat. He struck a figure that was both slender and powerful, and I swallowed down the sigh of appreciation that threatened to bubble from my lips.

"Good evening," he murmured, adjusting his cuff as he crossed the corridor toward me. The personal act of adjusting his sleeve was so ordinary a task that it leant a sense of intimacy to finding him in the narrow, dim corridor.

"Are you looking forward to the ball? We both know how deeply you enjoy dancing."

"I will enjoy it if I can claim a set from you."

I wanted to agree, badly, but it was unwise. If I allowed Benedict to be so handsome toward me, to touch me, I would never stop loving him. I cleared my throat. "I think my dances will be taken up by eligible gentlemen who are vying for the opportunity to court me." I gave him a flippant smile to match my facetious words, hoping they sounded more playful than cutting.

"That is precisely what I fear." His earnest tone made my stomach drop.

I doubled the defenses around my heart and gentled my voice. "We are not going to be together, Benedict. You must accept that."

"I do not have to accept anything I do not agree with. I told you I would prove myself, and I intend to do just that."

How unfair. It was not as though I had pushed him away out of spite. It was only days ago I had watched Mrs. Rossi hang on his arm possessively, and he had done nothing to indicate her attention was unwelcome. Neither James nor Henry acted in this manner around women, so Benedict shouldn't believe his lack of boundaries to be acceptable.

If that was Benedict proving himself, then he was only proving my fears to be valid.

I lifted my chin. "In the meantime, I will dance with kind gentlemen who do not reuse their compliments for every woman in their arms."

"You will make them all fall in love with you, too," he said in a low, gravelly voice. "Which is a special sort of torture when none of them will be able to have you."

"No one will be falling in love with me tonight, Benedict."

He stepped forward, his eyes dark and glittering. "One man already has."

My breath caught, and I hurried to cover the sound, all the while my pulse beat furiously. "You shouldn't say such things."

"How else am I to fight for you?"

"It is a fruitless battle. I do not know how many times I must say so."

"Because I am exactly like your father?"

"Yes." And, worse, because I was exactly like my mother. "We would not be good for one another."

"But you desire a love match."

"And I will have one."

His jaw clenched, the muscle jumping. "You already could, Thea. You are the only reason we are not announcing our good news and rejoicing in the possibility of a happy future. I want to be your husband. I want to kiss you, and I want to hold your hand under the table exactly like James and Felicity do when they think no one is looking. Why will you not let me love you?"

His plea was not without power. It filtered through my limbs, shaking me to the bones. A flicker of doubt rocked my perfectly constructed walls of protection.

Benedict seemed to sense my waning commitment to my goals. He took a step closer and reached up tentatively to drag his fingertips lightly over my cheekbone and trace my jaw. It sent shivers volleying down my neck, and my chest heaved while I tried to regain my breathing. He smelled so good, so familiar, and I wanted to inhale deeply so I would always remember this scent.

"I am not your father, Thea. I am different, and I will prove it to you." He picked up my hand, turned it over to reveal my naked wrist, and pressed a kiss to the tender skin there.

My body flushed with heat. I wanted that feeling forever, and the feeling of his lips made my thoughts swim. Snatches of memories flicked around in my head of Benedict with Miss Dodwell, him smiling down at his dancing partners, the opera woman hanging from his arm, and I shook my head and stepped back. I pulled my hand free and at once felt his absence. Did he not see how difficult this was for me too?

My voice was strangled when I spoke. "Even if you are not like my father, I would spend the rest of my life wondering if you were going to turn into him. I cannot live a life so full of angst and fear. I won't do it. It would be better to marry a man I did not love than to marry you and worry that I would lose you."

"It's foolishness. Can you not see that? Your reasoning isn't sound. It's ridiculous."

"And that is meant to change my mind?"

He stepped back. "Fine. I will stop trying to change your mind, Thea. It is clearly made up, and there is nothing I can do to alter it. So go off tonight and find yourself a man. In fact, you might as well shoot for a lord, for I know Keene or Hampton would fall for you in a heartbeat."

"Maybe I *will* find a lord. Then at least I will approach my marriage with complete expectations," I snapped, meeting his ire with equal exasperation.

"That is wise. You cannot be disappointed if you do not allow yourself to hope, yes? Is that the foolish mantra you choose to live by?"

My breaths came in heaving, vicious waves. I wanted to both shove Benedict away and pull him in and earnestly apologize for being so rash, but I'd dug this terrible hole, and I was now forced to stand in it. I turned away from him and marched down the stairs, careful to draw long, slow breaths and calm myself before facing Felicity.

I would master these feelings.

I would master my emotions.

And tonight, to prove to Benedict how little he'd affected me, I was going to dance with a lord.

CHAPTER 30
BENEDICT

I t was usually impossible to remain angry with Thea, but tonight I was doing a spectacular job of it. Her stubborn obstinance was going to be the death of me, and I wondered why I so fully loved a woman who drove me to such distraction.

Well, she was fiercely independent, for one thing, and I greatly admired her ability to work hard for the things she cared deeply about. Not very many women of my acquaintance would be willing to slum in the kitchens of a great house and wash dishes merely so they might chart their own path. There was also the way she teased me, which was awfully entertaining when it wasn't driving her under my skin. Or the way she carried such a passionate energy about her it was impossible not to smile in her company—even amidst the teasing.

But tonight I could not remove her resolute face from my mind when she announced we would never be together. Was it idiocy or hope that allowed me to persist in trying to win her around? I loved her. She as much as admitted that she loved me too. *Not* being together was utter nonsense.

I slid into the small study on the lower floor of our rented townhouse and found Henry there. I craved his steady company and reassuring stability. Perhaps I could convince him to go out with me and drown my frustrations in fisticuffs. I dropped into the chair beside him and leaned my head against the top of the padded cushion.

He waited a minute before speaking. "You are not going to the ball?"

My eyes were closed, and I kept them that way. "No. Thea does not want to admit that she loves me, so what is the point? I only came to London for her."

"I did tell you she would not wait forever."

I looked at him. "Such wisdom you showed, knowing how I felt before I was willing to admit it myself."

"Well, it was painfully obvious," Henry muttered. "What is less apparent is why you are running away from her now."

"I asked her to save a dance for me tonight, and she refused me. She is being stubborn, and I cannot make her see reason." I understood the validity of her fears. Indeed, after speaking with James and Felicity about Mrs. Rossi, I could see how Thea had come to the conclusions she had. But if she never allowed me to prove myself, how was I to change her mind?

"So you are leaving her to go off to the ball to dance with all the other gentlemen without so much as a fight?"

I blinked at my brother. "I've *been* fighting. It seems that is all I've done for the last few weeks. But she wants me to quietly accept that we are not good for one another."

Henry was thoughtful for a moment before speaking. "Have you let her win?"

"Yes. Constantly. She receives everything she wants from me."

"Not everything, not if you are still trying to convince her to marry you."

I stared at him.

"Let her win this," Henry said. "Agree to cease pestering her.

Give her room to believe you are stepping back like she's asked you to do."

"And let the other men have her?"

"No. It has nothing to do with the other men. It proves to her that you respect what she wants enough to give her what she asks of you. It provides you the opportunity to prove yourself."

His words resonated with me, and I sat up. "You brilliant man."

Time and again I had sworn to prove to Thea that I was different, that I was worth taking a chance on. I had begged her for the opportunity to prove myself. But I did not give her the one thing she had asked for, which would demonstrate how I valued her opinions and judgment.

Henry chuckled. "I would not go so far as that. I was merely pointing out the obvious."

I stood up and ruffled his curly hair. "Thank you, Hen."

He brushed his fingers through his hair to correct it, and I crossed the room quickly, hoping I had not missed the carriage. I stopped at the door of the study and looked back. "Are you certain you don't wish to come?"

He lifted his book. "Yes. Extremely certain."

"Suit yourself."

I made it to the door as the rest of the party was filing outside and took my hat from the table where I'd left it before fitting it to my head. Felicity looked surprised to see me. "I thought you'd chosen not to come."

"I changed my mind."

Thea scowled, and I smiled benignly at her. "You win," I said under my breath while we walked down to the waiting carriage. "I will leave you be."

She looked uneasy but nodded. "Thank you."

We rode to the ball in silence and mounted the steps to the tall, brightly lit townhouse. Mr. and Mrs. Hutton stood in the doorway of their ballroom, welcoming their guests, and I schooled my expression into general interest. The Huttons had been good friends of my parents, and James's godparents, so I had known them most of my life.

James leaned over to speak quietly to Felicity while we waited in line to greet our hosts. I did my best to leave space between Thea and me so I would not inadvertently touch her. Her familiar tangy floral scent wafted toward me, and I clenched my teeth together to keep myself from inhaling deeply.

"Good evening, James, Mrs. Bradwell," Mrs. Hutton said, curtseying politely.

Felicity performed the introductions. I paid them little mind beyond smiling and bowing when my name was mentioned, my attention drawn to the crowd already gathered in the ballroom. It was going to be a crush, and Thea was not going to be lacking for partners.

I pulled at my cuffs again, anxious to move on. After seeing the sheer number of gentlemen who could fall for Thea in a heartbeat, I regretted ever coming tonight. But I could not show Thea that I would respect her wishes unless I was here and not pestering her for a dance.

Our party moved into the ballroom and found a place to stand along the back wall.

Thea planted herself beside Felicity, and I strained to hear what she was saying. "I know you will not dance," Thea said, "but you do intend to provide introductions for me, yes?"

"I will aid you in whatever way I can, Thea, as promised."

She sagged a bit in relief. "I should like first to meet Lord Keene, and then Lord Hampton, if it can be managed."

I bit my cheek to keep from cursing. Was the woman bent on torturing me? She only knew either of their names because I had mentioned them in a fit of pique.

Felicity looked appropriately confused. "Who are these people? How do you know their names?"

Thea gave a little, unrefined shrug and avoided my gaze. "I have my methods."

"Oh, heavens, Thea. I wanted to help you make a match, but please promise me you will be wise. After what happened last year—"

Thea looked from Felicity to James. "That worked to your benefit, did it not?"

Good gads, she was acting ridiculous tonight.

"It did," Felicity said, "but I was fortunate that it was *James* whom I was found with and not a cad. It could just as easily have been my ruin."

Thea laughed a little, the sound hollow. "I intend to remain above reproach in all my behavior, Felicity. I promise. I do want to secure a good husband."

My stomach clenched again. "Quite impossible to promise a thing such as that, isn't it, Miss Northcott?"

Thea blinked innocently up at me. "You mean to say you don't believe I am capable of good behavior, Mr. Bradwell? How shocking of you. I had thought we were *friends*."

The word was sour, and I wasn't sure how much more I could take. Something between a laugh and a guffaw tore from my throat, and I cast my gaze about the room for a refreshment table. "Is there anything to drink here?"

This was far more difficult than I thought it would be.

Felicity grasped my sleeve in one hand and Thea's in the other, looking between us imploringly. "Whatever you do, promise me you will both remain in the ballroom all evening until it is time to leave. Promise me."

I promised. I loved my sister-in-law, and I would not do anything to hurt her if I could help it.

"Thank you," she said.

A woman in a violet turban and a long white feather approached and spoke to Felicity, and I stepped back and leaned against the wall, waiting for the matron to leave.

"We ought to find a few gentlemen to introduce you to," Felicity said to Thea once the woman had left. "James will know who is best."

"Lord Keene or Lord Hampton would be fine," Thea said, this time shooting a look in my direction.

I struggled to suppress my frustration. Was she trying to goad me? She did not even know them. They could be septuagenarians or missing half their teeth, and she would be none the wiser. I was a fool for providing her with any names at all. "Neither of those men would suit our purposes here very much."

"Because I am not worthy of a title?" Thea snapped, clearly still reeling from our earlier encounter.

"Because neither of them are in the market for a *wife*," I said. They were rakes, the both of them, and the most they would want from Thea would be to slink away to the library alone. Something she had promised Felicity she would not do.

Thea looked to the ceiling as though it would grant her serenity and patience. "Perhaps I could be the woman to change their mind."

"That is a lofty goal."

"But not insurmountable."

"Do I detect the possibility that you have now taken my warning to be something of a challenge?" I bit out between nearly clenched teeth.

"It does not sound like much of a challenge to me."

"Goodness," Felicity said, her widened eyes shooting between us. "Must I be forced to separate you like errant schoolchildren?"

Oh, what was I doing? The very opposite of what Henry had advised me, certainly. I shook my head, and a lone curl fell onto my forehead. I ran a hand through my hair to put it back where it belonged and trained my gaze on my sister-in-law. These social events were extremely difficult for her to manage, and I was certainly making it far worse. It was better if I put space

282

between Thea and myself. "Forgive me, Felicity. I have become carried away. I will remove myself to avoid any further disruptions to your evening."

"You are leaving the ball?" she asked.

"No. I have seen an old school chum, and I will greet him before Thea can light my cravat on fire with her evil stare."

Thea raised her chin.

Chagrined, I avoided looking at Thea, regretting my final words as they were leaving my mouth. I turned and walked away from them. Let Thea have her roguish lords and dance with every man in attendance. I would not bother her again.

The rest of the ball was a form of acute torture. Thea danced nearly every set after I left her side, and I passed the night by doing the very same thing, though I quickly found I made a somewhat disagreeable partner. None of the attempts by my dancing partners to bring me into a pleasant mood were rewarded with anything above a bland smile, and I walked more than one disappointed debutante back to her waiting mother.

Now that the drapes had been lifted from my ignorance and my excessive flirting was made known to me, it was clear to see that I was, in fact, half of the problem. This evening I had stepped away from more than one lingering hand on my arm, forcing them to drop their holds. I did not deliver a single compliment I did not feel with my whole soul, and the women appeared to understand the message I was attempting to portray. My behavior bordered politeness, remaining firmly in the realm of friendly but uninterested. It was not hard to do. The only woman in the room who had my interest was Thea.

Thea, on the other hand, was a smashing success, as expected. She twirled from one man to the next—never, I was pleased to notice, on Keene's or Hampton's arms—and radiantly lit up the ballroom wherever she went.

I had talked myself out of slipping from the room on more than one occasion, for I could not prove I would honor Thea's wishes if I was not there, could I?

Her laughter floated up over the group currently standing between us and lodged itself in my heart. She was a beacon, and I was a wayward ship. I only wanted to glide toward her. I moved to the refreshment table so I could see who she was speaking to and lifted a glass of something oddly colored, drinking it with little regard to what it tasted like.

Thea stood between two gentlemen, her dazzling smile displayed for both of them, while Felicity and James waited nearby. She looked up and found me watching her, her smile faltering momentarily. I lifted my glass slightly in a minor salute and tilted my head just a bit, but she received my message. Her mouth was flat, her eyes glued to me, and I wondered . . . no, I *hoped* she was altering her staunch opinion on the state of our relationship.

She turned toward Felicity and said something, and the next thing I knew, both women were slipping away from the gentlemen and coming toward the refreshment table.

Felicity looked up at me and smiled. "You have been busy this evening, Ben. I do not think I've seen you sit out a single dance."

"Put away your matchmaking ideas, please," I said with great boredom. "I have no designs on any of these young women."

"None of them?" Thea asked with wide, doll-like eyes. "Not a single woman in this room piques your interest?"

I held her gaze. "I do not desire a woman who does not desire me in equal measure, so at present I would have to say no."

She went still, but I was finished with these games. It hurt to watch Thea act with such little regard for my heart, and I was weary of the sport. A man could only fight so much or try for so long before he ran out of the desire to put himself through any more pain. I lifted my gaze to my sister-in-law. "I think I will hire a cab home. I am finished for the evening."

"It is no wonder. You've already danced a great deal," she said, smiling.

I gave her a weak smile in response, then looked to Thea. "I hope you enjoy yourself tonight, Miss Northcott."

With that, I turned and stalked from the room without looking back.

CHAPTER 31
THEA

I had done it now. I'd well and truly ruined any chance at happiness Benedict and I had ever had together—but I could not even allow myself to mourn a relationship I had not permitted to begin. His efforts last night to treat women with civility but not excessive attention had not gone unnoticed. He had listened to me, had tried to stem the charm that usually flooded from him.

I spent the morning roaming the house, waiting for Benedict to wake so I could apologize for my rudeness from the evening before, but he never arrived. After the entirety of the household had been awake for hours, I finally had enough waiting and paced away from the window in the drawing room. "Has Benedict gone out already this morning?"

Henry put his book down and looked at James.

James looked from Felicity to me. "He has. He went to find lodging."

"Lodging?" I asked, unable to be certain I'd correctly understood him.

"Yes." James cleared his throat. "He felt it would be best if he stayed in the bachelor's quarters we typically lease when we come to Town."

No one else spoke the words that lingered over us like an oppressing raincloud, that I was the reason for his sudden departure. I looked to Henry. "You did not wish to do the same?"

"I am comfortable here," he said simply.

The implication that Benedict was not comfortable here was then laid at my feet. Though I was certain Henry did not mean it that way, it was the truth nonetheless.

I lowered myself onto the cushioned window seat and leaned against the wall to look down at the empty street below. This was what I had wanted, wasn't it? For him to accept that we were not a good match and that our future was written in the stars. One only needed to look at my parents' unhappiness and how greatly we resembled them in order to be put off by the notion of Benedict and I together. But now that he was gone, my heart missed him, my eyes ached to see him, my fingers were desperate to be on his arm.

All of me wanted to be near all of him, and I hated that I was the reason he'd left.

Felicity stood and wiped her hands down her gown. "Are you ready, Thea? We may as well get on with it."

James looked between us with resignation, and I had no doubt his wife had informed him of our plans. "Are you certain you do not wish for an escort? I will remain in the carriage if the house looks respectable."

"The address is located in a respectable neighborhood," Felicity said, as though reminding him of something she had already said numerous times. "I asked my mother last night about the houses on that street, and she assured me they are perfectly acceptable. I have no doubt we will be safe."

James appeared as though he wanted to argue, but I think he must have known what Felicity guessed: I would need to do this on my own, without an audience. I rose and gave her a determined nod. "I am ready."

———

The street was quiet and clean, and our carriage stopped before a blue house with greenery hanging over the terrace. It was such a friendly, comfortable looking house that I couldn't help but be a little surprised by it. Not that I expected a mistress to live in a dark house with French gargoyles guarding the windows, but I might have expected something a little less agreeable.

"What shall we do if the solicitor wrote down the wrong street and this is not the woman we're looking for?" I asked.

"Then we apologize for our mistake and go to Gunter's for an ice."

I smiled. "I like your plan. Perhaps we should obtain that ice regardless of the outcome today." I faced the door and blew a breath out. "I think I shall need it."

Felicity said nothing more, but stood at my side and waited for me to be ready to knock on the door. This was a necessary introduction, for if I wanted Archie in my life, a *child*, I needed to at least be introduced to his mother. If she was a decent, respectable mother—and according to Archie, she was a very good mama—then she would not allow him to spend the summer with a complete stranger, regardless of the fact that we shared the same father.

But then there was also the ridiculous need deep within my heart for answers only she could give.

I curled my gloved fingers around the iron knocker and tapped it three resounding times, then stepped back and waited, holding my breath and absently pressing a finger to my mother's ring.

A maid came to the door, outfitted nicely, though plainly. "Can I help you?"

"We've come to call on Mrs. Danvers, if she is at home."

Felicity proffered her card and handed it to the maid, who took it with curiosity then closed the door.

"I took the liberty of writing your name on my card as well before we left," Felicity said quietly. "I thought we might need it."

We only had to wait a few minutes before the maid returned and let us inside, then down a corridor toward a brightly lit room. A woman stood at the window, an embroidery project discarded on the sofa, and she turned upon our entrance.

She was older than I'd expected for a mother of someone so young. Her dark hair was very near my own color, but shot through with strands of silver, and her face, though beautiful, was lined with age. She stared at me for a minute in silence. This woman now had control over half my inheritance. I had not been angry with Archie after meeting him, for I understood my father's desire to provide for both of his children. But this woman was a stranger and her hand in the situation irked me.

"I never believed we would have reason to meet," she said, her voice silky and lower than I'd expected. "But when we received word of the inheritance, I had hoped."

I stepped closer to her and met her at the window, while Felicity stood near the door. It seemed that none of us were willing to sit, for that implied the desire to remain. "I did not wish to meet you," I said bluntly. "But Archie changed my mind."

Her face softened with the affection of a mother. "You've been to see him, then? How is my boy?"

"Well. Thriving in his school." My words were as clipped and strained as my breathing. "Though I did wonder why you chose a school in Bath for him."

"My brother is the headmaster."

"Oh." Archie had not told me that.

She smiled. "So I know he is watched over. I considered living in Bath, too, but London is my home."

"He seemed well settled. I hoped you would grant him permission to visit me on occasion as well. Perhaps in the summer."

She hesitated, looking at Felicity, then back to me. "Perhaps it is better if we sit."

We obeyed, taking the sofa opposite her chair.

Nerves made her fingers flutter anxiously along the edge of the sofa cushion. "Archie is all I have, you see, so I am quite protective of him."

"That is understandable, Mrs. Danvers. But surely Mr. Danvers—"

"Does not exist," she said quietly, her hands motionless on her lap.

I had not expected that. "But Archie's name."

"Yes, well, I couldn't very well give him his father's name." She looked at her fingernails, then back at me. "Mr. Danvers was created years ago when I was struggling to find a way to keep other men at bay, to explain why I was unavailable. I met your father when I worked for a reputable faro club, and it was very nearly love right away, but he could not marry me because of my station."

"And because of my mother," I said.

She gave me a soft smile. "He did not yet know your mother."

The wind swept from my lungs, and I tightened my hands into fists on my lap. If she meant to imply that my father had been with her first . . . that he had carried on a relationship with her for decades, not even fathering her child until nine years ago . . . I swallowed hard and shook my head. "That cannot be true. My father loved my mother. He did not . . . he was not unfaithful to her in the beginning of her marriage."

"Of course he loved your mother," Mrs. Danvers said kindly. "He was a man with a full heart, and he loved many women."

Two women, if she was correct. But, of course, there were the others, too. The women he would sneak away with after balls or parties. He had not only been unfaithful to my mother, it would seem. But Mrs. Danvers seemed perfectly aware of that, if her response was any indication. *He loved many women.* Repulsion thickened my throat, making it difficult to swallow.

"How long did you . . ." I could not finish my question, but thankfully, she seemed to understand me.

"I never stopped loving your father, and despite his frequent responsibilities abroad, he never stopped loving me. He provided enough to remove me from the faro house and set me up in a little apartment in Cheapside."

That was a great expense that he needn't have gone to. Surely living on the Continent removed such a necessity, unless helping Mrs. Danvers was something he had wished to do of his own volition. "When I learned Archie was only a boy, I assumed your liaison was of a shorter nature."

She tilted her head a little, a mist present in her gaze. "There were other babies before, but I lost them. Archie was the first to be born healthy and strong, and I cherish him with all that I am."

It was evident in the way she spoke of her son that she was a doting mother and a kind soul. I wished I could like her, and I thought in any other capacity I would, but given her relationship with my family, I did not know if I would ever be able to find myself on pleasant footing with this woman.

I did not need a relationship with her, though. I only desired to have one with her son. "You will allow Archie to come to me, then? Perhaps for a few weeks in the summer. He is the only family I have, and I would like to know him better."

She was hesitant for only a moment. "Your father would have liked this."

Anger flew through me, but I tempered it with even breaths. My impulse to defend my mother's honor was strong, to reject anything that would have hurt her, but she was no more faithful than Father, so my defenses fell like sand on my tongue.

Mother had also hidden the will that would have supplied Archie with his inheritance six years ago, so she certainly did not need to be spoken of in this house.

"Can I ask what you have done since my father's death? If he provided for you, then . . ."

Mrs. Danvers shrugged. "We did what we needed to do. We've never been too hungry, if that is your fear. My brother took Archie on as a scholarship student before we could afford to pay."

The image of Archie, thin and hungry, had haunted me momentarily, but I allowed her to put my mind at ease.

I stood, having reached my limit for the moment. I was still reeling from the revelation that Mrs. Danvers had been with my father longer than he had known Mother. If that was the case, then I had been so wrong about . . . but no, I could not traverse that path at present.

Felicity rose beside me, silently providing her support.

"Can I ask," I said, watching Mrs. Danvers rise, "whatever happened to your fictional Mr. Danvers?"

"He was in the navy for a good long while, which provided me with the excuse to live alone or go on long journeys without inciting any questions among my neighbors. But then, six years ago, he died, leaving Archie and me with nothing."

I nodded, understanding. Father had been Mr. Danvers to her. He had provided the stories she supplied her friends and neighbors, and likely the letters she received as well. As my father's name was Charles *Daniel* Northcott, it was not a great stretch of imagination to discern where the Danvers name came from. Similar, yet subtly so.

We walked to the door and bade her farewell before Felicity led me to the carriage. "Will you be well?"

"Certainly," I said with more confidence than I felt. "She did not seem to be a terrible woman."

"No, not terrible." Felicity sighed as the carriage rocked forward. "She seemed like a woman deeply in love."

"I had the same impression." A woman so deeply in love that she lived a life alone, with snatches of attention, the veritable life of a widow long before the man of her affection died. But he must have cared for her in equal measure if he had provided for her for so long and split his inheritance between me and *her* son. He had cared for her long before he loved my mother, and this new information took all of my carefully erected walls and crumbled them to dust.

My fear that Benedict would be as Father was, that he would alter slowly over time, was unfounded. Father had not even done that. He was never honorable to begin with.

The truth rocked me, and every defense I'd built against Benedict's suit was now invalid. "My father was never faithful to my mother. It was not as I had imagined at all, that his willingness to flirt with other women had slowly distorted until he was an adulterer." I bent my head and dropped my face in my hands. "Oh, the things I've accused Benedict of. I have been such a fool."

Felicity remained quiet, and I lifted my head to look her in the eyes. I shook my head. "*Such* a fool. I am certain I've lost Benedict forever."

If she was surprised by my candid admission, she hid it well. "You have not lost him."

"You cannot know that. I was awful. He has tried to convince me that we would be good together, that our love is worth fighting for, and I pushed him away time and again because I feared ending up like my mother. He is so similar to my father, you see. They are nearly the same person. And I am my mother in both appearance and temperament. But now . . . now I see that I knew nothing of my parents' relationship." I groaned loudly. "I've thrown away my chance at happiness with him, and I will never be forgiven. I do not *deserve* to be forgiven."

Felicity laughed, drawing my attention. "As much as I find your dramatics a little amusing, you must cease. Surely you realize that if Benedict's heart was so fully engaged to you before whatever occurred between the two of you last night, then he will not be so easily changed."

"No, not *easily*. But if I have broken his heart, then it will not be easily mended, either. I've been a—"

"A fool? Yes, you said so. Now, instead of crying about it, we need to think through the situation logically."

"You will help me?"

"Of course." Felicity showed a quiet strength that I admired. I did not know how to be quiet in anything I did. "We will begin by forming a plan."

CHAPTER 32
BENEDICT

As difficult as it has been to stay away from Thea, it has also been something of a necessity. I could very easily have left London altogether, but I was seeing to the business of finding a land agent or a steward who might be willing to come work for me in Cumberland. I'd not yet finalized the sale of either house, but I had received letters from both of the solicitors I had inquired with, and now all that was left to me was to make a decision about my future.

But how could I make any such decisions about my future when the person I wanted to share it with was being obstinate and headstrong and dancing with ridiculous fops to wedge herself beneath my skin?

I deeply regretted the way I had left things with Thea last week. The sennight since the Huttons' ball had been miserably spent interviewing possible candidates and sitting in the damp room I was letting off of St. James Street. With great determination, though, I stayed away from my family's townhouse. I was not prepared to see her yet. I hoped the time away would make it easier to face Thea again next time I did.

I met James and Henry on the pavement before my rooms,

and we set off down St. James Street. Men walked past us, swinging canes and tipping their hats in greeting on the way to their clubs.

"We could go to Brooks," James suggested. "I could get you both in for dinner."

"I would prefer a brisk walk today," I said, delighting in the sunshine despite the cold. "Now will you cease making me wait, and tell me—"

"Benedict Bradwell," a deep, saccharine voice called from behind us. I turned to find Keller approaching us from behind, and Thea's friend Peter Seymour was beside him. His mouth curved into a foxlike smile. "I did wonder if that was you."

I turned and dipped my head politely to both of them. "Do you know my brothers? James and Henry Bradwell."

Mr. Seymour nodded. "We met yesterday. Good to see you both again."

"Yesterday?" I looked at James.

He nodded. "When Mr. Seymour called on Thea."

My chest tightened as sudden envy dashed through me. I knew Thea would have had suitors knocking at her door all week, but hearing about it did not sit well in my stomach. Mr. Seymour did not deserve her. I did not know the man, but I could sense that much. And he had *kissed* her all those years ago.

I had to clench my fists discreetly behind my back to remove some of the anger and jealousy now coursing through me.

"We recently heard of a new faro club opening on King Street," Keller said. "If you've any interest, I can procure you an invitation."

"I do not." I was not interested in losing my inheritance before I could secure an estate.

My brothers each gave similar answers, and Keller looked between us, annoyed. "You used to be reliable for a good time, Bradwell. Now you are only a disappointment."

I watched Keller walk away, Mr. Seymour in step with him,

and my shoulders lightened to a satisfied degree. "It is all very well being a disappointment to him, I think," I said. "So long as I make myself proud."

James clapped me on the back, and we resumed our walk to St. James's park. "You make me proud, Ben."

"I would add my pride to this as well," Henry said, "but I fear the moment has already grown far too tender for my comfort."

I grinned. "You mean you would prefer not to hear about how miserable I've been this last week?"

"You needn't share it," Henry said drily. "Thea has been miserable enough for both of you, and it is beginning to wear."

I stopped walking and both of my brothers turned back to face me. "She has been miserable?"

James laughed. "Undoubtedly. She has done nothing but mope and complain about the parties we are to attend. She smiles for any guests who come to call, but the moment they leave she returns to her morose melancholy. It is . . . quite depressing, actually."

A smile curved my lips. "If she is miserable without me, then perhaps she will soon see reason."

"I do not think you need to worry about that. She and Felicity are hatching some plan, and they will not allow me to know what it is about, but I have a hunch it involves you."

"A plan?" Why did the sound of that make me increasingly excited? "Perhaps I should make a point of attending the next ball you have on your calendar so I can see her."

"You could," Henry said. "Or you could—"

"If you tell me to let her win one more time, I am going to throw your books into the lake."

"Which books?" Henry asked, disturbed.

"Which lake?" James asked, amused.

I scowled and kept walking, my brothers falling into step beside me. "Any of them."

"For the sake of my books—whichever ones you are threatening—I will not say it aloud. But I do think returning now will be too soon."

"I do not wish to play games. I want to have a discussion with her, to communicate and know what she is thinking."

"This is not playing games," James added. "It is proving you respect Thea enough to give her what she asked for."

I ran a hand through my hair. "I wait until she comes to me, then? What if that day never arrives?"

Henry and James shared a look. "It will come. And, in the meantime, can we discuss the land agents you've met with thus far?" James asked. "Haversham told me you met with his younger brother, and I wondered if he presented well. Evidently he has a good head for numbers."

"But a lousy reputation among the money lenders," Henry said. "I heard he is over his head in debt."

"Blast. I liked him." We turned the corner and continued down the street toward the green park at the end. The sunshine and cool air was rejuvenating, and the hope my brothers had placed in my heart was encouraging. "What of Finch's nephew? He's a bit young, but he recently studied new irrigation techniques I found interesting."

"He wouldn't bring wisdom then, but perhaps ingenuity?" James mused.

"That was the measure I took."

We meandered into St. James's Park, talking of the various candidates I'd interviewed and then of the two houses. My brothers offered advice and gave me much to consider, but still I did not know what to do. My father, had he been alive, would have appreciated the grandeur of Kellinger. But Bumpton—as clumsy a house as its name—could not very well be out of consideration quite yet. I could not remove from my mind the way I'd felt Thea's presence when I'd stood on the front portico beside Henry and looked out over the fertile land.

My heart hurt, so it was with great pleasure that I welcomed a distraction in the form of two ladies coming toward us. Miss Marianne Hutton and her mother, Mrs. Hutton, who also happened to be James's godmother, both smiled at us, and the proper pleasantries were exchanged.

"How is your mother?" Mrs. Hutton asked. "I have been meaning to schedule a visit since the debacle last year."

"The debacle turned out to be a bit of a blessing," James said, referring to his marriage. It was at Mrs. Hutton's ball that he'd been caught alone with Felicity before they had married.

The matron smiled up at him with adoration. "That it did. How is your Mrs. Bradwell faring? I did not have much of an opportunity to speak to her at Marianne's ball."

"She is well."

"We are greatly looking forward to Miss Northcott's ball," Mrs. Hutton said warmly. "Her mother was my dear friend years ago when we were just girls ourselves, and it has done my heart well to see Miss Northcott. She looks like her mother did at her age."

"Will you also attend the ball, Miss Hutton?" Henry asked, surprising every member of the party. His eyes were bent on the young lady, and his mouth was trained in a faint smile.

She met his gaze with what appeared to be determination. "I intend to, yes."

"Then might I be so bold as to request that you save a set for me? I care not which."

Miss Hutton looked to her mother, then back to Henry and nodded. "I would be delighted to."

The women were shortly after on their way, and I did not know which of two questions was more pressing: why the devil did Henry ask that girl to save him a set, or when was this supposed ball to take place? Henry precluded me from needing to inquire on the first of the two.

"Do not think anything of that. It is merely business, and I do not have any romantic intentions where Miss Hutton is concerned."

"I did not know you were even aware of the chit's existence."

Henry turned a confused glance on James. "Of course I know her. She's a *Hutton*. Mother's particular friends."

Both James and I knew that, but this was Henry, a man so often lost in a book that he could not be counted upon to notice everything that occurred around him.

"Enough about the oddness of whatever that was," I said. "Why have neither of you told me about Thea's ball?"

"We planned to," Henry said.

"It is a week from Tuesday."

"Was I to be invited?"

"I believe that is part of the plan the women are hatching. You shall be notified of it shortly."

"Oh, good heavens."

"Indeed."

"Shall I feign surprise when I receive the invitation?" I asked.

"I do not think anyone intends to watch you receive it, so that is entirely up to you."

We continued on, and I felt the weight of the decisions I had yet to make crowd my shoulders. But when I closed my eyes and imagined the life I wanted to have, all of the answers were clearly before me. The land steward, the house, the estate itself were blindingly obvious, if Thea was by my side. The trouble was, if I bought the estate and Thea and I did not come to an accord, could I bear to live in the house without her?

CHAPTER 33

THEA

I was not prone to nerves, but tonight, while I waited for Hannah to finish my hair, I could not calm my trembling fingers. Felicity had kept her word to her mother-in-law and planned and executed a ball in my honor, but we had agreed to keep it somewhat small. Neither of us thought there was much worth in a lavish ball when I did not need to look for a suitor. I knew exactly whom I wanted to marry, and I planned to secure him tonight.

A soft knock on the door preceded Felicity's entrance, and she crossed the room as Hannah stepped back.

"You look darling, Thea."

"Thank you." The rose-pink silk ran luxuriously down my legs and paused just above my matching slippers, setting off the ivory pearls on my neck to advantage. "Is everything ready?"

Felicity smiled. "It is. Are you nervous?"

My stomach flipped at the thought of what I intended to do. "Yes, but I think it will be worth it. I cannot expect him to forget everything I have said or done, can I?"

Her smile softened. "Unlikely. But you can expect his forgiveness."

"I hope for it, at least."

I took my pair of long ivory gloves from the edge of my bed and followed Felicity into the corridor, pulling them on as we walked. She halted and turned to me. "Oh, I nearly forgot. We've had a late addition to the party." She screwed up her face in apology. "I'm afraid James saw Lord Claverley at Brooks yesterday and extended the invitation. Apparently his cousin did not leave him much choice."

"Am I permitted to refuse his request to dance?"

"You can refuse anyone you wish. That is entirely up to you. I will never force you to dance with someone you do not wish to dance with."

"You are the very best chaperone, Felicity." I slid my arm through hers and gave it a squeeze.

"It is an easy position when the woman in question hardly wishes to go out and already knows who she wants to marry. I do not think I would be such a good candidate for the position of chaperoning a woman who desired to attend every ball and meet every gentleman of the *ton*."

"Do not underestimate yourself. I am not easy to manage, and you have done so splendidly."

She shot me a smile from the side, and we descended the stairs to take our places at the entrance to the drawing room. The splendor was no less for the smaller guest list. The rugs had been rolled up and removed, the furniture pushed aside to create room for dancing. A string quartet James had hired for the evening was now tuning their instruments on the far side of the room. The chandelier was lit with rows of candles, and even more flames lined the mantel and tables, their light thrown through the room with help from the mirrors behind them. It was a ball to be proud of and a lovely backdrop for what I intended to do this evening.

It had been just over two weeks since Benedict had walked away from me, and each day felt more and more like my heart was being ripped from my chest, mishandled, then put back. My behavior that night had been childish and abhorrent, and while I did think I was justified in my insecurities, I could no longer allow such justification to hold after the light Mrs. Danvers had shed on my father's true character.

Whether or not my mother was aware of Mrs. Danvers, or the other women Father had been with, was irrelevant. I could not allow my parents' past mistakes to rule my life, and neither of them were blameless.

I could, however, chart my own future.

"You are certain Benedict received an invitation?" I whispered.

"Yes, Thea, for the twentieth time, he *did* receive his invitation, and he *did* reply favorably." She squeezed my hand. "He will be here."

Guests started to arrive at the top of the hour, and within thirty minutes the drawing room was mostly full. We were about to abandon our post when Lord Claverley started up the stairs toward us, and I exchanged a look with Felicity. James, who had taken his place beside his wife, now stepped forward a little, and I was glad to have such a stalwart chaperone.

"You are stunning this evening, my pet," Lord Claverley said, bowing over my hand. He pressed a wet kiss to my knuckles as I repressed a shudder.

"Lady Claverley does not join you this evening?" I asked, disentangling my hand.

"She was unable to leave the children."

"Of course, my lord," Felicity said. "We do know how she dotes on them."

"Quite."

Another set of footsteps mounted the stairs, and my heart sped in anticipation for the gentleman I had been hoping to see all evening.

"Might I humbly beg for the first set, Miss Northcott?" the earl asked.

The *first?* Surely he was aware that it held great importance, especially at my own ball. But the man I had hoped to dance with had not yet arrived. Lord Claverley was an earl, of course, but that did not mean he was the man of most importance in my life. He was not even a member of my family.

I cleared my throat. "Oh, actually—"

Benedict appeared at the top of the stairs then, his steps sure and quick, his appearance stealing my words. He took Felicity's hand first and kissed her knuckles with brotherly affection. "Sorry I am late. I had trouble finding a carriage."

"It is no bother," she said easily.

He turned to me, and my body flushed with the pleasure of being under his scrutiny, his blue eyes dark with some emotion I could not name.

"Actually," Benedict said, bending over my hand, his gaze never leaving mine. "I believe the first set was promised to me."

He bent his arm, and I placed my hand hesitantly on top of it. Tonight was not at all going to plan, but I was flexible and could still achieve my goal. It was hard, however, to focus with Benedict's muscles clenching beneath my fingers.

Claverley sputtered in shocked dismay, but we ignored him.

We stepped into the ballroom and the first dances were announced. To start—a waltz. I looked over my shoulder and found Felicity grinning. That certainly hadn't been in the plan, but I was glad of the change.

"I think my family is beginning a tradition of opening balls with waltzes," Benedict said.

"Are you disappointed?" I asked, taking my place beside him.

He held my gaze. "Not in the least."

The strings began, their music floating softly through the room like a caress, and we started our promenade. My heart reacted to being in Benedict's presence as though it was a desert and he was water. His absence had felt dry and lifeless, and now I wanted to bask in his gaze.

"You did not have to come to my rescue, but I thank you anyway."

"You are quite welcome," he said pleasantly.

The promenade ceased, and we faced one another. One of Benedict's hands circled behind my waist, and his other took possession of my left hand, lifting it above my head. I swallowed against my dry throat and put my right hand in position around his back. We were close, our arms entangled in such a way that I could hardly breathe. His scent tickled my nose, and I wanted to drop our position and fall into his embrace.

From the way his breathing grew shallow, I believed he might have felt much the same way.

"Can I ask *why* you stepped in when your cousin asked me to dance? You have every right to be upset with me."

Benedict smiled, and we began to twirl with the music. "I promised you I would always protect you, did I not? I will always be here for you, Thea. No matter what."

Warmth swept through my body, and I did not know how I would manage the remainder of the dance. We moved through the motions as two people did who felt deeply. Our eyes did not stray from one another, and his gloved hand held mine with such tenderness I felt cradled in his care. When the song came to a close, we walked from the center of the floor as if by mutual silent agreement that one dance was enough, and we would finish the set in conversation instead of dancing.

We did not have a terrace to escape to, so I turned to him and said, "I would like some lemonade if you would be so kind as to escort me to the parlor."

Benedict acquiesced, and we stepped from the drawing room, passing Peter Seymour near the door. He looked as though he meant to speak to me, but I turned away. Once we reached the corridor, I opened the door to the study, took Benedict by the arm, and pulled him into the dark room.

"I do not think Felicity would appreciate this very much," Benedict said quietly. The room was dark, but enough moonlight slipped through the window to show his expression, which appeared carved of stone. "We did promise her we would not sneak away."

"That promise was for another ball. I am certain, as long as we are not caught, she will not mind—"

Voices in the corridor passed by, and I closed my mouth at once so they would not detect us. I released Benedict's sleeve and faced the door, taking the bolt and sliding it into place so no one would be able to open it from the outside. "We cannot be found if they cannot open the door."

"We can be missed, however," he said drily.

"Please, Ben. Allow me to say what I have been planning so carefully for weeks, and then I will unlock the door and let you free."

"I did not say I minded being secreted away with you. I only wonder if it is the wisest choice."

"Because my choices thus far have proven extremely wise?" I countered.

"Fair enough."

I cleared my throat. "I first must apologize for my childish behavior."

"I cannot go through this," he said, raking a hand through his curls.

Cold dread slipped into my stomach. "Why not?"

"Because I cannot see your face. If you are about to grovel for my forgiveness, I would at least enjoy watching you do it."

I flattened my mouth, then looked about the room. "We should not light a candle. It could be visible beneath the door."

"We could move closer to the window."

"Oh, yes! The moonlight."

We carefully picked our way toward the single window in the small study, and Benedict pushed the drapes open further until the cool light streamed over us.

"You were saying?" he prompted, his smile widening.

"I really must start at the beginning." I inhaled, then began. I told him of going to visit Mrs. Danvers and the layers of truth she had revealed, of the way she had taken my beliefs about my father and spun them around.

"That must have been very difficult for you," he murmured.

"It was. But it was also freeing. My parents never changed. My mother might have, but my father had been unfaithful all along. He was not, as I'd feared, a flirt who grew out of his own control. I worried we would mirror my parents, that my heart would break again and again, but I realized how foolish that was. We are not them—"

"As I have previously stated."

"Yes, yes." I sighed. "Because you were much more intelligent than me."

"No, because I did not have the cloud of insecurity and concern hanging over me. While I did not like your opinions on the matter, I did grow to understand where they came from."

"I noticed your efforts at the Huttons' ball," I said, recalling the way he had stepped out of one partner's reach after her hand had lingered a little too long on his sleeve.

"I hoped you had," he said quietly. "Once it was made clear to me that your concerns were valid and my flirting was not delivering the correct message to these women, I subdued it. I am still working to find a balance between polite, friendly chatter and flirting."

"Your awareness does you credit, Ben." I cleared the emotion from my throat, my heart slamming in my chest. "You are thoughtful, and that is one of the reasons I would like to beg you, Benedict Bradwell, to forgive me for my foolishness, to accept me as I am today, and to agree to be my husband."

His mouth dropped open, and his head tilted a little to the side. Moonlight cast shadows over his face, but his surprise was evident alongside the mirth glittering in his eyes. "Is that not my responsibility?"

I blinked at him. This was not going at all how I expected. Surely he should be kissing me by now. "Well, you have already tried and were refused. I hoped, were you to learn of how my understanding had changed, that you would also accept my plea to become engaged."

"Yes, I did understand all of that." He rubbed a hand over his jaw. "But am I not meant to ask *you* to be my wife?"

"I did not ask you to be my wife. I asked you to be my husband."

"You should not be doing the asking at all."

"Whyever not? If I decide that I wish to marry you, to love you forever and cherish your heart and your mind, why must I wait for *you* to ask *me*?"

He smiled. "Because it is what is done."

"When have I ever done *what is done*?"

He opened his mouth to reply, looked to the window, then closed his mouth again. "Can I at least give my apology now?"

"You have nothing to apologize for. It was my childish, abhorrent behavior that pushed you away time and again—"

"And my inability to see how my flirtatious behavior with other women might hurt you. We both have faults," he said gently, drawing his fingers over my cheekbone and tracing my jaw much as he did before. "But now we will work together to overcome them."

"Together," I whispered. "I like the sound of that."

Benedict stepped closer, sliding his other hand around my waist. Moonlight bathed us completely, and I felt lifted from the dreary study and exalted by Benedict's touch. His lips hovered above mine, a whisper away, and my eyes drifted closed so I could savor every feeling, from the pressure of his hands to his warm chest against me. His lips lowered, and he kissed me slowly, tenderly, as though he wanted to stretch the moment forever. I lost all sense of time, wrapped in the explosion of warmth, and allowed my lips to lead, my hands to lose themselves in gripping his coat, my feet to feel weightless.

He wrapped his arms around my waist and lifted me, tilting his head to deepen the kiss, and I quickly realized Peter Seymour had inadequately prepared me for how utterly amazing kissing could be.

When Benedict lowered me again, he did not release me, but pulled me against his chest and slowly kissed my forehead, my temples, my nose.

"You never answered my question," I said, unable even to feign pique while in a state of such ecstasy.

His chuckle rumbled through his chest. "Fine, Thea. I will marry you."

"Do not bother yourself with sounding pleased or anything."

Benedict squeezed me tighter. "I would be honored to become your husband."

I sighed. "That is a relief. Felicity and I have been planning this for weeks."

"Planning what, exactly? The ball?"

I slid my hands up his back and spoke with nonchalance. "The right moment to beg you to consider me and forgive me. So yes, the ball. The dance. The quiet, secret conversation in a dark room."

"You planned to drag me to a dark room?"

"I thought it would be best for this conversation." And for kissing—but that had been the hopeful side of me.

"I am not surprised, actually." He grinned, lifting an eyebrow. "You also planned for me to ask you to dance?"

"No." I shrugged a little. "I planned to ask you to dance. But you did it first."

Benedict laughed again. He dropped a kiss on my head. "I think we ought to return now."

"Yes, we need to share our news with everyone."

But Benedict did not find this as urgent as he'd made me believe, for he kissed me once more, soundly, before leading me to the door. I unbolted it and peeked through a crack before ensuring that the corridor was empty and stepping from the room.

"Come," he said, taking my hand, and with it, my heart. "We have an announcement to make."

CHAPTER 34

BENEDICT

"My mother would likely appreciate it if the wedding took place in Bakewell," I said, my fingers absently running over the corded tassel on the pillow beside me.

"Well, of course the wedding *must* take place in Bakewell." Thea paced from the window in the drawing room to the fireplace and back, her violet gown billowing around her ankles as she walked. "When Felicity took me to the dressmaker, we ordered a pale pink gown that I now believe will be absolutely perfect for a bride. It is meant to be delivered in the next few days, which only leaves the wedding breakfast to be planned and the banns to be read."

I nestled further into the sofa cushion, watching her pace back and forth with amusement. "Have you already written out a menu for the breakfast, or are you considering allowing my mother any freedom there?"

"She can have complete freedom. Though"—Thea paused before the window and grinned at me—"I was hoping we could at least serve marzipan."

My heart warmed, and I nodded. "I am certain that would be acceptable."

Thea crossed to the writing table and sat down. "I will write to Lady Edith straight away." She turned on the seat and faced me, an adorable line marring her forehead. "Or would you rather share the news with her? I do wonder how she will take it."

"She will be overjoyed." I stood, crossing toward her, and she leaned her head back to hold my gaze. "She has wanted nothing more than to see me happily settled, and she has spoken of nothing but your Season, where she can find you happily settled, for the last few years. I do think she will be much relieved by our union."

"I hope that is the case."

Felicity and James had granted us many freedoms since our engagement, opting not to force us to remain in their sight at all times, but I kept my room on St. James Street anyway. My fingers trailed down Thea's arm, and she grew still in a way I had only noticed her doing when I touched her, as though I alone had the power to focus Thea's effervescent energy into calmness.

I took her hand and pulled her to her feet, and she came willingly. My stomach knotted, reminding me of the one thing I had yet to tell her. I was certain Thea would not be angry, exactly, but I did not know if she would be pleased, either. "There is something I wanted to discuss with you. I know there is much to decide about our future, but in regard to where we will live—"

"Oh, yes!" Her eyes brightened, and she took my other hand. "I hoped you would be amenable to spending some time in Bath? I do not have any great desire to live at the Royal Crescent or be fashionable, so I think we can find a place to let that is reasonably priced. When I left school and lived on my own, I learned to be very economic."

"Bath?" My stomach sank further. "To live?"

"I realize that it is more the place to go for those who are aging or facing difficult health, but Society appeared diverse when we attended the musicale. It seemed to me that many people go to Bath occasionally, even if they do not live there, so we would see a great deal of your friends and never want for invitations."

How was I to tell her now that I could not leave my estate in the state it was currently in? "You wish to live in Bath because you loved the town, or because of Archie?"

"Well, both, to be honest."

I nodded, looking to the window to best consider how to tell her my news. Her small hands slid around my waist, and she stepped into my arms, resting her head against my chest. My burdens lifted immediately. It mattered not if she wanted to live in Bath. I would go wherever she wanted to go. It would only take a bit of finagling to find a buyer for the estate, but perhaps if I made some of the repairs, I could sell the house or let it and redeem a portion of my inheritance.

Thea leaned her head back to look at me. "You look displeased. Did you hate Bath? I vow you will love Archie."

"I am certain I will. He seemed a good lad."

"Then it is Bath you dislike?"

"I liked Bath, and I only want to be where you are."

"Then tell me what is bothering you. Friends tell one another the things that bother them."

"Oh?" I chuckled. "Do friends also plan their weddings together and decide where they will live?"

"These friends do," she whispered, reaching up and pulling my head down for a kiss. I would never tire of Thea kissing me. Never.

I straightened, holding her to me. "When we were apart for those few weeks, I was interviewing land agents and stewards and even a butler, actually."

"Oh?" She slid her hands beneath my coat and locked her

fingers behind my back, seemingly content to be held. Then she looked up. "Are you planning to purchase an estate?"

"Not planning to." I cringed. "I already bought one."

Thea released me and stepped back, her round blue eyes wide. "You should have told me so. Where is it? What is it?"

"It is . . . a project. I am afraid it is what I can afford, but the roof has leaked a bit and will need a good deal of repairs before it is livable."

"But you are good at repairs. I am certain James and Henry would help."

Her immediate confidence in my brothers was sweet. "They have already agreed to, yes."

"We also have *my* inheritance, so we will not lack for funds. It might have been halved, but there was still a good deal of money left to me."

My smile widened. Her eagerness to share our funds made her feel like an equal partner—a woman I wanted by my side.

Thea frowned. "Your brothers have already agreed to help. Am I the last to learn of this?"

"I needed a home. I needed a distraction when I thought I'd lost you. I threw myself into planning my future, since it seemed void of you." I reached for her so she could be in my arms once more. "But I did not know how to tell you that. The estate can be sold, but will need the repairs done first. It sat vacant for quite a while, so I am not sure it will be easy to rid ourselves of. And . . . it is not in Bath."

"Oh, I do not care about that, not really. So long as we can spend some time there, maybe? Or invite Archie to stay with us for the summer, perhaps?" Her eyes became glassy. "A home of our own, Ben? I cannot believe it. Where is it?"

"Near the Westmorland border, not too far from Chelton. Though I would not call them neighbors."

"Close enough."

"Would you be happy living up in the wilds of Cumberland forever?"

"I think of little children running about Chelton's gardens or picnicking in our mysterious park and I cannot do anything but love the idea of living in the wilds of Cumberland with you." She lowered her voice. "I would live anywhere with you."

I kissed her then, deeply, infusing it with all the love and affection I had not been previously able to show her in recent weeks. "Even at a home called Bumpton Hall?"

"Even there."

"You know it will be work."

She grinned. "I was a kitchen maid, darling. I'm not afraid of work."

I could not help but feel complete and utter joy, for I knew her to be telling me the truth.

"Now," I said, "about those little children you were imagining . . ."

Thea

I would live anywhere, so long as I lived with Benedict. It would be even better, I thought, to bring Archie to our estate for a summer holiday than to try and catch snippets of time with him while he was in school. Once again, Benedict had pleasantly surprised me when he shared news of the house he had purchased. A home we could build *together*. I reached up to kiss him again and show him my utter appreciation when a polite knock on the door warned us of impending company, and we stepped apart.

Benedict scowled at the door, waiting to see who it was, and

I wondered if he knew how imposing he could look.

"You've a visitor, ma'am," the footman said. "Lord Claverley."

"Bring him up," Benedict said.

"For me?" I whispered. "The earl no longer has business with me."

Lord Claverley entered the room shortly, his ruddy cheeks mottled from the cold outside or the exertion of mounting the steps to the first floor.

Benedict took a step forward, angling himself a little before me in a protective stance, and I wondered if it was intentional or natural. "Cousin," he greeted politely. "Whatever can we do for you?"

Lord Claverley's gaze flicked to me. "I'd hoped for a word with Miss Northcott."

"Of course," I said gallantly, then swung my arm toward the sofas. "Please be seated."

He hesitated, but I did not move forward. He must have sensed that I would not step toward the seats until he did. I waited until he lowered himself onto the sofa before opting to sit across from him, Benedict beside me.

"You must be anxious for the wedding," Lord Claverley said, looking from me to Benedict. His eyes narrowed. "The union came as a complete surprise to me."

I arranged my expression into a smile, though it fought to scowl instead. "Indeed, we are very anxious. Is there something you needed from me, my lord?"

He cleared his throat. "Yes, well, I came to offer my assistance. I would like to host an engagement ball in your honor."

"I only just had a ball, so we do not feel it necessary—"

"Ah, but you had a ball in London, not in Cumberland. Surely Lady Edith will desire to celebrate your union at home with your neighbors."

"She might," I admitted. "I intend to reserve that honor for her."

The earl looked exasperated. "Should I be offended that you do not seem to desire my help, Miss Northcott? I have been nothing but dismissed from you since you returned from school."

Benedict cleared his throat. "I believe if a woman rejects your advances, Cousin, it is wise to cease making them."

"Advances?" His cheeks flushed. "I am offering *assistance*."

He was doing so with the motive of dancing with me, I knew it. The man was prideful, or bored, and wanted to find a way to put his hands on me. Benedict knew it as well as I, if the anger glittering in his blue eyes was any indication.

"We no longer need your assistance, and I will thank you for respecting that," I said.

Benedict stood to punctuate my point, and I rose beside him, curling my hand around his arm.

Lord Claverley sputtered. His blush crept to the edges of his ears and along his neck, making his pallid face brighter than an apple. He did not do us the courtesy of taking our leave, but trudged from the room with angry, humiliated steps.

"I fear that will have consequences," I said mildly.

"Indeed, like keeping my cousin away from Chelton?"

"And Bumpton, potentially," I added.

Benedict turned and took me in his arms, heedless of the open door and potential of being spotted by Felicity or James. He tipped my chin up to kiss me squarely on the lips, then leaned back and spoke softly. "That man will never set foot in Bumpton, darling."

"You will turn away your own cousin?"

"I will turn away anyone who causes you to feel unsafe. Like I said, Thea . . ." Benedict broke his words up with a succession of kisses along my jaw. "I will always be here for you."

EPILOGUE
THEA

L ady Edith glowed with palpable pride, her smile a lit candle, beaming ceaselessly. The wedding was over and we stood in the courtyard at Chelton, admiring the tables laden with food and drink and the various friends and neighbors milling about.

"Is it safe to assume you never thought this would happen?" I asked, looking over her shoulder where Benedict stood with James.

"I think it is safe to assume even you did not believe it possible," Lady Edith said. "Though I am ever so glad to be surprised in this case." She reached for my hand and squeezed my fingers affectionately.

I sipped from my lemonade glass and scanned the occupants of the courtyard, glad to find Lord Claverley's ruddy face absent. It had been a spot of unease for Lady Edith to agree to withhold the earl's invitation, but in the end Benedict had remained firm, and his mother relented.

"If I'd known you would be happy with Benedict, I would not have worried so deeply about finding you a match in Town." She sipped her lemonade and looked at me over the rim. "In fact, at one point I did wonder if I could contrive a match between you and Henry, but your personalities are so different that I did not think you would suit one another."

I lifted an eyebrow and each of us sought Henry out. Unsurprisingly, he was missing.

"Someday he will find a woman to love," I said. "When he is ready. Love cannot be rushed."

"No, it cannot," Benedict said, coming to stand beside me. "Even if one tries exceedingly hard to rush it." His smile was unrepentant, and his hand snaked around my waist, pulling me close to his side.

"I should go in search of Henry," Lady Edith said, worrying her lip.

Benedict leaned down and whispered in my ear. "We should leave while Mother is occupied."

"We cannot leave our own wedding breakfast."

"Whyever not? We've eaten, accepted well wishes, and fed our neighbors. What more do they need from us?"

"Very well," I whispered. "But do not forget the valises."

Benedict looked down at me, confused. "I've already had your trunks delivered to Bumpton."

"Yes, but we'll need *valises*."

"Whatever for?"

"For the bed," I said, keeping an innocent expression on my face. "I will line them up in the center. It is the only way I'll entice you into it, correct? Of course, I know I promised I would never again mention when you failed to be a gentleman and forced me to sleep on the cold, hard, ground—"

Benedict swept me off my feet, carrying me from the courtyard and into the house without any care for who was watching.

"Put me down, and I promise I will not speak of your utter lack of chivalry again."

"You vowed never to bring it up in the first place," he muttered. "But now that you have, I am of a mind to hide tomatoes beneath *your* bed and allow them to stink up your room."

I flattened my lips, drawing my arms around my husband's neck and holding on. It seemed he had no intention of putting me down as we made our way through the house toward the front door.

"I only did that once. I was *very* angry at you for flirting with that girl at the fete."

He stopped walking and looked at me. He was so close I could see the varying shades of blue in his eyes. "That was why you hid the tomatoes beneath my bed? Because I flirted with that girl?"

"I had thought you cared for me, Ben, and I was extremely jealous."

"Not sure I deserved the tomatoes, though," he muttered.

"No, probably not." I wrinkled my nose. "I expected an odor, but I did not realize they would smell quite that awful."

Benedict carried me through the front door and down the curved, stone stairs to the carriage awaiting us.

"You had this escape planned?" I asked.

He shot me an unrepentant smile. "They have been waiting for a quarter hour now. The poor horses need to walk."

"We ought to hurry them along to Bumpton, then."

Benedict's blue eyes glittered. "My thoughts exactly."

The sun reached the edge of the earth and threw gold light over the clouds streaking the vast sky. From the front portico we could see a vast majority of our land, rolling in hills and fields in all directions, sliced down the middle by a long lane. Benedict had already completed a good portion of the work required on the roof prior to the wedding, and now it was up to both of us to style the house in a way that suited our tastes.

Benedict's knuckles grazed my cheeks. "You look much healthier now than when I first saw you in the Fullers' garden."

"It is all the marzipan and morning chocolate filling my cheeks again."

"Whatever the cause, I'm glad of it. The thin, gaunt Thea I found that day frightened me a little."

I leaned into his side, and his arm wrapped around my shoulder. "I thought I would miss the folly at Chelton, but we have such beautiful views from our front door that I do not think I will miss it too much."

"I imagined this, you know."

"The views?"

He drew in a shaky breath and pulled me against his chest, my head turned so I could hear his heart beating and look out at the sunset at the same time. "No, the view. I stood here with Henry when we first came to see the house—"

"Not in this position, I hope."

"—and imagined standing here with you, looking out at our land."

I stilled, glad he had ignored my joke.

"It was why I chose this house over the other one."

"I cannot imagine another house meeting our needs better than Bumpton. It is so full of character."

"Exactly like you."

I reached up on tiptoe and wrapped my hands around Benedict's neck, pulling him down to meet my kiss. Warmth exploded within my heart, so full of love I could not contain it in the one small organ.

"Now, there is one last place we have not yet visited in the house," Benedict said, leaning his forehead against mine. "I think you will want to make yourself intimately familiar with it."

I screwed my eyebrows together. I'd been to visit the house a handful of times before the wedding and thought I had seen everything from the attics to the bedchambers to the parlor. We'd even spent a good deal of time in the servants' quarters, making a list of what we needed to purchase to make their rooms more comfortable and choosing paper for the walls so they were not as dreary.

"What is it?" I asked.

"The kitchen, of course."

I started to pull away, a smile spreading over my mouth, when Benedict tugged me back in. Amusement was thick in his smile and sparkling like mischief in his eyes. "In case you ever feel the need to run away again, I want you to feel comfortable in the kitchen here."

"Once you've tasted my overbeaten bread, you will regret giving me that option."

"I have witnessed your ability to scrub a dish, so I think we can find a place for you helping Cook."

"Are you certain that is a good idea? In the kitchen I will have access to all the tomatoes."

"Hmmm." Benedict rubbed his chin, making a show of thinking over what I had said.

I leaned up and kissed his chin, stealing his attention. Disentangling myself, I took his hand and pulled him into the house.

"Where are we going?" he asked.

"To the kitchen, of course," I said, as though it was the most reasonable thing.

Benedict's loud, rumbling laughter sent prickles over my skin and a wide smile to my face. He yanked me to a stop and pulled me into his arms, kissing me soundly. "We can get to the kitchens tomorrow."

"Oh, very well." And I kissed him again.

HONORABLY ENGAGED

Henry Bradwell has a secret, and Marianne Hutton is the only person who knows what it is.

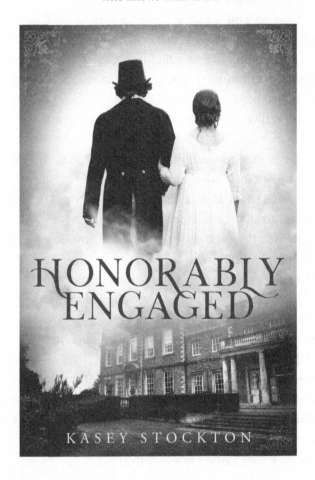

ACKNOWLEDGMENTS

From the moment I begin drafting my manuscript until the book releases, there are many, many stages of the process and people who give me feedback in a variety of ways. I'm so fortunate to have the support system, editors, early readers, and author friends I do, because they all work together to support me in different ways through this process.

But I wouldn't be able to write without the support system I have outside of the reading world, too. My sweet children, amazing husband, friends, and family make all of this doable, and I'm so grateful for every one of you. But most of all, Jon, because you mop the floors when I'm on a tight deadline, and I really hate mopping floors.

To my beta readers: Heidi Stott, Brooke Losee, Nancy Madsen, Emily Flynn, Teah Weight, Melanie Atkinson, and Karen Painter, thank you for your insight and taking the time to read my messy draft! Anneka Walker and Deborah Hathaway, thank you for taking time out of your own crazy lives and writing time to read my book and give me valuable feedback. You are both the best!

My editors, Jacque Stevens and Karie Crawford, I'm so glad you help me work out story kinks and delete my 500 that's. You polished my story and manuscript and made it reader ready. Thank you, ladies!

Finally, and most importantly of all, thank you to my Heavenly Father. I would not have finished this story without divine support. Love stories have a magic all their own. They pull us out of difficult, real situations and give us a few hours of hope, happiness, and escape. God cares about each of His children, and He cares about the little things we care about, because He loves us. I know He supports my writing, and I know He loves you, too.

ABOUT THE AUTHOR

Kasey Stockton is a staunch lover of all things romantic. She doesn't discriminate between genres and enjoys a wide variety of happily ever afters. Drawn to the Regency period at a young age when gifted a copy of *Sense and Sensibility* by her grandmother, Kasey initially began writing Regency romances. She has since written in a variety of genres, but all of her titles fall under clean romance. A native of northern California, she now resides in Texas with her own prince charming and their three children. When not reading, writing, or binge-watching chick flicks, she enjoys running, cutting hair, and anything chocolate.

Made in the USA
Coppell, TX
01 September 2024

36690793R00198